Winter

CW00497683

Folly

VIVIENNE SHANNON

CHAPTER 1

From her mother, Miss Violette deVere received the blessings of a pretty name and a tender heart; from her father, the curse of unladylike height, a strong nose, a determined jaw and a mop of flaming hair that would succumb to neither comb nor curling iron. Entirely her own was a wild, romantic and yearning soul; and despite her best efforts to subdue it with liberal applications of common sense and logic, her soul, like her hair, could be neither tamed nor ignored.

Her mother's dying words were, "*Ma petite*, all who know you cannot help but love you, but an aristocratic husband will look for a beauty to grace his table. *C'est triste, mais vrai, non?* Expect nothing – for if you do, you will be broken-hearted by it." With that, she expired, as pretty in death as she had been in life, her dark curls an artless tangle on the crisp white pillow and her blue eyes closed

1

forever. She was joined, some eight years later, by her devoted husband, and in the early spring of 1800, Violette crossed the English Channel to take possession of the deVere family home, Sumbourne Manor in Kent. And being a single young woman in possession of a large fortune, Violette had the good sense to retain the companionship of her father's sister, Miss Felicia deVere, to be her chaperone.

Sumbourne Manor was an ancient house, white-washed and half-timbered with a deeply sloping roof of weathered red clay tiles. It sat in an expanse of neglected parkland, with, closer to the house, a dull garden of low hedges and gravel walks. Beyond the stable yard was an expanse of the apple orchards for which Kent is renowned; gnarled and twisted old trees giving a late crop of small yellow apples, their unprepossessing appearance belying their richly perfumed sweetness.

The house was not the grand affair that Violette had been expecting. It was a maze of small, inconvenient rooms leading one into the other, with unexpected odd steps here and there. Just as these seemed designed for the express purpose of sending the unwary flying headfirst into every room in a most undignified manner, so Violette flew headfirst into loving her new home.

The panelled hallway was dominated by a wide, shallow staircase adorned with elaborate carvings, and if the trees in the orchard invited climbing up, so the stair bannisters positively encouraged sliding down. A pair of bears formed the newel posts, their coats polished to a high shine by the loving hands of previous generations of small children.

Running her own fingers over them, Violette could not help but say to herself, 'Even with my plain face, and being, at full five and twenty, upon the elderly side for marriage; and even though I loom over the heads of most men, I might still meet someone who will love me. For I should like nothing better than to see my own children running pell-mell through this creaky old house, sliding down these bannisters and climbing those trees.' She put these thoughts from her with a sigh of regret. 'It will not happen. I cannot expect love, and I will not be married for my fortune. I must reconcile myself to spinsterhood. I shall take a lesson from my aunt, and learn to live as she does, counting my blessings.

'And if I yearn for romance, then I shall find it in the pages of a novel!'

The late summer of 1800 was particularly wet, day upon day of rain, and for weeks the two ladies had been largely confined to the house. Left to her own devices, Violette would have been content to sit by the fireside and read, but her aunt could not comprehend how Violette could enjoy her own company to such an extent. And she was nervous about the wisdom of a young lady reading novels, a subject upon which her own father had held a very strong opinion.

Miss Felicia therefore embarked upon a schedule of amusements for her niece, with cards and quilling, silhouettes and scrapbooks, all accompanied by a constant stream of light chatter. But as much as Violette had grown to love her aunt over the preceding months, and appreciated her attempts to entertain her, there were times when she yearned for silence and solitude. So it was that on a particular Thursday morning in the last week of September, her aunt came hurrying out into the stable yard where the boy was hitching up the pony and trap, calling to her niece in some distress.

"Lettie! My dear!" She was still in her morning wrapper, with her cap awry and ribbons fluttering. "Whatever are you about? Hill tells me you are taking a nuncheon with you and intending to – well, I don't know quite what! Walk somewhere! Whatever for? Who is to accompany you? I shall come with you, of course I shall, we can walk down to the village together after breakfast by all means, though I beg you to wait for me. I am still *déshabillé* !"

"No, Aunt!" Violette drew in a breath, and spoke more gently. "Thank you; but I do not wish to walk sedately down to the village. It's such a gloriously lovely morning, and it seems to have done nothing but rain since I have been here. I shall enjoy striding out –."

"Striding out? Good gracious child, what a horrid expression!"

4

"Walking briskly, then. Exploring. Looking at views. On my own!" Violette had become most sincerely attached to her aunt, but this conversation, as to how fast she might walk or in which direction, served only to infuriate her.

"But, my dear, take a groom with you, at least – let John Hill come with you. A young lady cannot go gallivanting about the countryside alone! Whatever would people say? You might get lost, or stolen away by the gypsies, or even the French, if they were to come ashore with murder in their hearts – for we are not above a half-mile to the coast, and the French are all rascals and not to be trusted to stay on their own side of the water, as we well know."

"But I shan't get lost! Even if I were, I daresay the pony can find his way home when he wants his dinner. I see no point in taking John from his duties here to watch me walking back and forth across the Downs. It's hardly out of our own park, Aunt!" Observing Miss Felicia's stricken face, Violette added, gently, "I shall keep my wits about me, I promise you." With this, she smiled brilliantly at her aunt and clicked her tongue encouragingly to the pony, and the trap rattled out of the stable yard.

At some point in the past, a distant deVere had planted an avenue of elms. These splendid trees stretched away from the house to give onto a narrow road, leading to Canterbury – and thence to London – in one direction, and in the other, to Sumbourne village. This was little more than a handful of cottages surrounding a tumbledown old inn by name of The Dragon. The inn was perched upon a rocky promontory, from whence a narrow stair cut into the cliff face led down to a cove where a fishing boat or two could be found drawn up onto the shingle. But Violette turned the pony's head away from the coast, heading along a grassy track that wound uphill through patchy woodland. It was early in the day but already hot and the shade was welcome, despite the clouds of midges that made the pony twitch his ears and toss his head.

After a mile or so, the trees thinned out. The trap emerged into sunshine with a high blue sky dotted with gentle puffs of white cloud. Before Violette spread a vista of low hills and distant valleys, shadows chasing the clouds as they moved idly across the sun. Here and there were thickets of beech and sweet chestnut, their foliage hinting at the advent of the shimmering reds and golds of autumn.

Cresting a rise, Violette saw that the gentle swell of the grassy landscape was bisected by a deeply indented gully, perhaps the site of a long-forgotten river, now overgrown with grasses and wild flowers. At its centre, a shallow brook splashed its way down the hill in a series of pretty falls and fern-fringed pools, and on one bank stood the remains of an ancient church; one of the walls fallen away to a heap of stones, and the roof caved in. She halted the trap, and sat for a moment with her eyes closed and her face turned to the sun. It was profoundly quiet, save for the soft repetition of the horse tearing tender

6

mouthfuls of the short grass and larks singing somewhere high above.

Violette jumped down from the trap and set off uphill, following the path of the stream. It was a steep climb. She was breathless when at last she rounded the final group of boulders and found herself at the top of the hill, on a long, level stretch of grass affording a spectacular view across hills and valleys in all directions. Here was the source of the stream, a bubbling spring forming a dark, deep pool at the base of the stones. Violette knelt, and drank from her cupped hands. The water was sweet and bitter cold, and she splashed some over her hot face.

This pool had overflowed to mingle with the waters from the recent rains which had not drained away, and had transformed much of the plateau into something approaching a shallow lake, reflecting the clouds scudding across the sky, and Violette stood for a moment admiring the view. In a gentle fold of a distant hill she could make out the roofs and chimneys of some remote hamlet, a few lazy wisps of smoke rising into the air. Turning her head, her eye was caught by a gleam of silver, more distant still. A river had spilled its banks and flooded the park and gardens of a striking house constructed of shining white stone. Flat roofed and with its massive-columned portico, it had the look of ancient temple, such as could be found in the ruins of some once-great civilisation. Before it, a statue of a winged woman clad in draperies held aloft a sword, and behind her stretched a long terrace where a row of tall windows caught the early morning sun in a blinding sheet of gold. This majestic edifice was perfectly reflected in the swathe of unmoving water before it like something from a dream.

From her vantage point, Violette could make out a series of outbuildings and courtyards. There was no sign of life. No dog barked, no rider swung himself from his horse in the stable yard; no boy went clattering across the courtyard with a bucket or stopped to talk to a maidservant.

'It has the look of something enchanted; frozen in time, like Sleeping Beauty's castle,' she thought. 'It's grand, and no doubt the latest fashion, but I don't like it much. It seems so very cold and forbidding.' A cloud passed over the sun and Violette shivered, and a pang of hunger reminded her that she'd had no breakfast.

She turned away, and retraced her steps downhill.

She settled herself on the grass, with her back against one of the tumbled stones of the church ruins, and a slice of pigeon pie and an apple laid out upon her handkerchief. From her reticule she drew out a novel. With a sigh of pleasure, she prepared to spend an hour or two reading in the sunshine.

Lost entirely in the adventures of Rosalia, blackmailed into marrying the manipulative Count Orsinio, escaping his cruel intentions by stowing away on a pirate ship and currently concealed behind

8

a curtain with a dagger clutched in her hand, Violette absently noted a single drop of rain form a perfect circle on the page, and then, that the larks had stopped singing.

She looked up from her book. The sky had assumed a mantle of cloud of so dark a hue that it was nearly black. At her feet, the little brook was become transformed into a fast-running stream, its picturesque little falls and fern-fringed pools subsumed into a rush of water spilling across the width of the gully. Violette watched, fascinated, as another wave of muddy water came churning down the hill. It brought with it a cascade of small stones and clods of earth torn from the stream's grassy banks and these went whirling away in the water's race downstream.

The pony raised his head, his ears pricked.

The air was still. Nature held its breath; and then a blast of white-hot lightning flashed across the sky.

The ground shook with a cannon-fire boom of thunder. The pony went back on his hind legs with a scream of pure terror. And before Violette could jump to her feet, he'd bolted, the trap bounding behind him as he skittered this way and that, down the hill and out of sight.

The rain fell like water poured from a bucket. Within moments the stream had swelled to fill the gully, a thunderous torrent ripping away great clods of mud and grass and stones as it swept relentlessly onwards. There was a deep-throated rumble. Violette turned her head, to see a great shelf of earth and stones detach itself from the hilltop above her, and, borne upon a massive wave of thick brown water, come plunging down the hill towards her.

She screamed, and staggered backwards, desperate to get out of its path. It smashed into her, battering her with stones and clods of earth and knocking her feet from under her. Flailing her arms, she touched solid rock – the fallen stones of the church – and scrambled into their shelter, clinging to them for safety and sobbing for breath as the water churned around her.

And then she heard the desperate barking of a dog.

He was far out in the middle of the stream, a great black animal, his ears flat against his skull, eyes bulging with terror as his paws scrabbled uselessly against the current. It was to no avail. He was beyond all help, caught in the maelstrom sweeping him downstream to his doom.

Violette stumbled to her feet. The thin muslin of her dress was thick with mud and had wound itself round her legs like the winding sheet of a corpse. She grabbed at the hem, and pulled her dress up as high as she could manage, ripping it in the process. She knotted it around her waist and, hardly knowing what she was doing, she threw herself into the torrent.

The water was over her knees, and she staggered and fell; righting herself, her hair plastered across her face, sobbing for breath, she fought her way through the raging water, desperate to reach the terrified animal.

He saw her. He turned his head towards her, his eyes rolling. She grabbed at his collar and was swept along with him. The water exploded over her head; the dog was a dead weight, pulling her down below the surface. She screamed at him, "Come on, *come on*, you *damned* stupid animal! Come ON!" and hauled at his collar, fighting to get them both to safety.

There was a great shout. "This way! Loki! Here boy! This way!" A man came racing down the hill, and flung himself into the water. The dog's head broke the surface once more. With a final, despairing effort he thrust his body towards his master. One hand still clutching at the dog's collar, Violette reached out the other, and the man caught her hand in both of his, and hauled them into shallower water.

Violette scrambled her way onto higher ground. There she sank onto the muddy grass, her head on her arms, sobbing and retching. At last she could speak. "Is the dog alright?" As if in answer, the dog licked her cheek. Violette burst into tears. Then all went into black … and she knew nothing more.

She was wrapped in something rough; a coarse blanket that scratched her skin. She opened her eyes to a dim, reddish light. She lay quite still, disoriented. She could hear the rapid thrumming of rain on a roof, and its counterpoint, a slow drip, drip from a leak somewhere close by.

'Is this my room? Is it morning or night?' Fear took her in its grip, and she moved her head fretfully from side to side. 'I am not at home. This is not my bed.'

She tried to call out for her maid to bring her a drink, but her voice came out as nothing more than a croaking whisper. Then she came more fully awake, and knew that she was not in her old bedroom at St Cloud sur Mer, that pretty room with the flowered paper upon the walls; nor at her new home in Kent, where the bed had barley-twist posts and a cover of midnight blue wool, and the window casements rattled in the wind. With difficulty, Violette turned her head. Pain throbbed at her temples, and she closed her eyes, overcome with nausea.

When she opened her eyes again it was to make out rough stone walls. She was in a small room, no more than a hut, and empty save for the bed, and a stick-back chair drawn up to the hearth. A dog was asleep in front of the remains of a fire, burned down now to little more than grey ash with a few last vestiges of red embers still showing. A man was sitting on the chair. Draped across the back of it were some torn and muddied rags. To her horror Violette realised that they were her clothes - her dress and her undergarments, too. Beneath the blanket, she was naked.

With a gasp of horror, she sat up, clutching the blanket to her.

The man by the fireside looked up. "You saved my dog. It was a ridiculous thing to do. To risk your life, for the sake of a dog. But he means a lot to me. I am in your debt." He stood, and came towards her. Violette could see nothing of him, silhouetted as he was against the dying light of the fire, other than that he seemed a giant of a man.

She shrank back. "My clothes. Did you – what did you…?" She could hardly formulate the words.

"Did I undress you? I did." The embers shifted in the hearth, and a last dying tongue of flamed leaped up, sending his shadow leering across the wall. His voice was a throaty rasp. "You were near frozen. I thought to save your life. Letting you perish for the propriety of a few damp petticoats seemed a poor trade."

"I'm so cold." Violette's teeth rattled in her head.

"There's no more wood. I've used what there was. All that's left is this chair," he indicated the chair he'd been sitting on. "I broke the other to burn it. And I could break this one, too, but then where would I sit? I'd have to sit upon the bed beside you." He chuckled. "Perhaps you would prefer me not to."

Violette was racked by a sudden burst of coughing, and his amusement vanished in an instant. Two rapid strides brought him to her side. "You have taken a fever." He reached out his hand to lay it upon her forehead. She gasped with the shock of it. His fingers were the cold of winter snows and in the shadow his eyes glittered with a pale light. The strength ebbed from her limbs. She could only whisper, "Please don't. Please – I beg you…." before she sank back, helpless.

The last thing she heard, as she drifted into the delirium of a fever dream, was his voice "Death, at your service."

CHAPTER 2

"It was the very strangest occurrence, my dear! For we were beside ourselves with fear for her, and had sent the servants out to look for her when she didn't come home for her dinner, but the rain, well, I had never seen rain like it! Close to midnight there was a hammering at the door and it was the stable lad saying that the pony had come home all alone, dragging the remains of the trap behind him, still harnessed up but smashed to smithereens. And John says that it is beyond repair, and we shall have to send to Canterbury to order a new one, and what that will cost I do not know!

"So I sent the boy off for the constable from Larkham, but he came back as quick as he went to say that he could not get through, for the Winterbourne was in full flood! I heard later that it had gone smashing through the village and pulled down the bridge and the millwheel broke clean away and was found the next day half-way to Dover. And no flour to be had until it is mended, so the villagers will have to send out for flour and that will be a nuisance for them all.

"And we thought her drowned, or taken by the gypsies, or smugglers even, for what with the taxes on every blessed thing – salt, indeed! And soap, too! They say Cornwall is the place for smugglers but do not be deceived, for the Kentish coast is a veritable haven for them. And I have such a fondness for Orange Pekoe and the tea merchant in Folkestone charges such a price for it, so that you can hardly blame – I mean – that is –."

Having talked herself into something of a difficulty, Miss Felicia deVere broke off, and offered her guest a ratafia biscuit to distract her attention from the brimming tea caddy.

Her guest, equally tactfully, changed the subject. "But the poor girl was found alive and well. Thank heaven." Mrs George leaned closer, and her voice dropped to something of a whisper. "In a shepherd's hut, you say. And her clothing all ripped to shreds? And no ... no gypsy had... had... ."There was no way of finishing this sentence delicately, and Miss Felicia determined to ignore it.

She and Mrs George had been young ladies together and had remained the firmest of friends these thirty-five years or more. Mrs George had enjoyed the great good fortune to have married a most considerate man who had died young and left her a comfortable income for her lifetime. And upon Miss Felicia's visits to Bath – sadly, not as often as she would have liked – she had passed many a happy hour with her friend at her pretty house in Milsom

Street. But enjoyable as it was to spend a darkling winter afternoon discussing the activities of the young ladies of the Ton over the teacups, Miss Felicia felt that impugning the reputation of her own niece was a step too far.

"No indeed!" She took a reviving sip of her tea. "As I was saying – well, the next morning, after I had been awake all the night in such fear as I cannot describe, there came such a knocking at the door! It was the constable to say that she was alive, and at an inn over towards Little Hougham.

"How she was found is something of a mystery. The innkeeper had some story of a great tall fellow, 'a black-chinned ruffian with a great black dog to match' is how he put it - hammering on his door at dawn when the rain had stopped. He said he'd found a young lady taken shelter in one of the shepherd huts, and that she was in a poor way and someone should go for her. By the time the innkeeper had roused his wife and got brandy and blankets and harnessed up his cart, the fellow was gone, so it's not known who he was or how he came to find her."

"A big fellow with a beard! So it *was* a gypsy!"

"She had a dreadful fever, and was abed a good two weeks and slow after that to mend, so the physician recommended Bath. Tunbridge Wells is closer but the waters are not considered as efficacious, and the doctor said that the hot bathing spring will restore her admirably, and she will quite get her complexion back – thank goodness. For it is the poor girl's only claim to beauty; though she has a sad tendency to freckles."

Mrs George was sympathetic. As a girl she, too, had been plagued by the freckles and knew what a burden they could be.

"And so here we are. I for one will be very pleased to escape a winter in Kent, for the winds blow something bitter, and it can snow something quite considerable. And now we shall be staying in Bath right through until the spring. Oh - for dear Lettie's sake, of course. Not for my own pleasure, for indeed, the snow can look most picturesque. But I declare I *do* enjoy Bath considerably more."

Miss Felicia deVere adored Bath. Bath was the prettiest of places altogether. With its buildings made from the local golden-coloured sandstone, it seemed to be filled with sunshine on even the dullest winter day. There was so much to see! The delights of the milliner's window and that of the dressmaker and the rattling carriages of the Ton passing by - the ladies in their barouches, the whips in their curricles, the rakes in their colourful high-perch phaetons. Here was the stage coach disgorging passengers from London and the mail coach arriving with its blare of trumpets, and the crowd that greeted it, and the parcels being unloaded.

The fashions, the parties, the gossip, the scandals. Drinking chocolate in the Pump Room, selecting marzipan shapes and sweet biscuits at Mollands. Nothing, in Miss Felica's opinion, could compare to these delights.

Many years before, her brother had fallen in love with a dancer in the French ballet and decamped to live with his young wife in her native country.

This had sent Sir William deVere into an apoplexy, and he had left London upon the instant, commanding his daughter with him to keep his house, and had sunk himself into the querulous, demanding temperament of the invalid. And it was only the delights of a fortnight's sojourn in Bath each year, where Sir William went to take the waters in the hope of easing both his gout and his dyspepsia, and the eventual dream of living there, that had sustained Felicia deVere through those long years of exile.

She had always assumed that, upon Sir William's eventual death, her brother would return from France, bringing his wife and child with him. And when that happened, she would have asked him for an allowance, upon receipt of which she would have moved to Bath to keep rooms with her friend Mrs George.

But her brother never had returned from France. Miss Felicia knew very little of finance other than fretting over the household bills once a month (for the numbers never did seem to come out as she thought they should) but she was aware that her father had made no provision for her brother that would induce him to return to England. Accordingly, the conversation about the allowance and the scheme for Bath had never taken place. She had stayed on at the Manor quite alone but for the servants. And if she sometimes caught herself reflecting on the different life she might have had, she would give herself a shake and roundly count her blessings.

'I have a comfortable home, and dear, loyal servants in John Hill and his sister Sarah; good food upon the table and really as many fires as I wish through the colder weather – though coal is a dreadful price. And a shopping trip to Folkestone once a month is pleasant enough.' Though try as she might, she could not help a little voice in her head that *would* add, 'Though it truly cannot compare with the delights of Bath!

But now she was here once more! And not for a mere fortnight, but for three whole *months* – for it would be well into the New Year before they returned to Kent! Miss Felica was thrilled. She was in the company of her niece, and Mrs George had found them a delightful house to rent in one of the more fashionable streets. There might not be balls, for of course she and Violette were still in the last few weeks of mourning for Violette's dear papa, but that was no matter; there would be balls enough when it was known that Miss Violette deVere was out of mourning. And for now there would be card parties, and promenades in the Pump Room and musical entertainments a-plenty.

"…. so we must arrange a visit to the *modiste!* The poor child's clothing – my dear! They say the French are a fashionable people, and perhaps her gowns were considered elegant in that dreadful backwater where my brother set up home."

"I thought he lived in Paris?"

"To start, yes indeed. They did not move in society, of course; my sister-in-law was not quite ... but then of course – events... ."

The French had had the temerity to rise up against their King and Queen, and the events of the last ten years or more had been shocking beyond belief. Even though he was a bully and a warmonger, perhaps there was cause to be grateful to Monsieur Bonaparte who had stopped the choppings-off of heads and the stormings of Bastilles and all the other mad excesses in which the French had indulged.

"So they left Paris and travelled to the South, quite away from all civilisation as far as I can understand, for my brother had some notion of being an artist and painting the beauties of the countryside. Really! No wonder the silly child felt she could go romping about in a rainstorm and take no harm. My sister-in-law has been dead these several years and I suppose my brother employed some housekeeper to be in charge so the child has not had wise counsel from a sensible sort of woman, and most assuredly not an English gentlewoman. As for clothes – well, a French housekeeper can hardly be expected to understand clothing suitable for English society." Miss Felicia shuddered at the thought of Violette's unsuitable wardrobe. "No indeed. So while we are here I intend to take dear Lettie to Madame Audabon's establishment, and we shall fit her with everything suitable for an English winter in Bath."

Miss Felicia concluded with a determined nod of her head, and helped herself to the last ratafia biscuit. She felt that Violette needed her, and she would 'step up to the mark', or whatever sporting slang it was that those dreadful Corinthians were so fond of using.

.

CHAPTER 3

For the first two weeks that they were in Bath, Violette had been ordered to rest, and not to set foot outside the house but to be taken in a closed chair to the hot springs and lie in the water for an hour a day. After the first time of doing so she refused to return.

"Aunt. Have you seen the hot bath? I was wrapped up in a brown sheet and dropped in the water along with all the other hapless souls. With the steam rising off the water, I declare that we looked like so many lumps of gristle floating around in the stewpot. I most assuredly will not go back!"

Violette undertook her own convalescence by sending to the confectioners for Turkish Delight and to the subscription library for novels, and lying on the sofa in her room in front of a blazing fire – for although the weather was sunny, there was a biting east wind – with Mrs Edgeworth and Mrs Radcliffe for company.

With her niece confined to the house, Miss Felicia was set free to gad, and pay calls and leave cards, and enjoy the delicious novelty of inviting her friends to drink tea in her own – or at least temporarily her own – house, as much as she desired. It was a division of labour that suited them both perfectly.

The fortnight of Violette's convalescence was soon over. She was released from her imprisonment, and so it was that one bright morning, she found herself standing on the corner of Quiet Street and Milsom Street, the destination of choice for all ladies of fashion, for here was situated Madame Audabon's establishment.

The door was opened for them by a personage of so superior a mien that Violette took him for a gentleman. He bowed, and Violette was only saved from the dreadful faux-pas of a curtsy in return by her aunt's vice-like grip upon her wrist and a discreet, but vehement, shake of the head.

Upon enquiring of them their names, and establishing that they were expected by Madame herself, he beckoned imperiously, and a young lady assistant clad in sober blue bombazine arrived to escort them to Madame's *atelier*.

Violette was positively wide-eyed as she and her aunt made their way through the busy salon. It bore no resemblance to the cramped handful of shops to be found in Sumbourne village, dark, low-beamed and always with a faint aura of dust and mould; and the delights of linen-drapers and milliners in busy Folkestone were as nothing compared to the enchantments of this positive emporium of fashionable taste.

It was not the frantic rush of the weeks immediately leading up to the start of the Season, when new gowns were ordered by the dozen, but nonetheless the salon was crowded. There was a space set aside for the gentlemen who accompanied their wives or daughters on their shopping expeditions. Sprawled upon a low sofa or upright in a winged chair, and with a glass of Madeira to hand, they could be observed laughing over the latest gossip sheet or scurrilous cartoon lampooning one of their fellows who had been caught out in some indiscretion. Here, too, could be found those redoubtable dowagers who made it their business to know everyone else's; and rapturously considering the delights of silk ribbons and lavender-scented gloves, the young ladies of the Ton fluttered becomingly beneath their bonnets. Lastly were the mammas, high upon the hunt and staring quite frankly about them, eager for news of engagements and weddings, balls and routs and the doings of eligible bachelors who might be new to the charms of Bath. And over all was the industrious hum of light chatter embroidered with a little well-bred laughter, as reputations were torn to pieces and stitched back together again.

The walls were lined with shelves stacked high with boxes and interspersed with gilt-framed mirrors. These reflected the light of a chandelier that would have graced any aristocratic ballroom. At intervals upon the shining wooden counter tops were elaborate displays of lace and embroidery, beadwork and silk flowers. And as Violette and her aunt passed by, an assistant shook out a fine paisley shawl in a sumptuous swirl of green and gold, for the benefit of a little group of elderly ladies seated upon delicate gilt chairs, a footman standing discreetly to one side.

One of these dowagers turned her head as Violette passed by, and Violette distinctly heard her say to her companions, "I declare, that's Felicia deVere. That lady with her must be Sir William's granddaughter, you know! Brought up in the *Bohemian* style, so I've heard. Artists and their models and so on. Shocking!" Out of the corner of her eye, Violette saw all three ladies turn and stare at her quite unashamedly. Another of the ladies responded in a carrying whisper with a strong Scottish lilt, "Och, that puir lassie. She really is quite the lanky beanpole!" Violette's face burned.

At this moment, the footman threw open the door to Madame's *atelier*, and Violette plunged thankfully into its hushed interior. And here she spent a miserable half-hour staring at her reflection in the looking glass while Madame Audabon and her aunt discussed her as if she were not there at all.

Between them – and in the most circuitous manner, which had avoided any mention of Violette's prodigious height, advanced years and single status – they eschewed the prevailing fashion for white muslin as being too girlish, and were embarked upon a search for something a little more, as Madame Audabon put it, "*Sophistique.* A little more *classique*, shall we say?"

"The young lady 'as a beautiful figure; and so striking 'er colouring!" Madame Audabon had been horrified to be addressed by her client in incomprehensible rapid-fire French, and was saved, to some extent, by Miss Felicia, who informed her that her niece had grown up in the south of that country.

"Zees explain so much. She 'as the dialect of that part of the country, which make eet difficult to understand for me, from ze north," but even so Madame was left with the hideous dilemma of having to continue the pretence of her French birth in front of her staff and other clientele while knowing that Miss Violette deVere was aware that this was a lie.

But if the session was uncomfortable for her, so it was a torture for Violette. Being forced to stare at her reflection made her even more miserably aware of all her faults. The first was her age, for she was very aware that the discussion about the suitability of white muslin was merely another way of pointing out how ridiculously elderly she was, at five and twenty, to be entering into fashionable society for the first time. The second was her height, for she towered over her aunt, Madame herself, and her assistant who was reaching here, there and everywhere with her wretched tape measure. Last, and perhaps worst, was her hair. "Such a mass of golden curls! What the French call *blonde au frais*. Strawberry blonde," said Madame Audabon, archly.

'Orange. Ginger.' Violette stared at her hair in the mirror. 'There is no such thing as this idea of strawberry-coloured hair! Carrot-colour, rather. And as for curls? What nonsense. It's more like a mane.'

No matter how tightly wound were the curl-papers at night, Violette's hair would not fall in smooth ringlets in the morning, and no matter how much pomade Hill, her aunt's maid, applied, it would not lie close to her head. Violette had given up trying to control it, and merely wound it into a tight and unfashionable knot at the back of her head, and fixed it with what felt like a hundred pins that dug into her scalp all day.

"And such a figure – so slender. Like a classical goddess!"

'I am as thin as a twig,' said Violette to herself, miserably. Unbidden, her mother's words came back to her. *An aristocratic husband will look for a beauty to grace his table and bear his children.* She swallowed back the tears that threatened.

"If we are finished with the measuring, Madame Audabon, perhaps we could go and look at some gayer fabrics." Miss Felicia put down the length of figured grey silk Madame Audabon had handed her, and looked with disfavour upon the samples of fabrics draped elegantly across the pretty gilt-framed daybed upon which she was seated. "These are so very – so very *effacing*! It's just coming up the year since my brother died, and for the past few months we have been living most quietly in half-mourning. But I think we can move into some gayer fashions now. My eye was caught by some pretty striped satins as we came through the door. What do you think, Violette dear? Shall we look for something a little less sombre?"

Madame escorted the two ladies back into the salon where they were found chairs in a quiet corner and a footman summoned to bring refreshments. Miss Felicia bore an assistant away in the direction of the striped satins which had made such an impression upon her, and Violette sipped her lemon cordial, and amused herself by watching the door and observing who came in and out.

She was rewarded soon enough. The door opened to admit a very pretty young lady, her glossy dark ringlets peeping from beneath a pink velvet bonnet trimmed with swansdown, and carrying a matching muff. She was delivered into the establishment by a pair of gentlemen. Both were strikingly tall and equally broad of shoulder; one clearly the young lady's brother, being just as dark-haired and sharing a pronounced family resemblance. He was clad in the distinctive high-collared, cut-away dark blue jacket of a Navy midshipman and his sparkling blue eyes and ruddy countenance spoke of an outdoor life and a happy disposition, unrestrained by a society which held that overt displays of emotion were to be discouraged.

The other gentleman – 'Their father?' wondered Violette; 'No. A somewhat older brother, I suspect, though the resemblance between them is not so pronounced,' was striking in the extreme. His nose was aquiline, his expression supercilious, and his own hair, curling slightly above his high-starched shirt points, was as silvery pale as the moon, at startling odds with his dark brows and lashes. He was as disdainfully languid of manner as his companion appeared lively, and most exquisitely tailored.

His cravat was starched to perfection, knotted and folded and held by the simplest of pins, a single freshwater pearl the size of a robin's egg. His quizzing glass was looped around his neck on a fine gold chain; his boots were shined to within one inch of their lives. And he wore a coat of the deepest indigo, with the merest hint of a silken blue sheen.

This article caused Madame to stiffen. She snapped her fingers, and an assistant materialised beside her instantly. French accent disregarded in the moment, Madame Audabon hissed, "I don't care how you do it, but get yourself to his lordship's valet and find out where that coat was made. That is a London cut if ever I saw one. I would put money on it being from Weston and Shultz. And find out where the fabric comes from. The colour is something new, I have not seen the like before. Once his lordship has taken even one more step along the street, we will have every young lady in the town in here, demanding such fabric for a riding dress or a Spenser jacket!"

Her assistant hesitated. Madame snapped, "Go! Go!" and she scurried off to fetch her bonnet.

From her corner, Violette stared, fascinated, as the exquisite gentleman made a slow, hood-lidded survey of the salon. He acknowledged an acquaintance or two with a nod and the merest suggestion of a lifted finger; found a seat to his liking upon a yellow velvet sofa and sat, brushing an invisible speck of dust from his otherwise pristine buckskins. Finally, he arranged himself with one arm laid carefully across the back of the sofa, displaying the requisite inch of gleaming white shirt cuff below his jacket sleeve, and one leg outstretched to display a muscular calf.

'Quite as if he is sitting for his portrait,' thought Violette, smiling broadly at this performance. Her amusement was suddenly stilled. His gaze swept the room once more. This time it alighted upon her. His mouth moved fractionally, as if in a *moue* of disgust, and he immediately glanced away.

Violette blushed horribly. 'He is like a hunter searching for his prey. He reminds me of the falcons I would see over the fields at home, seeming to hang quite effortless in the air, but in a moment dropping from the skies like an arrow to snatch up some unsuspecting prey.' Behind her she fancied she heard some stifled laughter. She felt instinctively that she was the joke. And with all her heart she wished herself anywhere but here.

Having found several bolts of fabric which appealed to her, Miss Felicia had them carried across to Violette. "Stand up, my dear, and look in the glass, and see what you think of this." She flung a length of pea green satin around her niece's neck, saying to the assistant, "We are invited to Mrs Fitzallen's for next Saturday evening, and this will mark the entry of my niece into Society. I wish for her to make the best impression. Do you not think – for an evening party?" She turned back to study

Violette's reflection in the mirror. "I like it. It makes a most striking contrast with your hair, Lettie dear."

Violette heard a muffled snort, and could feel eyes burning into her. A dreadful compulsion made her look across the salon, and sure enough, the exquisite gentleman's glance had lighted upon her once more, his quizzing glass to his eye. Violette turned her burning face away.

"Not the green, aunt," she whispered, but her aunt took no notice. She had followed Violette's glance across the room.

"Good gracious, it's Richard Taverner – Lord Winterbourne! And his brother and sister with him, I believe. I declare, Lettie, he is our neighbour in the country, not five miles from us if we were to take the coast road, and a deal quicker across country, if one were so minded. He has a new house built which is the very latest fashion, and a marvel to all who see it; that is, not a new house built exactly, for they are a very old family indeed. The previous Lord Winterbourne, his father you know, was a rake of the first order and known for a gambling man. He it was tore down the house that had stood there since who knows when, to build this new one. It's said to be a veritable palace, all in the most beautiful white stone.

"I was acquainted with Lady Winterbourne when we were young, but upon her marriage – well, her husband did not encourage callers. And then my own circumstances... but enough of that. Come child, we will step across and introduce ourselves!"

Her voice was a whisper, but a shrill and carrying one.

"No indeed, we may not! I beg of you, Aunt, do not –," but it was to no avail. Violette had no choice but to follow behind her aunt, and make her curtsy. Lord Winterbourne rose reluctantly to his feet as they approached.

"Lord Winterbourne – forgive me." Miss Felicia nodded merrily up at him, making the feathers in her bonnet dance. "We are not acquainted, exactly, but I would introduce you to my niece, Miss Violette deVere. Violette, dear, this is –."

He cut her off, abruptly. "We reside in the same county I believe I heard you say. A great many people are situated in Kent. I can hardly be expected to know each one of them, madam." He spoke in a drawl so considered it was on the verge of insulting; his tone was icily correct. He gave the tiniest bow of his head, his eyes averted – the most minimal gesture of acknowledgement, finely judged to be both courteous and dismissive.

"Come, Kit, Clara." His brother raised his head from his newspaper, and turned towards the door and the young lady joined him. "We are finished here, I think."

Miss Felicia blushed deeply. Tears started to her eyes. It was the most appalling snub, and so very public – by dinner time, everyone in town would know of her humiliation.

Violette was furious. How *dare* he slight her aunt in this way? She would force him into a conversation whether he wished it or not! She would *make* him be civil! She stepped directly into his path.

"Lord Winterbourne." She afforded him her most brilliant smile. "I wonder if you are familiar with the recent events regarding the river that bears your name? I myself witnessed its seasonable flooding a few weeks ago and nearly drowned. It made for a most thrilling adventure!

"I had not heard of it before and had to look it up in the encyclopaedia. It is a natural phenomenon, it seems. The river rises as if from nowhere after prolonged heavy rainfall, and –."

He stiffened. Over her head – it astonished her to notice that he was tall enough to look over her head – but over her head, as if speaking to himself, he murmured in a thoughtful undertone, "Quite extraordinarily plain. Argumentative, it seems. And worse than that – educated. Whatever were the parents thinking?"

And with that he turned, and stepped away and into the street.

CHAPTER 4

According to her aunt, Mrs Fitzallen's party was to be a simple, pleasant gathering of old friends. Violette had mixed feelings about it.

By now she was so well recovered from her illness that she was perfectly capable of spending an evening in company, and the novelty of doing nothing but read all day in her own company had worn thin. The thought of dancing filled her with dread, but her aunt assured her that if there were to be any dancing, it would be only for the young ones, and simple country dances at that, nothing too difficult to master, and in any event, no-one of any consequence would be attending.

'In other words,' thought Violette, with a wry smile to herself, 'I should not worry about the dancing. It is simple enough that even a dunce such as myself can manage, and in any case I will not be expected to stand up, for I am so very old for it. And even if I were to be asked to dance, I should not worry about making a fool of myself, for there will be no-one there to see it.'

She consoled herself that there was bound to be a good supper and it was rumoured that at her last party, Mrs Fitzallen had served ices. Violette played a strong hand at whist, so she was sure to be in demand at the card table. And she was very fond of music, and the Spanish Quartet would be playing; so all-in-all, it would be a deal more pleasant than another evening spent practising at the piano and listening to her aunt turning over the events of her day.

She wished that she could do something with her appearance, but what that would be she could not conceive and she went up to dress on Saturday afternoon with a heavy heart. Although she hoped against hope that somehow between ordering it in the shop and finding it in the box now lying upon her bed, the gown would have transformed itself into a thing of beauty, she doubted it greatly. 'If it is truly too hideous,' she thought, 'I shall do one of two things; cry off with the headache and spend another evening indoors, or wrap myself in a very large shawl and sit in the darkest corner I can find.'

Miss Felicia had been deeply distressed by Lord Winterbourne's behaviour at Madame Audabon's establishment. Upon his departure, she had sunk into a chair, dabbing at her eyes with her handkerchief. "It is my own silly fault, Violette dear; he is known as quite the most terrifying man in London. He is so very haughty that he hardly appears in public. It's said that for every ten invitations he receives, he refuses nine of them. To have Lord Winterbourne at one's ball is the very highest mark of distinction, and even then he stays only for the minimum number of dances that etiquette demands. His silence; his hauteur; his hair; his height! It is said that even the Prince of Wales is cowed by him, and Mr Brummel was recently heard to remark that Winterbourne's elegant simplicity of dress put him quite in the shade."

A footman materialised beside them, and Violette ordered a glass of Madeira to be brought for her aunt. Miss Felicia took a few reviving sips, and continued, "How I had the temerity to approach him I do not know. Whatever was I thinking? If I had been a man – well, it is a mercy that a gentleman cannot cut a lady, for I perfectly deserved the put-down."

"Aunt, you sound as if you are grateful to the horrible fellow! This talk of cuts and put-downs – I do not understand it at all!"

Miss Felicia explained. "A cut is an indication of being offended by another's behaviour. There is the cut indirect. A gentleman might see another gentleman walking towards him, but turn his head or cross the road, feigning ignorance of his presence. A gentleman can cut only another gentleman – not a lady, and not his social inferiors.

"A lady can cut a gentleman but it calls for extreme provocation. It suggests that his behaviour has been so insulting that he has quite overstepped the bounds of decency. The very worst thing is the cut direct. One looks a gentleman full in the face, and pretends to neither see nor hear him. It is the very height of insult, comparable to the slash of a sword, dividing them forever. It's dreadful to witness; the person being cut can never recover their reputation. It can lead to one gentleman calling another out!

"I have never forgotten seeing –," her voice shook, and she dabbed at her eyes with her handkerchief, "I saw your own grandfather give the cut direct when he came upon – someone – in the street. And that person departed immediately for the Continent, and never came home more."

All around them was gossip and laughter and chit chat, but Violette and her aunt sat as if in a quiet bubble. After a moment, Violette asked, "Was it my father?"

"It was. My brother Charles, whom I loved dearly. We came upon him walking through Pall Mall with your mamma upon his arm. She was wearing a hat with a purple feather. I remember it so well; for some reason it seemed the hat was what inflamed papa the most."

Miss Felicia sipped at her wine, and managed a tremulous smile. "My goodness. I don't know why I should be so upset; it was such a very long time ago and hardly the same as Lord Winterbourne's behaviour. He snubbed me, that's all. No doubt my humiliation will be spoken of, but it will have no lasting effect. It was nicely judged on his part; he is the absolute master of etiquette."

"It seems perfectly ridiculous, and almost sounds as if you admire him for it, Aunt!" Violette couldn't help but laugh at her aunt's earnest expression.

"I didn't like it. But it is how society functions, and perhaps I deserved it."

Violette's smile vanished. "No, Aunt! You did not deserve such treatment, and I despise him for it!"

Violette had not possessed the heart to be firm with her aunt after that. Miss Felicia had lost all delight in her shopping expedition by now, saying only, with a sad attempt at gaiety, "Perhaps we are not quite ready to look at these new designs. A shade of mauve will be perfectly suitable, and it is after all a pretty conceit, to match the colour to your name."

Violette had therefore acceded to an evening dress of a dull slub, in a shade somewhere between magenta and purple, with puffed sleeves and a trim of cream-coloured lace. So it was with a sigh of resignation that she untied the string around the box, and took away the paper. But her gown was not there! There was nothing in any shade of violet at all, not mauve, not lilac, not lavender, heather, purple, heliotrope, ashes of roses or anything else.

Instead, she shook out a gown of heavy silk crêpe de chine, champagne coloured, with short sleeves in a tailored style; the whole thing quite astonishingly plain. The beauty was in the fabric, and the colour, and the cut. In short it was a truly lovely garment, and Violette's heart sank with something like despair. 'Such a beautiful gown,' she thought, 'and delivered to me in error. No doubt some other poor girl has taken delivery of the ghastly purple monstrosity, and is even now in floods of tears and being consoled by her maid!'

But it was not an error. It was not from Madame Audabon's establishment, at all. The label on it was that of a fashionable London dressmaker and it was addressed in the firmest of hands; *Miss V deVere*, and with the correct address. And there was a note. *To honour my debt - D.*

Violette stared at the note in some bewilderment. "What debt? Who is D?" and then she remembered the leaping flames, and that voice, low and urgent, "I am in your debt."

"Death," he had said.

She quivered at the memory of those cold fingers on her face, and looked around her, as if he might be watching her from some corner of the room; and she felt the heat spread throughout her body, turning her limbs liquid.

Nestled in the tissue paper were gloves, and there was a bandeau of bronze and gold striped silk, to be fastened with a gold pin, and a fan painted in the oriental style, with a design of white birds upon a gold ground. The final touch was a long length of fabric in sable-colour velvet, to drape across her arms as an evening stole.

Violette held the dress in front of her, and stared at her reflection in the mirror. There was a tap at the door, and Hill entered. She stopped in her tracks. "Why – Miss Lettie! Is this your dress for the evening? How elegant!"

Violette held out the bandeau. "This came with it. To tie up my hair, I suppose. But I have no idea how to do it, for the dress is so beautiful, and my hair is not and never would be!"

"But the colour – oh, Miss Lettie, the colour of the dress brings out the colour of your hair something lovely!" It was true. The combination of soft candlelight and the champagne shade of the gown brought a warm copper-coloured glow to Lettie's hair.

Sarah Hill was of an age with Violette's aunt, and had been with Felicia de Vere since she was a girl of fourteen. Hill had fond memories of Miss Felicia's London Season. She had been the prettiest of young ladies, with a complexion of peaches and cream, as light on her feet as a fairy, and with a passionate fondness for clothes and the latest styles. Those thrilling days had come to an abrupt end, following her father's rage at his disobedient son, and poor Miss Felica had been sequestered away in the Kentish countryside. But she had never lost her taste for the London fashions. She still subscribed to *The Lady's Magazine* and other periodicals, and she and Hill would often spend a pleasant hour looking over the fashion plates together. And now Hill was seized with an outrageous and astonishing idea.

"Miss Lettie. I have an idea for your hair. I think we should cut if off."

"Cut off my hair?" Violette gaped at her. "But it is grown down to my waist!"

"Miss, with respect, who's to know how long is your hair? You wear it every day tied back in no style at all. Your hair does not exist. Perhaps if there was not the weight of it, it would curl more naturally.

"It is the very latest thing for ladies of fashion to wear their hair cropped! *A la victime*, they call it, or sometimes a guillotine cut, or a Titus cut. They say that when the poor noble ladies in Paris went to have their heads chopped off, they chopped off their hair first. Lady Caroline Lamb has hers so, and Lady Rutland has followed the fashion as well. And – oh!" Hill stopped dead. "I'm so sorry Miss. I clean forgot. You probably knew someone who had their head chopped off. I didn't mean to offend."

"No. I didn't know anyone who – who died like that." Violette hesitated a moment. "Do you think it would suit me? What if it looks dreadful?"

"I'll cut it short – shorter, that is. To begin. And you can see if you like it. If not, there will still be enough to tie back, and no-one will be able to tell. Or we could fashion a turban style headdress, perhaps," finished Hill, doubtfully.

So it was done. Violette's hair was released from its pins and it tumbled free, a crackling bright mass that stood out around her shoulders like a veil. Hill gathered up a great handful of it. Violette held her breath, and perhaps Hill did too and at the first loud rasp of the scissors they both let out a little scream of shock. But then Violette felt the heavy weight of her hair depart, and a breath of cool air on her neck. Her head felt unnaturally light, as if it would float away from her shoulders. She stared at her reflection in the looking-glass. Her eyes were

42

bright, her cheeks flushed. "More! Cut it off! Cut it all! The whole lot!"

Hill wielded the scissors again. Released from its crippling weight, Violette's hair sprang into soft curls that framed her face and softened her jawline. Hill took the bandeau and fastened it around Violette's head, teasing the curls through. Then she helped Violette into her gown.

The rich fabric slid across Violette's body in one fluid, heavy movement, cool and caressing. Her breath caught in her throat as she stared at her reflection in the glass. Could this truly be her? Here was a woman of sublime poise and refinement. Not beautiful – something more. Seductive. She was transported to the world of the ballroom; the yearning sweetness of the violin as the bow slid smoothly across its strings; the intoxicating perfume of hothouse lilies, their unsullied white petals gleaming in the light of a hundred candles. She shivered at the thought of a man's eyes upon her and his hand taking hers and leading her away to the dance.

Hill clapped her hands, and the spell was broken. "Miss Lettie, you look so very elegant, I would hardly know you for the same – oh, beg pardon Miss! I didn't mean no offence!"

Violette smiled at her through the mirror. "Don't worry, Hill. I scarce recognise myself!" She turned back to the box, and took out her gloves and drew them on. Her eyes were caught by the note.

"I always pay my debts," he'd said. "Death, at your service." Who was he, this Captain Death? And how had he known where to find her?

CHAPTER 5

Mrs Fitzallen was thrown into a spin. Her musical evening was intended to be an informal gathering of twenty or so of her close acquaintance. They'd listen to the Spanish Quartet and enjoy a lavish supper before the card tables were set out; this was the real point of the evening, for Mrs Fitzallen had developed an absolute passion for the newly fashionable game of Commerce. It had as many variations of play as one could wish, and having been recently introduced to yet another, she was eager to impart this knowledge to her fellow enthusiasts.

No doubt a few of the young ladies would entertain the company with an air or two at the pianoforte; and if a set could be got up, there would be some dancing, but this was not in any way an event that would attract the attention of the upper echelons of the Ton. So she was astonished – appalled, in fact – to learn that Lady Clara Taverner was a fervent admirer of Spanish music, and would appreciate an invitation, and that should such an invitation be forthcoming, Lady Clara would be escorted by her brother, Lord Winterbourne.

This gentleman was notorious for his scathing put downs and considered the very arbiter of taste. He was known to be scrupulous in his choice of entertainments on offer to him and said to turn down any invitation for an entertainment taking place upon a moonless night, on the grounds that he would not risk his wardrobe at the hands of some random footpad or highwayman who might be lurking under cover of darkness. Why he should wish to attend a simple musical evening with cards, Mrs Fitzallen could not begin to imagine.

Upon receipt of this news, relayed over a cup of chocolate at the Pump Rooms by an old school friend whose daughter knew someone who was acquainted with the Taverners – for so these things are arranged – Mrs Fitzallen gasped herself into the vapours, and had to be revived with the liberal application of salts and the consumption of a large glass of sherry wine.

She rushed home and screamed at her cook to arrange for strawberry ices – "But, madam, there is not a strawberry to be had in the whole of the country, for it is December!" – and screamed at a somewhat bemused Mr Fitzallen to send round to the wine merchant and order his best champagne. She screamed at her maid to revive her ostrich feathers by whatever means possible, or else to run – yes, *run*, to Madame Audabon's to obtain new – "No matter the expense! If they have them dyed in a sort of honey shade to match my gown that would be best, or if not, then perhaps a blue, but white will do at a pinch!" and screamed at her husband again, to go to his safe and fetch out her good sapphires. And if he had pledged them to the bank, as he had been wont to do upon occasion, then he was to find whatever means necessary to retrieve them.

Violette and her aunt arrived at Mrs Fitzallen's to find that lady in all splendour with her sapphires in full attendance and ostrich feathers waving. They were greeted in an absent sort of way, as if Mrs Fitzallen was preoccupied with who might come in the door behind them, and helped to champagne, and seats were found for them. The Spanish Quartet struck up with a loud crash of chords on a guitar, which made Mrs Fitzallen jump and let out a strangled scream.

Listening to these rustic airs, Violette was reminded of the narrow, heat-soaked streets of St Cloud. It had been a shock, upon her father's death, to discover that she was heir to her grandfather's fortune, a condition of which was that she was to take up residence in England; but she was excited to embark upon the adventure of this new life with an aunt she had never met, in a country she had never visited.

She mourned the loss of her father, as she had her mother before, genuinely, but with no very great depth of emotion. They'd been fond parents, but too much wrapped up in their affection for one another to have much time for their only child. They'd lived a merry life of entertainments and pleasures with their friends which had hardly included her, and with no governess or nurse to answer to, Violette had been left free to immerse herself in her father's library or roam the countryside with the village children. After her mother's death, her father had become a more distant figure still, devoted to his hobbies and passions, and so in many respects her life had been one of some solitude.

But it was a sweet memory to picture the village square of St Cloud; a central fountain surrounded by narrow houses constructed of pale stone that glowed in the sun, their balconies flower-bedecked. There was always some acquaintance of her father at work here with his easel or sketchbook, and the warm evening air would carry with it the scents of oregano and thyme. A musician would be playing, for the simple enjoyment of it, and maybe a glass of wine or two, the plaintive thrum of his guitar echoed by insistent chirrup of the cicadas.

Violette lapsed into a pleasantly nostalgic half-dream, but after a while she became aware of the strangest of sensations at the back of her neck – a prickling feeling, as if eyes were upon her. She could hardly twist around in her seat to look; her enjoyment of the music was spoiled, and she began to feel more and more uncomfortable. In the end she could not bear it, and could think of nothing else but to wonder who it was that was staring at her so intently. A footman was moving among the guests with a tray of champagne, and upon the pretence of catching his eye, Violette held her fan to her face and twisted somewhat in her seat to look about her.

Leaning nonchalantly against the doorframe with his eyes fixed upon her was the unmistakable figure of Lord Winterbourne. When Violette caught his eye, he gave the most imperceptible of nods.

Violette looked away immediately, and then wished she had not. 'I should have played him at his own game and cut him dead with an icy stare!' she thought. 'And it's too late now. Oh, how very vexing!'

For someone who delighted in Spanish music, Lady Clara was a surprisingly inattentive listener. As soon as the last chord was played, she jumped to her feet with an audible sigh of relief. The party went in to supper, Violette determinedly not looking to see where Lord Winterbourne was or what he was doing. 'He may stare at me all he likes,' she said to herself, in a fury, 'But I most assuredly shall not give him the satisfaction of noticing!'

After supper, the party broke up a little. The card tables were set out, and one of the Fitzallen daughters crossed to the piano and started upon a Scotch ballad. A gentleman of portly stature and dressed much in the fashion of the previous century, resplendent in satin breeches and powdered wig, joined her at the piano and sang along tunelessly with the chorus, much to her bemusement. After she had brought the Scotch ballad to a rapid and thankful end, her place was taken by a young man employed for the purpose of providing music for the dance. He launched into some gayer airs, and there was a scurry to and fro as partners were secured and assembled themselves into a set.

No-one asked for Violette, which she minded not at all. Happy to sit and observe, to her surprise she found the chair beside her taken by none other than Clara Taverner.

"I hope you do not mind if I address you, even though we have not been introduced. We arrived so late and the music had started and we had to creep in like mice. My brother would fuss so with his hair, which would not fall to his liking! But we have met, though you may not remember, at Madame Audabon's. That is, not met, precisely. You were engaged in conversation with my brother, and I thought you looked a most interesting person, and wished that we could speak. But I was only there to collect some ribbon, and it was such a crush of people and you seemed very engaged. I cannot think your gown from that establishment? It really is of the most decided taste; I would have it for a London gown, to be sure." This was delivered in a rush, between mouthfuls of coffee ice.

Upon leaving the supper table Lady Clara had congratulated her hostess on the ices. "I declare I never had a coffee ice before, only ever strawberry in the summer, which everyone serves, so very dull; and this is delicious! 1 shall tell our cook to send round for the receipt, and have it served at our next entertainment, and make sure to tell everyone that I ate it first at Mrs Fitzallen's!" Mrs Fitzallen was quite overcome, and had sent a maid straightaway to the kitchen to fetch another serving and pressed it upon Lady Clara.

She was now holding the bowl in one hand and wielding the spoon in the other, and laughing all the while. "I declare this is such a novel way of eating, perched upon a chair quite like Miss Muffet upon her tuffet, though what a tuffet could be I have no idea.

"In French, the expression is *la touffe d'herbe*. It means a little grassy hill," volunteered Violette.

Lady Clara looked startled for a moment. "My goodness – I had quite forgot you are French. You don't sound it at all, for you speak English beautifully."

Violette laughed. "My father was English, and we had English visitors to our home all the time."

"Oh – the artists! Yes of course." This was said rather doubtfully. Lady Clara continued, artlessly, "But I don't mind that. You seem a very respectable person all the same, and my brother said you were very clever."

Violette was taken aback to think that Lord Winterbourne had mentioned her to his sister, but she had no opportunity to ponder on it, for Lady Clara continued, "Who knew it could be such fun to eat an ice and watch the dancing at the same time? I shall make it quite the fashion, I daresay. Though if anyone comes to ask for me, I shall have to refuse most decided, for I do not know what I should do with my spoon!"

This last was delivered in a cascade of giggles. Violette decided that she rather liked Lady Clara. It suddenly occurred to her that she had been leading a very quiet life since leaving her home in France and that the company of her aunt and her aunt's friends in Kent was, perhaps, a little dull.

"Do you know," Violette ventured, "I believe I have seen your house. It was but a few weeks since. I was walking up on the Downs and looked over to see a most magnificent white house, though the park and gardens were sadly flooded."

"That is our house! But we have hardly been there this last year or more. Lord Winterbourne has such dealings in Town, you know and so he travels a great deal, and my brother is gone to the Naval Academy in Portsmouth. And since our mother died some eighteen months ago, I have been staying with some cousins – distant in nature, for I never met them before arriving on their doorstep, and distant in geography, too, for they are in Scotland.

"But at long last I am let out of the schoolroom and am here for the winter to make some new acquaintance. It will be my birthday in the spring, and I shall be eighteen, and then I shall embark upon my first London season with all the parties and balls and I cannot wait!"

Their conversation was interrupted, for at that moment Mr Fitzallen arrived before Violette's chair to effect an introduction to a man of middling age dressed in his scarlet and black, who would engage her to stand up with him for the next dance. Violette was too startled to refuse, and stood, to discover that he was also of middling height, and she a good head taller than he. Courteously enough, he bowed over her hand and led her to the floor. The music started up again and away they went down the line.

A travelling show had once arrived in St Cloud sur Mer, with a dancing giraffe. Upon seeing it, a friend of her mamma's had let out a scream of laughter so that heads had turned, and in a loud voice she had cried, "*Voila! C'est Violette, non?* The legs going in all directions!"

This unhappy memory returned now in full force, and the more Violette attempted to concentrate on the steps and the changes of partner, the clumsier she found herself. Her embarrassment was made worse by the fear that she might raise her head to see Lord Winterbourne lolling against the wall and examining her performance through his quizzing glass. Torn between fear of the quizzing glass and frustration at the steps, she scowled her way through the set, trying her best to choke back tears of humiliation.

The line consisted of a dozen couples or more, and long before the end was in sight she wished herself anywhere away and for the torture to be over. There was one more change to be made before the dance came to its conclusion. She turned away to her left to join her new partner. He took her hand in his. A shock ran through her. She raised her head to meet his eyes.

"Lord Winterbourne!" she said.

"Miss deVere," he answered.

His eyes were the palest of pale grey, the colour of a clouded sky reflected in a pool of still water, and the black lashes that framed them were such that a girl would envy. His white hair was arranged so that the curls fell, as if by happy accident, in a deceptively tousled arrangement. And he smelled delicious; not of the heavily perfumed colognes that other men adopted, but as if he had stepped indoors from a frosted winter's night.

He cleared his throat. He clasped her other hand in his, and away they went down the line once more. If Violette had thought that her embarrassment in the dance could be no worse, she was wrong.

Even though Violette was completely taken up with what her feet were doing, she could still appreciate that to either side of her, couples were smiling at one another and exchanging remarks as they met in the dance and separated again, and there were flirtatious glances exchanged, but she and Lord Winterbourne danced in excruciating silence. She chanced a quick look at his countenance when, yet again, she stumbled and clutched hold of his hand to steady herself, and saw his perfect composure ruffled with a raised eyebrow.

Violette racked her brains for some witty comment, and then for any comment at all. The lack of conversation between them began to loom larger and larger in her mind until she felt her lips frozen in a rictus smile, as if no words would ever escape them again. With one more change, she found herself back with her original partner. He escorted her back to her aunt, found her a glass of punch, and made his departure.

Violette fanned herself violently for a moment or two. When she had regained her composure, and dared to lift her head once more and look around her, it was to note that of Clara Taverner there was no sign; and none, now, of her brother.

Next day, Lady Clara paid a morning call, accompanied by a sour-looking lady.

"This is Miss Flint. She and my mamma were cousins by marriage or some such, and poor Miss Flint has come all the way from the north to keep me company, which must be a most vexatious task!" Lady Clara laughed, but her cousin seemed unamused, staring into the middle distance with a disapproving expression on her face. "Oh, and do call me Clara, I beseech you – Lady Clara is such a mouthful. Or even Clarrie, which is what my naughty brother calls me. He says it's because he once knew a cow by the same name. He is the most ridiculous tease!"

Violette could not imagine the haughty Lord Winterbourne calling his sister such a name or for such a reason, but Clara hastened to add, "Oh, not Richard, he is so frightfully stiff, he would not countenance it. No indeed, my brother Christopher – Mr Kit Taverner. He's my twin, and when he finishes his studies at the Academy next year, he'll be joining his ship as an officer. It's his dream to travel right around the world, and I'm sure he'll do it! He has the most adventurous nature. When we were children he was always leading me into terrible scrapes."

Her visit was brief, as was the custom when calling for the first time. She had come to say goodbye. "It's a shame, when we have just met so recently; but for the first time since our mother died we shall all be together for Christmas and spending the holiday in the country. I hope we shall meet again, either in London during the Season or in the country perhaps. Oh, Miss deVere, I *do* hope we shall be the very greatest of friends!"

And with that, she took her leave.

CHAPTER 6

Violette and her aunt returned from Bath remarkably refreshed, and life settled back into its usual routine. The days lengthened into spring, and Violette began to assume the mantle of the lady of a large house; talking to the gardener about repairs to the disused hothouse, with the idea of growing grapes and peaches, and discussing menus with the cook. In truth, she felt something of an imposter, and was soon happy to return these responsibilities to her aunt, who had been running the household for so many years. But at the start of March, John approached her.

"It's coming up the first Friday of the month, Miss Violette, and the horse market will be at Canterbury. We have the pony for the pony-and-trap, and we have the carriage horses, but I have two lads beneath me in the stables with hardly enough to keep them busy. I wonder if you had thought of a mare for riding out? It's nice exercise for a young lady and I know you to be fond of the fresh air. Or hunting perhaps? Back in your grandfather's day, begging your pardon, the Boxing Day meet would start from Sumbourne Manor. It was the custom then for her ladyship to ride out with the gentlemen to the first jumps and back. I have a friend who tells me there is a nice-behaved mare and a couple of good hunters going up for auction." He tapped the side of his nose, knowingly. "From a big house. A quiet sale, if you get my meaning. The gentleman owner is said to be in dibs to the bank."

Miss Felicia was all excitement at the idea of a trip to Canterbury. "We could stay overnight at The Falstaff Inn. It's a respectable establishment, my dear, or so John tells me, and quite suitable for ladies on their own. It's a coaching inn, so we shall see the London stage come in. There are some pretty shops in the town and I shall be able to match my embroidery silks; and I should like to find a new bonnet for the summer. We shall take Hill with us, of course."

So it was decided. Early the next Thursday they set out, and by midday they were drawing into the courtyard of The Falstaff. It was everything that could be desired. It was a solid square sort of place, half-timbered in the style that was the fashion in the days of Good Queen Bess. Between it and the great stone archway of the West Gate leading into the city centre, was a fast-flowing tributary of the River Stour, so that the entrance into the town was approached over a picturesque little bridge. The narrow riverbank had been planted with flowers to make a garden and the whole had an air of antiquity and romance that appealed greatly to Violette. "This is most delightful, aunt," she said, looking about her with pleasure. "It seems to me that the inn here and our own home at Sumbourne must be of an age!"

The two ladies spent a happy afternoon looking at the shops and visiting the Cathedral. Violette purchased a copy of Master Chaucer's book of *The Canterbury Tales*, set in a heavy black type and written in the original ancient English tongue. So authentic was it in appearance that it was virtually impossible to read; luckily on the facing page was a translation provided for those of a less scholarly disposition.

They looked at the place where the knights were said to have struck down the saint, Thomas à Becket, and looked at the tomb of the Black Prince, and admired the views from the old city walls; and found a delightful milliner with styles said to be the latest from London.

Violette purchased a chipstraw hat for the summer, trimmed with lemon-coloured ribbons and with gloves to match. Miss Felicia admired the hat, but Violette felt that her admiration was somewhat subdued, and the answer was quickly discovered. For as they were moving towards the door, Miss Felicia drew Violette's attention to a leaf-green silk confection fantastically trimmed with velvet cherries. "I have been admiring this beautiful bonnet, Violette dear. Is it not the prettiest thing you ever saw?" Almost without knowing she was doing it, Miss Felicia put out a wistful hand to stroke it, as one would pet a beloved lapdog or a kitten.

"Aunt, that bonnet is perfection itself. You must have it!"

"Oh, no! It is the most dreadful extravagance! I cannot think of it!" replied her aunt, firmly, and Violette said no more. But when they arrived back at their lodgings and her aunt slipped upstairs to her room, Violette found John and sent him back to the shop.

The two ladies were in the parlour with the tea tray, when there was a gentle knock at the door and the maid entered. "Miss," addressing Violette, "your groom is below and asks me to tell you that he has collected your parcel and asks what he should do with it."

"Tell him to bring it up!" Violette returned, and clapped her hands with excitement. When John arrived with the hatbox, she couldn't wait, but presented it to her aunt as a gift.

Miss Felicia was quite overcome. "My dear! You are generosity itself!" She lifted the bonnet from its box, running her finger lovingly over the gay white and pink striped ribbon that accompanied the silk cherries, "Oh – but I can't accept it! I can think of no occasion when I would wear it!"

"Nonsense," said Violette, firmly. "Try it on!" Miss Felicia needed no more encouragement. She stepped across to the looking glass hanging above the mantle, and put the bonnet on. Violette clapped her hands. Quite without knowing she did it, she called to John, "Is it not the prettiest sight? Tell my aunt, John, that she must have it!" and to her aunt,

"It might sit in its box for a while; but one day it will be the absolutely perfect bonnet for the occasion!"

"It's most becoming, Miss," John answered, stiffly; "but if you'll excuse me, I must go and see to the horses."

They rose early next morning to attend the horse market, which was situated just at the old St George's Gate on the southern side of the city walls. John being a Canterbury man, he told them of the outcry when it was recently decided to demolish the old gate to make way for a new water-works to supply the city.

"There were two great round towers here, and when I was a boy, this was a gaol, and men were taken from it to be hanged at the market cross. There are those who pride themselves on being new and ahead of the times, and those who wish to preserve the past; and I suppose there will always be a clash between them."

Builders were hard at work constructing the new drain, and what with the noise of their banging and crashing, and the sheep baaing and the cows lowing – for it was a market for cattle just as much as horses – and horses neighing and the pieman shouting – "Hot pies a penny! Hot pies a penny!" and what seemed, all-in-all, a general mayhem, Miss Felicia wondered that perhaps it was not a suitable place for ladies, and somewhat regretted this part of the outing.

"There are no other ladies here at all, Lettie dear! That is – I mean ladies of – of quality." She turned her eyes hurriedly away from the early-morning girls in their flounces and feathers, yawning at the entrance to the alehouse. "And I see why, for it really has a most unpleasant odour to the air. Perhaps we have made an error in coming. I beg you, let us remain in the carriage, and John can go and see the horses, my dear."

Violette had no such qualms. "It's all very well, Aunt, to wish we had a gentleman with us to undertake such matters, but the fact is that we do not. I quite understand that John Hill and his sister have been with you for so many years that you consider them almost as part of the family, but the truth is that we cannot expect them to help us run our lives. It's vulgar to speak of money, but I shall. I have come into an inheritance, and am determined to see with my own eyes how it is to be spent.

"I shall go and look at the horses with John. I'll be perfectly safe in his company and you may stay here in the care of the coachman, who is armed with his whip. Indeed, Aunt, the crowd is composed of respectable gentlemen. There are no ruffians here to worry you!"

Violette alighted from the carriage, leaving her aunt with a scented handkerchief to hold to her nose, and went with John to inspect the horses herself. She was hardly a horsewoman; she was content enough to take John's opinion on a purchase, and listened with half an ear while he talked of withers and hocks and goodness only knew what else. She decided against the hunters. "I would not know how to hunt, and would feel most sorry for the poor fox," she said, consideringly, but was very taken with the look of the glossy bay mare, and stood back a little to allow John to negotiate a price for her, and arrange for the horse's delivery.

The carriage stood a good distance away from the worst of the hustle-and-bustle. Upon spying Violette making her way back through the throng, her aunt stepped out of it to join her and was given a great start upon being addressed by name.

"Miss deVere! It is – is it not? Miss Felicia, if I may make so bold! I vow I would know that pretty smile anywhere!" This startling declaration was delivered by a gentleman of fine bearing, with a hearty set of grey whiskers. There was something about him of the Military, perhaps. As Violette joined them, he bowed deeply to both ladies, and laughed at Miss Felicia's look of puzzlement.

"You do not know me. Perhaps I have changed so very much. But you knew me once, and looked upon me most fondly, my dear."

"Lieutenant Jennings? Can it be you?" There passed across her aunt's face such a look of astonishment – and something like joy – that of a sudden Violette could see the young girl she once had been.

"Indeed. Though Major Jennings I was when I left the service."

"Not wounded out, I hope?"

"No, my dear. Pensioned out. I had done my thirty years, and seen enough of the world."

"And you live here?"

"I do. I have a house not so very far distant. And I wonder – I am engaged upon business just now, and must away. But I should so like to see you. Perhaps I might invite you, and your companion, of course, to dine with me this evening? If you would care to."

The exchange had been so rapid, and her aunt so very flustered, that Violette had not been introduced. Now she spoke up. "I must introduce myself, it seems! I am Violette, Miss deVere's niece, and I am sure I speak for us both when I say we should be very happy to dine; but do you not need to consult Mrs Jennings? I am sure your wife would be somewhat startled to have guests thrust upon her, so out of the blue!"

It was clear that Miss Felicia had not considered the presence of a Mrs Jennings. Her face clouded over in an instant and then brightened upon his reply. "I am not – I never did marry!" accompanied by a most meaningful look; only for her expression to give way once more to doubt, at the propriety of two single ladies dining with a single gentleman in his own home.

Major Jennings recollected himself. "My sister will be there. You will remember Sally, I am sure, and she keeps house for me now. And who could object to an old friend wishing to renew a long ago – and if you will permit me to say, much cherished – acquaintance? Miss deVere, pray impress upon your aunt how very proper it will be."

So it was decided, and John was sent to arrange for another night's stay at the inn.

Major Jennings lived at Oare, a tiny hamlet on the coast about halfway between Canterbury and the next town of Faversham. The ladies alighted from the carriage, looking about them with some interest. It appeared that Oare consisted of nothing more than a few houses and an inn, situated on a spit of pebbly land jutting out into the water and surrounded by marshes. Gulls screamed overhead, and there was the plaintive two-note cry of the curlew, but other than that, and the sound of the waves lapping gently at the stones, all was silence.

Miss Felicia murmured to her niece that it seemed a most desolate place; but Major Jennings was all enthusiasm. He escorted them towards the end of the spit, where some small boats were moored, and pointed out his own. "I like to fish and I potter, by which I mean, I row a little this way and a little that. After all those years in the Army, it seems I have joined the Navy, now!"

The sun low on the horizon made the waves gold-tipped, and a skein of geese winged overhead, their honking cries fading behind them. Despite her aunt's distaste for the place, Violette felt that there was something bracing about the salt air blowing off the marsh. To her it seemed a wild and lonely habitation, filled with the promise of adventure, and vastly romantic.

Major Jennings' house was surrounded by gardens, though with not a flower to be seen. "I see you are questioning my gardens. Not pleasure gardens at all but all filled with vegetables! This is my hobby, and I am intent on developing a new type of onion which will prevent that stinging of the eyes that is such a problem in its preparation."

Neither lady had ever had cause to deal with an onion, and knew not quite how to reply to this ambition. But although his hobby might be humble, his house was something grand. It was a veritable mansion, built of red brick and the roof positively festooned with chimneys in a variety of decorative styles. Major Jennings ushered his guests into a darkly panelled hallway, and thence into a drawing room richly furnished, though in a distinctly old-fashioned style. Elaborately-carved oak furniture and high-backed settles cushioned with faded embroideries in dark colours gave a decidedly oppressive air.

"You are surprised at my style of living. But if you remember," he nodded at Miss Felicia, "I had expectations from my great-aunt. Though your father thought them no more than moonshine – well, enough of that, my dear, things are as they are, and we cannot help them. Oh, and Miss Felicia, you will remember my sister! Miss Violette, allow me to present Miss Sally Jennings, my sister, who keeps house for me, and a good job she makes of it, too!"

Miss Jennings was a wraith of a woman; thin and small, with a long nose which reminded Violette of a beak. Her resemblance to a bird was emphasised by her manner of nodding her head when she spoke in a kind of pecking motion, as if to emphasise that she was correct in her opinions and no-one should think to disagree with her.

They were served a dish of oysters. "From Whitstable, just along the coast from here, and fresh today," said Major Jennings.

"A dreadful price, and the man who sells them has a reputation as a cheat, but he knows how to deal with me, he does!" Miss Jennings' head bobbed.

There was a roast chicken and peas. "From the garden. Last year's crop, but my sister is skilled in preserves," said Major Jennings, proudly.

"Delightful, so sweet and delicious," offered Miss Felicia, to be greeted by a dismissive snort from Miss Jennings; "You would not be so complimentary if you had to pick over a bucket of peas, Miss Felicia, indeed you would not!" Just as she had never dealt with an onion, so Felica deVere had never picked over a bucket of peas and no reply was forthcoming.

Violette thought she would contribute to the conversation. "It is so very quaint here, and quiet. We drove through the prettiest of woods, with a positive carpet of snowdrops to each side of the lane, yet I understand you to be but a mile from the next town?"

Miss Felicia turned to Miss Jennings. "I daresay Faversham is a pretty kind of place, and is there good shopping there, and a reputable tea merchant? We have a very good pastry cook in Folkestone. They make an exceedingly delicious Scotch shortbread. I seem to remember you fond of Scotch shortbread, Miss Jennings, when we were girls. The next time I am there, I shall procure you some."

Miss Jennings stared at her. "I have enough to occupy myself here," she said with finality, "and I do not see the sense in gadding about and wasting money. We are not all cursed with the sin of gluttony, nor blessed with a bottomless purse."

With that, she rang the bell for the girl to come and clear the plates away, and Miss Felicia, who was enjoying her dinner and had not finished eating, hastily laid down her fork with no little regret.

After dinner, they repaired to the drawing room and tea was brought in – 'a very inferior blend,' Miss Felicia noted, sadly – and Major Jennings told them of his new post. He was with the Excise office in Faversham, and travelled all over Kent from inn to inn with his two officers. "Known as 'gaugers', for they are employed to taste the beer and calculate if it had been watered down, 'gauging its strength', if you like. And that is an occupation that many men like to apply for, thinking it to be a very merry task indeed; but it is a difficult life, for we are roundly abused in our office." He stopped to take a mouthful of tea.

"Why should you be abused?" asked Violette.

"We are catchers of smugglers, my dear young lady! Those men who infest the coastline in these parts, and bring in goods from the Continent under cover of a moonless night. Aye, and a cargo or two of escaping Frenchies when the Terror was at its height!"

"Why should they smuggle? I understand how they would wish to save those fleeing the guillotine. That sounds to me a most heroic and compassionate deed! But I do not understand about the rest."

Major Jennings frowned. "They didn't save those Frenchies out of compassion, my dear, but for the jewels they were paid in. Scoundrels, to be profiting by others' misfortunes."

"But were they not putting their own lives in danger? Doesn't it suggest the old maxim that the end justifies the means? By which, I mean that the smugglers took a great risk to save lives, so maybe they were justified in taking payment for that risk? If they had families of their own to provide for, surely?"

"You are very decided in your opinions, Miss Violette!" Miss Sally Jennings frowned at the sight of Miss Felicia helping herself to a second lump of sugar. Miss Felicia dropped the sugar tongs immediately, and stirred her cup vigorously to hide her confusion.

Violette bit her lip. She felt that they were on the verge of a disagreement, and it was not her place to be so outspoken and to argue with her host. The memory of Lord Winterbourne, and his voice – appalled, dismissive – came into her mind. *'Educated. What were the parents thinking?'* She subsided into silence, blushing hotly.

Miss Felicia steered the conversation away from this philosophical powder keg. "It's the taxes, Lettie dear. They really are quite fierce upon the pocket, and each year the tax is imposed upon something new, so that every single thing, from bricks to buttons, is more expensive by the day. It can have a most disastrous effect upon a household budget."

Major Jennings laughed. "I cannot see you purchasing bricks, Miss Felicia!" He turned to Violette. "But your aunt is quite right about the taxation. It's everyone's patriotic duty to pay their taxes. They are determined by the King himself, and we have seen in France what happens when the King's authority is undermined!

"The smugglers wish to evade the tax, d'you see. They buy goods on the Continent at a low price, and bring them to sell here. By evading the customs' tax they can make a good profit by undercutting the reputable and law-abiding tradesmen. And yes! They do indeed undermine the authority of the King, which in my mind is something close to treason! And what is worse, they are helped in this treasonous law-breaking by the ordinary people of England. They are given shelter by those who should know better, and even the most respectable of people buy their goods and support their wicked trade."

"Goodness me!" Miss Felicia felt quite faint. Who would have thought that sending John down to The Dragon to purchase a pound of tea would be – in Major Jennings' words – '*something close to treason*'? She thought of the rose-scented soap she liked, and cook's liberal use of sugar and sherry wine to make a Tipsy Pudding, of which she was very fond.

It suddenly came to her that she would like nothing better than for this conversation to be at an end, and for her to be at home in her own bed, with the covers up to her chin and the front door firmly shut and bolted. 'From this day on,' she resolved, 'I shall give up rose soap and sugar, and we shall economise our housekeeping. It is my patriotic duty! For I most assuredly do not wish to be clapped in irons and taken off to the town gaol!'

Major Jennings was fired up. He was not to be stopped. "I am out to catch the wickedest of them all; a great dark fellow with a great black dog, name of Cap'n Death – the fellow, not the dog. And I'll find him, aye, you may be sure of it. There's a bounty on his head, one hundred guineas for the fellow that catches him and takes him to justice, dead or alive, it's no matter! And that fellow will be me!"

Violette let out an audible gasp, and covered it up by swallowing a great mouthful of tea. Such was her haste that it went down the wrong way and led to a furious fit of coughing which left her with streaming eyes.

With attention successfully diverted from this unfortunate subject, and Miss Felica fussing Violette for fear of a chill, the carriage was sent for and the two ladies took their leave. And they sat side by side, each in an appalled and reflective silence, all the way back to the Falstaff Inn.

Violette had never told anyone of the true nature of the adventure that had befallen her, that day up on the Downs. She had given out that she had simply lost her footing and fallen in the river, and then, cold and lost with the rain falling so heavily, she had stumbled upon the shepherds' hut and taken refuge there. As to the story of being found by a black-chinned ruffian, she said, stoutly, that she had no recollection of any such thing, and the first she knew was the arrival at the shepherds' hut of the innkeeper and his wife.

But now Violette passed a sleepless night.

"I am in your debt," he'd said, his voice as dark and rich as spiced rum, and his laugh, a wicked, rasping chuckle. With burning cheeks, she recollected her nakedness beneath the blanket and something more – something she had resolutely refused to believe, let alone admit, even to herself.

She had woken in the night. The fire had burned away. There was not even the last glimmer of red embers to bring some light into the room, and with no moon to cast its glow, it was so black that if her eyes were open or shut, she could not tell. Her senses were all about; her eyes could see nothing, but her ears were attuned to the smallest sound. A tiny scratching rustle – a mouse, somewhere in the wall. Breathing at her feet, the dog. He whimpered in his sleep, and shifted his weight a little.

There was the whisper of a breath beside her as well, and a sensation of the most absolute comfort. Hardly knowing if she was awake or dreaming, she could tell it was Captain Death beside her. His arms cradled her, and beneath her cheek, his naked chest rose and fell with each sleeping breath.

'Any respectable woman would have extricated herself and left – or slapped the blackguard's face!' thought Violette. 'But I did not. I buried my face in his shoulder, and fell back to sleep as if it were the most natural thing in the world.

'I have told myself all these long months that it could not possibly be the way I remember; that I was in a fever – which is true, and I was ill for days after – and it was a delirium dream. But now I wonder. It seems too real to have been my imagination! I hardly know what to believe!' Her body burned with heat. All unbidden rose the memory of his naked body against hers, and she thrilled again at the thought of it. And then another, dreadful thought crossed her mind.

'If it was real … and if people found out – it would be the scandal of the century! I would be an object of the most despising ridicule. Not just dead to society, not just shunned, but abhorred; utterly repudiated by all who know me." Her stomach churned at the thought. The gossip, the jests made at her expense, the pointing fingers and the skirts pulled to one side as she passed by in the street. 'And my poor aunt, as well! She has led such a difficult life, and now she is enjoying herself so thoroughly, and with another chance at love, it seems. I could hardly live with myself if my foolishness and – and headstrongness – doomed her to return to the lonely life she led before.'

She closed her eyes, only for them to fly open again at the thought of something worse. 'I've been supposing him a gentleman, but Major Jennings knows everything about him, and describes him as the lowest type of ruffian. How could such a fellow be acquainted with the fashion establishment of

London? How would he have known my identity, or where to find me? For it must have been he who sent the gown – and he must have been at Madame Audabon's establishment! Watching me, and I knowing nothing of him! There were a dozen gentlemen there, as well as the assistants in the shop, the servants, the footmen, the coachmen in the street. How dreadful. It could have been absolutely anyone!'

CHAPTER 7

When the butler brought in the letters at breakfast a day or so later, one, addressed to Violette, proved to be a note from Clara Taverner.

"Aunt! we are invited to Lady Clara's cotillion ball for her birthday!" Violette read the invitation aloud.

Having been born in a most inconvenient month which allows us neither the festivities of Christmas nor the enchantments of The Season, it is to be but a little local event for neighbours and close friends only. We are neighbours already and I hope that you will allow me to call you my friend, and to hope also that you and your aunt, Miss Felicia deVere, will attend. I long for you to meet my brother Mr Kit Taverner, for of course it will be his birthday too

Violette laid the letter aside. "I shall order myself a new gown. The invitation asks us to stay overnight so that I may join Lady Clara when she rides out with the hunt the next morning. I fancy I require a new riding habit; I shall go to London for them both." And to herself, she added, 'And I shall quiz that establishment about the ordering of my champagne gown at the same time, and find out the identity of that mysterious fellow who calls himself Captain Death!'

Violette helped herself to a slice of caraway seed cake and lifted the lid of the chocolate pot to discover it empty. "Why is there no chocolate, Aunt? Could you ring the bell, and get the maid to fetch some?"

Miss Felicia bit her lip. Her attempts to deal only with reputable tradesmen were thwarted at every turn. It appeared that the whole grocery establishment of Sumbourne and Folkestone was in the pocket of the smugglers' trade.

"Madam, the tea merchant has no chocolate nor Orange Pekoe this week, so the order came back with black tea only, and that such a price!" Cook was not best pleased. Arranging the menus with Miss Felicia was usually straightforward, but with this new scheme of hers it was become virtually impossible. "Sugar is three times the price of the sugar we normally purchase. And Mr Figgis the chandler has no spermaceti candles in stock, and so offers beeswax, which are a dreadful price and last but a minute, or tallow, as if a refined household would want the smell!" She sniffed, disdainfully, and after a moment, she added, as if in afterthought, "John tells me that there are good candles available, and chocolate too… if we wished for them."

Miss Felicia would not be swayed. 'At least,' she thought to herself, 'I am making a good effort, and Major Jennings would be proud of me, if he knew how patriotic I am become!' But her resolve was tested beyond endurance the very next morning, when the maid delivered hot water to her room along with a small container of some slimy brown substance. She rang the bell for Hill.

"Hill, why have I no soap? And what is in this pot?"

"The cakes of rose soap you like, Miss Felicia, are not available and so we have this brown soft soap, which I fear is not good for the complexion. Or they had green soap by the pound, but that was a terrible price."

This was the last straw. "Take away this horrid concoction and send John down to The Dragon to fetch me a box of good soap. And a pound of Orange Pekoe and a pound of chocolate, while he's at it!"

'Patriotism is all very well,' she said to herself, looking in the glass. 'But the King – and Major Jennings – cannot expect me to sacrifice my complexion to it!'

Lady Clara's ball may have been considered a simple, local affair by the lady herself, but upon arrival at the house – as astonishing close to as it had appeared when she viewed it from afar, those few months ago – Violette could see at least a dozen carriages disgorging passengers, and another two dozen or more lined up along the avenue waiting their turn.

Violette and her aunt were shown upstairs to their rooms, accompanied by Hill and their luggage, and tidied their hair before returning to the ballroom. Here they were announced into a scene that had Miss Felicia gazing about her in wide-eyed astonishment. "My dear! How beautiful! And how – how – *vastly* splendid!"

Splendid it was, indeed. There must have been a hundred guests already assembled, and easily room for a hundred more, for the room was generous in its proportions. The walls were a soft shade of blue, and at regular intervals were gilded mirrors, each with its matching pair of lustres. Here was the great array of tall arched windows leading out onto the terrace, and fluted white columns in the classical style flanked the entrances into the card rooms at one end and the supper room at the other. The ceiling was an extravagance of complicated plasterwork. Flowers and grapes and festoons of vine leaves clustered with bunches of grapes twisted around a trio of chandeliers, each abundantly layered with crystal drops throwing rainbows across every surface.

"Such a quantity of candles! I vow there must be fifty or more in each of those chandeliers – not to mention the wall lustres, too!" Miss Felicia recollected her manners enough to pull herself together and stop staring about her with her mouth agape; but she could not restrain herself from hissing at Violette, "Lettie dear, I have heard it said that Lord Winterbourne's father spent his way through the entirety of his fortune and that of his wife as well and even," she lowered her voice to the merest whisper, "cheated at cards in order to rob his friends of their wealth, so determined was he to have a house that outshone any other. But this! I can hardly believe – oh, my goodness!"

Unable to clearly articulate her thoughts on this matter, she stopped speaking altogether. It was as well, since coming towards them was their hostess, ready to greet them. But Miss Felicia could not help but consider the cost of so many good candles, and since the complexities of mathematics was not her strong point, this was a challenge that occupied her thoughts a good deal for the next hour or so.

Lady Clara was escorted by her twin. They were so alike that their relationship was unmistakable, though Mr Kit Taverner was a good head-and-a half taller than his sister. Like his twin, his hair was dark and his eyes blue; though if hers were the deep colour of cornflowers, then his were more akin to the same grey shade as his brother's. Unlike that gentleman, however, he had nothing about him of the foppish Dandy.

'Rather,' reflected Violette, 'his height and build suggest something of the Corinthian,' and her supposition was proved right upon conversation, where he spoke at length of his career in the Navy.

"I discovered pretty quick that I was not cut out for university life nor a career in the church or the law, as so many of my acquaintance prefer. It's an active, outdoors life for me. Sailing and rowing! Boats and the open sea are my passion.

"I think nothing of swimming a mile before breakfast, and am at home in the boxing ring – which explains my appearance!" for he was sporting a shocking black eye which gave him a most raffish air.

He had nothing of the disdainful expression of his older brother, and none of that gentleman's drawling arrogance of speech. Indeed, he seemed an enthusiastic and sensible conversationalist, most genuinely pleased to meet his sister's new friends. He made a good impression upon Violette with his first remark to her, "Why, Miss deVere, what a charming gown – so unusual a colour! You think it strange that a man should notice a gown, but I often accompany my sister to her dressmaker. Clarrie always asks my opinion and I am pleased to give it!"

Lady Clara added, "If Kit were not so determined to be a sailor, I say he could open his own fashion establishment, though I cannot quite see him posturing about with a silver-topped cane and flattering all the ladies!" All about them laughed at this idea, though it gave Violette a moment's fleeting apprehension; could Mr Kit Taverner be … 'No,' she said, firmly to herself. 'He is at home on the sea and has an understanding of ladies' gowns but I cannot suspect every man I meet of being a smuggler; it's simply too ridiculous for words! And anyway … if he – or anyone – was Captain Death…. surely I would know? I'd feel … something.'

Violette was happy with her appearance. She had gone to the London dressmakers as she had planned, though she had been unable to discover the identity of the person who had sent her the champagne gown.

The owner of that establishment, Mrs Bell, had been charming, but firm. "I am sorry, Miss deVere, but I was told the gown was for a gift and meant to be a surprise, and I was ordered not to reveal the identity of the person who arranged for it. My reputation is for complete and utter discretion in all my dealings, as I am certain you will understand."

Violette did understand. 'There will be another way of finding out,' she said to herself.

Mrs Bell's establishment was as different from Madame Audabon's as it could possibly be. Tucked away in a quiet side street in Mayfair and as discreet as the lady herself, there was nothing much more to see than a black-painted door with a brass knocker and a small brass sign upon the wall.

A footman opened the door and escorted Violette to a small parlour to sit with a glass of Madeira. Mrs Bell came forward, accompanied by her assistant and a small man with an elaborate coiffeur and a pince-nez. He was introduced, "Mr Timothy is our expert in the construction of the tailored riding-dress for ladies," and, having made his bow, that gentleman excused himself just as fast. The discretion of this establishment, compared to the very public atmosphere of Madame Audabon's, was much more to Violette's taste, and she spent a happy hour with Mrs Bell, discussing styles and fabric. They settled upon a charcoal-colour broadcloth for the riding dress, trimmed in the military style with black and white braiding and silver cording.

When Mrs Bell left to go and discuss the pattern with Mr Timothy, Violette turned to the assistant. "I see no-one with a tape measure fussing about me. How can you know what size to fit my gowns?" The assistant was perhaps new; she was certainly young, and eager to show off her knowledge. "We already have your measurements – from the gown before."

"And how did you get those?"

"They arrived by messenger, Miss. I thought you had them sent from your dressmaker in Bath?"

So Violette was no nearer to resolving the mystery. She turned her attention instead to the matter of a gown for Lady Clara's ball. A shimmering silk velvet as light as thistledown was settled upon, in a rich shade of chestnut.

"You are lucky, Miss deVere, to carry your clothes with such ease and elegance," said Mrs Bell. "There is something in your carriage which gives you a most superior style. I have many young ladies in here who would envy your deportment, and your looks are so striking, that you cannot help but attract notice. And I think you will find that this gown will do you justice!" She was most sincere in her words, for unlike many of her profession, she was not given to false flattery. Miss deVere was certainly not a beauty in the conventional sense but her face was interesting. 'It is,' thought Mrs Bell, 'what the French call *jolie laide* – plain features that somehow form a fascinating whole.'

She hesitated a moment, for she intended to ask a delicate question. She had taken a liking to Miss deVere and knew something of her history. Indeed, who could not know of it? Violette might have thought of herself as hidden away in the furthest reaches of the Kent countryside, and of no interest to any, but once more the story of her family was upon everyone's lips, just as it had been when her father had given up everything to marry a fortune-hunting dancing girl.

Mrs Bell was fully conversant with the story of Sir Charles deVere's exile to the Continent. It might have been thirty years ago or more, but it had been the most shocking event of that Season or any other in memory, and many a dowager remembered the scandal very well. Over the last few weeks these redoubtable ladies had started returning from their country residences or the delights of Bath or Ramsgate to gather in London in preparation for the Season, just as flocks of twittering birds return from their exotic winter locations. Where better to renew acquaintance than over a glass of Madeira at Mrs Bell's establishment, while their granddaughters fretted over the choice of gowns for the coming Season? And so it was that any hope that Violette might have had for a discreet entry into society was futile.

Pretty little Felicia deVere forbidden a marriage of her own, "... and she as set to be engaged to an officer in the East Kents as makes no difference!" remarked Lady Andover.

"A most respectable regiment," added her companion, Miss Rhodes, "why, my own dear brother was of that company!"

"The father was quite maddened with rage!" chimed in Mrs Baxter-Lees, who might not have a title, but had wealth enough from a good marriage, albeit into trade, to make up for it. "He drank himself into an apoplexy, or so it was said. I danced with him three times at the Haversham's ball you know, during my first Season. A most charming young man; and with that flaming hair of his, so very handsome!" Sophia Baxter-Lees was known to have been rackety in her youth, so the intriguing revelation of three dances with the same partner was passed over with some delicacy, other than, "Och, but he was a carnaptious piece, sure enough; perhaps you were lucky to escape him, my dear!" from Mary Abercrombie, down from the Highlands for the Season and who prided herself on speaking plain.

"Perhaps." Mrs Baxter-Lees was doubtful. Sir William might have had a temper but he had also a vast fortune, and she reflected that a vast fortune could compensate for many things. She was reminded of her own husband's unfortunate foray into speculation, with the subsequent loss of a very nice parure of diamonds which had found its way to the bank and was unlikely ever to be redeemed from those clanking vaults.

"Well, he disinherited his son, that much is certain I heard that Sir Charles lived in really quite abject poverty, hardly a *sou* to his name. And the place simply overrun with theatrical types and artist's models!"

"Taking their clothes off at the drop of a hat!" This, again, from Miss Rhodes, in quite a fluster of excitement.

"Shocking! The girl seems to have been brought up in an absolute den of iniquity. No wonder she's said to have no idea of the manners of an English lady or the conventions of polite society. She'll never find a match. No respectable family would want her rampaging about in their midst!"

"Terribly rich, though. The richest heiress in England, I've heard it said. And all from some worthless farmland that had been in family for generations and then found to be simply stuffed with coal!"

"And not trade, either. Discovering value in one's land is a perfectly respectable source of income. Unlike, say, owning a mill."

This last was definitely directed at Mrs Baxter-Lees, who felt that the conversation was concluded. She moved away to look at some pattern books, leaving the other ladies to reflect upon the competing interests of vast wealth, a far-from-respectable upbringing and an unfavourable countenance.

Lady Abercrombie was not finished. "Och, but I saw her, you know, when I was in Bath. That puir lassie was aye as skinny as a besom broom. And examining some hackit green cloth for an evening gown; she'd have been a rare sight in it. Enough, now, I must away."

Lady Abercrombie took her leave and Lady Andover remarked to Miss Rhodes that it was a relief. "The woman hails from a perfectly respectable family in Hampshire and merely married into Scotland. She is no more Scotch than I am myself; and I find most of what she says to be utterly incomprehensible!"

All in all, it was no wonder that all of society was agog to see Miss Violette deVere. And Mrs Bell felt it her duty to try and give her some advice, as far as she was able and without being thought presumptuous.
She narrowed her eyes at the fabric pinned here and there about Violette's person.

"Miss deVere, I would suggest that your gown needs a long stole to be worn across the body – to drape across the hip, and fasten at the shoulder to remind us of the classical statues of antiquity." She turned to her assistant. "Go and fetch a length of the crimson sea silk for Miss deVere." When her assistant left the room, she turned back to Violette. "Pray excuse me, Miss deVere, but your grandmother was known for her rubies. They would be perfect with this."

"My grandmother's rubies?" Violette was startled. She had not thought of jewels other than those that had accompanied her from her home in France; pearls that her father had given her mother on their wedding day, and a pair of diamond clips that he had presented to Violette for her sixteenth birthday.

Mrs Bell bit her lip. "Forgive me. I should not have presumed – ."

But Violette was too surprised to be offended. "No-one ever said anything to me about … that is, it did not occur to me to ask anyone …" her voice tailed off.

Mrs Bell murmured in a delicate undertone, "The bank, perhaps? I believe it is quite the usual thing."

Violette was amazed. 'What a ninny I've been!' she scolded herself. 'I just arrived here and fitted in with my aunt and her way of life, and I knew that I had an inheritance but thought of it as being enough to live on and buy some clothes and not much else at all. How much this fortune truly is or how it is administered, I have no idea!

'I doubt my aunt knows, either. She does speak so often of economy, and perhaps she worries about the household expenses, but does not think it appropriate to discuss them with me. I shall make an appointment for the bank forthwith, and find out what I have, and if I have some rubies to wear with this dress, then that will be all to the good!'

There were rubies, indeed. Mr Chapman at the bank in Folkestone led her into a strong room, and took out case after case, and the contents glittered like a pirate's treasure in the candlelight. There were midnight blue sapphires and grass-green emeralds, diamonds flashing rainbows of fire and, indeed, the fabled rubies – an elaborate necklace of them, claret-colour, gleaming with brown and purple lights, set with pearls and with long drop earrings to match. Case after case contained hatpins and bracelets and brooches and rings in semi-precious stones, suitable for day wear – coral and turquoise, topaz and aquamarine and amber, all set in gold and silver. Violette had looked about her in baffled wonderment.

"Why are they all hidden away here? Surely upon her mother's death they should have gone to my aunt."

"Ah. Well." Mr Chapman hesitated. "After Sir Charles left in such – as my client, your grandfather saw it – unfortunate circumstances, he became somewhat … Sir William again, if you take my meaning, he became a little, er, that is, your aunt did not have …"

"She has lived in somewhat reduced circumstances, perhaps this is what you are implying?"

"Indeed." Mr Chapman was grateful. "I think your grandfather was under the impression that Miss deVere would fall prey to fortune hunters. Which is, forgive me, how he viewed your father's marriage. Though I am sure that Sir Charles was very happy, very happy indeed!" he finished, hurriedly. "Of course, Miss deVere then was not of an age to concern herself overmuch with the arrangements that your grandfather made. And we were placed under strict instruction not to discuss such matters with her. Not that such a nicely brought up young lady would have thought to question …". He felt that he had said quite enough. He was unused to having young ladies quiz him about matters financial and legal, and thought it most inappropriate that Miss Violette deVere had cornered him in this way. But his discomfort was not yet complete.

"And as for the money?"

"The – the money?" Even the wording of her request – he was quite shocked. A young lady to use such language. He gulped, a little.

"Yes. 'The blunt', as I understand the sporting gentlemen to say. And indeed, I shall be blunt about it. How much do I have? Do I have enough to settle a sum upon my aunt? When she wanted to buy a bonnet – I mean, it's shocking that she has no capital to call her own. She may wish to marry. Or travel. Well, I don't know what she might wish to do, but to keep house for me for the rest of her life cannot be it, surely.

"I have bought a new mare, and some clothes. Do I have enough to pay for repairs to the house, or to hire another gardener? And I have a fancy to plant tulips, and I am sure they must be quite the price."

"Buy a horse – pay for a gardener? My very dear young lady." Mr Chapman mopped his brow. "You are one of the richest ladies in the whole of England. You can do anything you wish. Buy a dozen horses if you will. Pay a hundred gardeners. Have tulips as far as the eye can see!" He could not quite bring himself to say aloud how much Violette was worth. He took his quill, and dipped it in the inkwell. His hands shook as he wrote a figure down on a scrap of notepaper. He dusted it with a little sand before pushing it across the table to her.

Violette stared at the paper in silence for a moment. Then she folded it into her reticule.

"I shall take the rubies with me. Perhaps I could have one of your clerks to come with me in the carriage to carry them. That will do for now, I think. Good day."

This conversation had taken place a fortnight before the ball. Violette had been in something of a state of the most profound shock following her visit to the bank, and slept badly for several nights, for it seemed a terrible responsibility had been placed upon her shoulders. Instead of rushing out to spend lavishly, she was almost afraid to spend any money at all. But one thing she did decide upon was to employ the services of a dancing master.

Violette had cast off the mourning garb she had worn since her arrival in England. The dark mornings and afternoons of the winter were slowly departing. The first tender blossoms were appearing on the apple trees in the orchard; snowdrops were replaced by the bright faces of primroses. And something within her was changing, too. Perhaps I am not ugly, as I have thought all my life, but something else instead. I am rich, and I shall enter into society and spend the Season in London. And as for Lady Clara's ball, why, I shall be wearing rubies and chestnut-coloured silk velvet. And there will be no more dancing giraffe!"

The dancing master arrived, complete with beribboned shoes and a silver-topped cane, accompanied by a lad with a violin to provide the music. Perhaps he was expecting a young lady who wished to refine her technique; perhaps someone who had heard of the new dance called the waltz, lately arrived from the Continent and danced by the scandalous Lady Caroline Lamb – not at a public ball, thank heavens, only at a private affair, but even so, one attended by a hundred guests or more.

What he was not expecting was a very tall young lady who could not dance a single step, and seemed in constant danger of falling over her own feet to come crashing to the ground, bringing her partner, and possibly others in the dance, with her.

"This is the first ball I have ever attended, and I am something nervous. It is to be a cotillion ball, but I don't know what that means."

"It's the new fashion, Miss deVere. Before this, we had the dress ball, very formal, which opened with a minuet, a very slow and showy dance. The cotillion ball is less formal. If it's in a private house then all the guests are presumed to be acquainted, so there's no need of formal introduction before being asked to dance – unlike at a public ball at the Assembly Rooms, for instance. And, of course, it opens with a cotillion, so we shall start with that.

"So; we start with four couples, in a square. Take your partner's hand with your left hand, Miss deVere – no, no, your left hand in my right. That's it. Turn to me and I bow, and you curtsy. Not down to the floor, Miss deVere, I am not His Majesty! Just a small dip, will do. Then we circle to the right; sixteen steps, *la la, la la la la*, that's it, you are doing very well. Oops, just a little stumble, keep going, *la la la*. Then we drop hands, and you dance to the left – your left – *left,* Miss deVere – and join the next gentleman along. Hands crossed behind the back, circle round, dance to the right; your *right*, Miss deVere …!"

The hour seemed interminable to Violette, and no doubt to the hapless young man instructing her but he was patient and she was determined. They stopped for a glass of lemon cordial, and Violette asked a question that had been much upon her mind.

She could not help but think of the evening at Lady Fitzallen's and Lord Winterbourne's strange behaviour. How she had caught him staring at her in a most ungentlemanly fashion; how in the dance she'd raised her eyes to meet his, and how his gaze had instantly slid away from her look; how very silent he had been, and how he had departed without a backward glance. It was most odd, and she could not fathom it out at all.

She couldn't ask the dancing master to explain Lord Winterbourne's peculiar manner, but it did strike her that she could hardly blame him for not speaking when she had failed to speak a single word herself, 'and that is something I must address.' So she put the question to the dancing master.

"I feel that there is an art to conversation in the dance, and I fear I am sadly lacking in that skill; what to say and when to say it. One can hardly start a conversation about, say, philosophy or politics during the Boulanger, no matter how much standing about there might be waiting for one's turn on the floor."

The dancing master was too professional to throw his hands up in the air with a despairing cry, but they certainly twitched; it was with a great effort of will that he spoke in a gentle, modulated voice. "Ah, no, Miss deVere, we do not discuss such weighty matters in the ballroom. ('Nor, indeed, as ladies, anywhere else,' he would have liked to have added, but did not.) "You are quite right; light conversation in the dance is an essential part of the proceedings. It is always a nice idea to offer the gentleman the opportunity to answer a question. For example, the music. Does he care for it? What does he think of the playing? You might comment on the weather or the arrangement of the flowers, or the number of guests, for instance.

"Let us resume our lesson. We shall try the cotillion once more, and we shall accompany it with some pleasant conversation here and there as we proceed."

Violette tried her best but soon concluded that she could master steps or conversation but not both at the same time, and the few comments she did manage to gasp out seemed to horrify her partner. After a particularly energetic series of steps, her remark, "I am horribly hot!" was met with an appalled reprimand.

"A lady never draws attention to her physical being, Miss deVere! I beg you, never say you are hot – or cold, for that matter!"

At the end of the hour the maid entered, curtsied to Violette and said, "Please Miss, there are callers in the morning room with Miss Felicia, and she asks if you will come and join them."

With that, the dancing master was let go, but instructed to return at the same hour the next day, and every day until the day of the ball. Violette hummed her way into the morning room, dancing a few steps here and there, and feeling quite pleased with her progress.

So it was that, upon arrival at Winterbourne Hall, she felt confident in her mastery of the steps of the cotillion and able to make at least a minimal number of comments about inconsequential matters. She thought, also, that she looked well in her velvet; and standing beside Mr Kit Taverner she even forgot to be self-conscious about her height. He was most attentive. He summoned a footman to bring glasses of punch for Violette and her aunt, and then took it upon himself to escort them around the room, introducing them to one person after another, nodding at his friends here and there, some of whom engaged Violette for dances or offered to fetch her champagne.

All-in-all it was a most amusing promenade, and Kit Taverner a most charming companion. He treated Violette as if she were a piece of fragile porcelain, staying close to her side and engaging her in a positive flow of light conversation which put her entirely at her ease, saying, 'I know, Miss Violette – I hope I may address you so, for I feel that we are destined to be close friends – that you are but lately come into society, and are perhaps not well acquainted with many of our guests.' He accompanied this with a smile of such genuine warmth that Violette instinctively placed her hand upon his arm; and to her surprise, he placed his own hand over hers and gave it the lightest of squeezes.

Violette hastily removed her hand, wondering if she had been rather forward, and reflecting that he was several years younger than she, 'though why that thought should trouble me, I do not know.'

Of Lord Winterbourne there was no sign, but to Miss Felicia's evident delight, they came to a small group of gentlemen seemingly deep in a discussion and among these gentlemen was no other than Major Jennings.

He bowed over Miss Felicia's hand, and asked her for the first; blushing, she accepted. When Mr Taverner had seen them to chairs and made his bow to them and departed, she turned to Violette. "My dear, do you think I did right in accepting Major Jennings for the first dance? I feel that perhaps – perhaps I should not stand up. And at my age, too. Perhaps it is not appropriate. And I cannot leave you sitting unattended with no chaperone!"

Violette looked at her aunt most tenderly. With her cheeks pink and her eyes sparkling, she looked as excited as a girl at her first ball. Violette felt a sudden rush of anger at her grandfather, who had stolen her away from her first season to bury her in the depths of the countryside, and her own father, too, who had taken it for granted that he should purchase his own happiness at the expense of that of his sister.

'Well,' thought Violette, 'things are going to change for my aunt and I am going to make it up to her one way and another. And if a romance with

Major Jennings is still possible then I shall do everything I can to make it go forward!'

Aloud, she said, "Why should you not stand up with the Major? I think him a very personable gentleman, and it seems to me he has never forgotten you. Go, dance every dance with him as far as I am concerned, and I wish you happy!"

This was too much; Miss Felicia was appalled. "Two dances, dear! Never dance more than two dances with the same gentleman for fear of the rumour-mill. Bear that in mind, I beg of you."

Violette laughed. "Do not fear for me, Aunt. I hardly expect such attentions from any of the gentlemen here. No doubt my gawky performance in the dance is spoken of already, and I am perfectly content to sit and watch. It seems most unfair that you should pay the price for my lack of partners!"

But lack of partners seemed not to be a problem at all. Up came Kit Taverner and asked her, if she was not engaged, if she would stand up with him for the first. This was a great honour, for it was his ball as much as his sister's, and although Lady Clara would open the dancing, to be upon the arm of her twin set Violette only second in consequence. They danced the cotillion, and Violette managed very well, with her head held high and a determined smile upon her lips. And after that, requests came thick and fast, as one gentleman after another invited her for the next, or the second after that.

Violette smiled her way through one dance after another, feeling quite light-headed with it all. 'It is delightful to be in such demand. I declare I have danced every dance! I would never have thought to enjoy myself so much!' If she wondered at it at all, Violette might have assumed that all this attention was the result of her acquisition of dancing skills, or the flattery of her new gown or the confidence engendered by the cool weight of her grandmother's rubies around her neck, reminding her that her parentage might have been scandalous, but that she came from a distinguished family with a long history and of some consequence. But just before supper was announced, she was suddenly – and horribly – reminded that dancing lessons and new gowns and the respectful gleam of her grandmother's rubies were as nothing when weighed against her fortune.

It happened that she was not engaged for the supper dance. The ballroom being grown very hot, she stepped out onto the terrace for a breath of air. The shadows in the garden shifted and changed as the feeble light of the new moon, hardly more than a finger-nail paring of silver, was obscured by the drifting clouds.

The ballroom was richly perfumed with the scents of hothouse flowers, added to by the heavy colognes and pomades worn by the men and the oriental perfumes of the women, but the air here was sweet and fresh. Violette closed her eyes and breathed in the cold green scent of leaves and grass, and then made her way further along the terrace. The music and laughter of the ballroom were left behind, replaced by the sounds of the night. She heard the soft rustle of leaves in the breeze and the haunting cry of an owl. From somewhere nearby a nightingale started up with a sudden cascade of liquid notes.

Violette paused at the top of a flight of shallow steps, and leaned on the balustrade, listening. The nightingale's song ended as quickly as it had begun. And in the sudden silence she heard the whisper of voices coming from somewhere below. Her dancing slippers were soft and made no sound. Violette took a cautious step or two further along the terrace and looked over the balustrade to see two gentlemen below her. The pale moonlight briefly illuminated the head and shoulders of Mr Kit Taverner. His companion was hidden in the shadows.

Kit spoke in a low, furious voice. "You must do something. I mean it! She is the richest prize on the market, and you yourself made sure she was invited tonight; yet you have spent the whole evening at cards and done nothing to catch her! Others are fishing in the same waters, Richard. If you would set but one foot in the ballroom you would see them eying her with the most covetous of attentions. You need to bait for her! She will not leap from the water and into your net of her own accord!"

"Enough!" The light, drawling tones of Lord Winterbourne were unmistakeable. "Begod, Kit, I wish you would not involve yourself in this affair! There are not enough guineas in the bank to compensate me for looking at that face over my breakfast each morning."

"You find her ugly; and she is a country hobbledehoy, or so reports would have it. Argumentative, you say. But these things do not matter! You are three and thirty, Richard, and any number of wealthy mamas have dangled their daughters in front of you, yet you refuse them all. We need the money, Richard, and we need it soon. If I were of age I'd play for her myself, you may be sure of it!"

A couple had come out onto the terrace a little further along, and there was a snatch of laughter. Violette stepped back from the balustrade and moved along the terrace on shaking legs to take shelter in a dark corner behind a planting of flowering shrubs. She sank down upon the rim of an ornate metal jardiniere, and covered her face with her hands, in an excess of mortification.

She had looked for Lord Winterbourne, she admitted it to herself. All this evening, while she had been dancing with this partner and that, she had thought she would look up and find him quizzing her, or might reach out her hand to a new partner and find it taken by Richard Taverner. The thought of it had made her feel quite deliciously nervous, an intriguing, breathless anticipation – dread or delight, she could not tell which. But now she was reminded of those words of her mother's, that had impacted upon her so forcibly when she was but fifteen, and beginning then to dream of a husband and children, and wondering what life would hold for her. *An aristocratic husband will look for beauty… expect nothing, for you will be broken-hearted by it.*

She had not understood what her mother had meant, but now it was become clear. I have been laughed at for being such a maypole of a girl, and pitied for my years, being so far past the first flush of girlhood. Maybe I have some wit, or a kind heart. Perhaps I would be a good companion and a gentle mother, and provide a loving home for my husband. But not one of the gentlemen who have danced attendance upon me this night cares a jot about any of those things.

'All who look at me see only my fortune and nothing else. Kit Taverner is just the same, no matter how warm his manner might be. And as for his brother, well, maybe he does look beyond my fortune; but it could not be made clearer that what he sees fills him with repugnance. I did not understand it – but I understand it now!'

She gritted her teeth. 'No!' She took a deep breath. 'I will not allow myself to be broken-hearted by it! I have been a fool, and I thank heaven that no-one but me knows it.' With this, she stood, brushing the dust from her gown. Straightening her shoulders, she made her way back into the ballroom with a smile fixed upon her lips, and her head held high.

CHAPTER 8

Despite her rousing words to herself, Violette could eat no supper. She smiled at her aunt, though her eyes were bright with unshed tears, and answered remarks addressed to her by her neighbours at the supper table as much as she was able, but after a while she made her excuses and slipped away to her room, there to pace the floor in an agony of shame.

'I am so ugly that he would not marry me even for my money; that's the truth of it. Even for a fortune, he could not bear the sight of me!' Hot tears of humiliation streamed down her cheeks. She tore off the velvet dress that she had thought suited her so well, and the rubies of which she had been so proud, and threw them on the floor, and flung herself on her bed. 'Richard Taverner presents an exterior as chilly and forbidding as this house he lives in. All is outward perfection with no warm heart within. I have spoken but a dozen words to him, and he even fewer to me, and what he has said to me – and about me – are of a most shocking kind of arrogance and cruelty. Why? What have I done to him that warrants such abhorrence on his part?'

Violette sat up and pummelled her pillow, and threw herself back down upon it in an agony of frustration.

'And as for his absolute refusal of me – why, I wouldn't marry him if he were the last man alive and he begged me upon bended knee! He is the haughtiest man in the world! Why should I not read the encyclopaedia? Why should it disgust him that I have an enquiring mind? He snubbed my aunt and made her cry. How dare he! I shall think no more of Lord Winterbourne – other than to hate him!'

With this, Violette closed her eyes, and tried to turn her mind to pleasant thoughts in the hope of falling asleep, but her mind would not be still. Lord Winterbourne's words played themselves over and over in her head, until she thought she would scream aloud with the torment of it, and she sat bolt upright again.

'I will never get to sleep.' She pressed her hands to her head, clutching at her hair. 'Oh! What is the point, what *is* the point of thinking of this again and *again*!' She climbed out of bed and found some eau-de-cologne to bathe her forehead and her hot cheeks. She opened the window, and sat upon the window seat looking out across the gardens.

The last carriages had departed, and now Violette gave up all notion of sleep. 'It must be close to dawn,' she said to herself, 'and every person is gone to their beds. But I am so very thirsty. Hungry, too, for I ate hardly any supper. Should ring for the maid? But I can't start ringing bells and wakening the servants, what will they think of me?'

The longing for a drink began to grow in her mind and overshadow all else to the point where, even though it might be the height of bad manners to roam at will through someone else's house in the small hours of the morning, Violette decided to take the risk. 'I shall creep downstairs and wake no-one. Surely there will be drinks left in the supper room, or if I must, I shall find the kitchens and fetch myself something; some milk, perhaps.'

Violette pulled on her wrapper, and lit her candle. Her door opened with a resounding creak, and she stiffened, but no-one put their head out of their room to see what she was about. She took a deep breath, and crept cautiously down the stairs to the first floor. The house was silent, but for the faint chime of bells somewhere – a clock, marking out the hour. Four in the morning. When the last note sounded, the silence was profound. A dead, still calm seemed to settle over the house.

Here was the ballroom, deserted. The candles had been snuffed, and through the row of tall windows the setting moon sent ghostly fingers of pale light across the floor. She took a cautious step towards the supper room and hesitated. There was light showing beneath the door of the card room, and she heard a low laugh. Players, still at table, and deep in some game.

She tiptoed noiselessly away, and down the next stairs to the entrance hall. It was a cavernous space.

The black marble floor stretched away into pure darkness, upon which the meagre light of her single candle made no impact.

Shadowy alcoves housed life-sized marble statues. There was a Madonna with her head bowed, and a weeping angel; a crouching child in rags, playing with a kitten, and an old blind beggar with his hand outstretched. They too, caught the flickering light of her candle as she moved past them, looking for a way into the further parts of the house. 'The man who built this house – old Lord Winterbourne – must have had a positive mania for statues. It's a shame he chose such – such horrid ones!'

Violette moved on. Her feet made no sound. All she could hear was her own ragged breathing, and the thud of her own heart. Before her yawned black emptiness. Behind her were the statues, unmoving and silent.

'I'll turn back. I don't need a drink. I wish I had never got out of my bed.' But she couldn't move, for with that thought came another; that if she turned around, it would be to see the Madonna raise her head, and the angel turn her tear-stained face towards her. Her heart gave a sickening lurch in her chest.

'I have heard of people being frozen with fear,' she thought, wildly, 'and I am; too scared to move even an inch!' Tears sprang to her eyes; she dashed her hand across her face to wipe them away and her attention was caught by a movement over her shoulder – she looked, to glimpse a wraithlike white figure moving behind her.

She dropped her candle and plunged forward, propelled by pure cold terror. Along one dark corridor after another she fled, whimpering with fear. Finally, she came to a halt, her breath coming in quivering gasps, her heart pounding in her ears.

She leant against the wall, drawing in a shuddering breath, and gave a shaky laugh. 'I vow, I am behaving like some silly girl in a novel, thinking of malevolent spirits. I believe that ghostly white figure was nothing more than my reflection in a looking glass!

'I'm utterly lost, and I feel quite extraordinarily miserable and not like myself at all!' With that, she sat down abruptly upon the floor and burst into a storm of weeping.

When she'd had her cry out, she felt a little better, and spoke roundly to herself. 'I give up. I shall sit here until the early morning servants start their day, and they will find me – sitting on the floor in my nightgown with my hair on end like some madwoman escaped from the attics!' She wiped her eyes on the hem of her nightgown. 'Someone will show me back to my room and bring me some hot chocolate and bread and butter. And when I tell this story to my aunt, it will be nothing more than an amusing anecdote, though she will be most dreadfully shocked.'

The thought of her aunt's horrified face when she recounted this story to her brought a smile to Violette's lips, and she felt a deal better. 'I hope I do not have to wait too long, for I am very cold. There's a terrible draft coming from somewhere. Why! Here is a door open!' Her eyes had adjusted to the gloom, and there was indeed a narrow strip of something paler. 'There must be someone else awake. I'll find them and they'll help me find my way back.'

Violette slipped through the doorway and found herself outside in the stable yard. The moon gone and the sky was a dazzle of stars. Somewhere near at hand a horse whinnied.

Violette called, softly "Hello? Is someone here?" In an instant she was seized, a hand clasped over her mouth, and pulled into a stall.

A voice in her ear – low and urgent. "Make a sound at your peril. I have a knife at your throat! Nod your head if you understand!"

She gave a jerky nod. She could tell nothing of her captor other than that she could smell the sea and the salt spray upon his clothing and hear his breath heaving in his chest. His horse, lathered up from fast riding, was huffing and blowing beside them. And something else again. Hoofbeats, distant but coming fast, and voices. At her feet, a dog whined, low and soft. His master gave him some whispered command, "Loki! Stay!"

Violette's heart rushed into her throat. It was he! – the man who called himself Death, the man that Major Jennings spoke of as a dangerous criminal. That unmistakeable rasping voice, urgent and low. "Who are you? What the devil are you doing here?" The hand was removed from her mouth, just enough to allow her to speak.

"It's – I'm Miss deVere." Her voice was a tremulous whisper. "You know me."

"What the –?" His grip on her relaxed. Violette turned and put her hands out towards him, blindly, encountering the rough wool of his jacket. He caught them in his own. "You are trembling – and your hands are cold as ice." And then his mouth was firm and compelling upon her own, as he pulled her against his body.

Violette melted into him. His arms encircled her, crushing her to him as his kiss deepened. He moved fractionally, as if to pull away from her, but she clung to him, returning his kiss with a passion she never dreamed she possessed. Her hands twisted in the collar of his jacket, pulling him closer still.

Between one heartbeat and the next, their embrace was over. Three horses came clattering into the stable yard; three riders, the gold braid of their uniforms glinting in the faint light. Captain Death pulled her further into the shadows.

"Why are those men following you?" Her voice was the merest whisper, but even so he placed his hand against her lips to silence her.

His own words were but a breath in her ear. "I was a fool to go out in the moonlight and hope to escape detection. They came upon me quite by chance. I rode as fast as I could but these damned hills offer no shelter or hiding place. I saw this house in the distance. I thought I'd lost them. If they catch me, I'm done for!"

The first rider dismounted from his horse. To Violette's horror, Captain Death's dog shot out from beside him and flew at the intruder, coming to a halt crouched low upon his haunches, growling and snarling.

The man raised his pistol.

Violette stepped out of the shadows, a glimmering white figure in her night clothes. "Loki! Here boy!" She walked towards the men and the dog, untying the sash from her wrapper, and she knelt and tied it around Loki's neck and grasped the end of it with trembling fingers. "You have found my dog, gentlemen. Thank heavens." She gave a shaky laugh. "But what do you here in the middle of the night? I am a visitor to the house, but can I help you in some way?"

The three men looked startled, as well they might. She appeared from the shadows as if some ghostly apparition. Free of its sash, her wrapper was fallen open and her nightgown, of the finest lawn, was not so very concealing as she might have wished in the circumstances. But her terror had turned into a sort of boldness, and she was seized with the spirit of adventure, and she laughed aloud at the sight of their shocked faces.

The first rider doffed his hat, and bowed. "Captain Malone of the Excise, ma'am. We are searching for a man who has escaped us and we thought he had come in this direction." His gaze lingered upon the dog. "He is known to have a companion; a great black dog. Very like this one." He paused. "Not what I would call a lap dog for a lady such as yourself." There was a slight, but unmistakeable emphasis on the word 'lady', as if he doubted that she was any such thing.

Violette drew herself up to her full height, and pulled her wrapper closer around her body. "Captain Malone, you say. I am Miss deVere, of Sumbourne Manor. I think you will be acquainted with Major Jennings, your superior, I believe, and a close friend of my family. And here you are at Winterbourne Hall, and I wonder if you perhaps need to speak to his lordship? If so, let me call the servants, and Lord Winterbourne's man will rouse him from his bed and he can come and shiver in the stable yard and listen to your impertinence as well. What is your pleasure, sir?"

Captain Malone hesitated for a second. Then he bowed. "My apologies, Miss deVere. Though I will say – the man we seek is a ruffian of the first order. It is not in a young lady's interests to be wandering about outdoors in the middle of the night – half-dressed and unchaperoned."

With that he wheeled his horse about, and the men departed.

Dawn was on the horizon, and the stars were fading. Violette untied the dog, and he disappeared out of the stable yard, to who-knew-where. She looked about her, but Captain Death was gone. Violette went back indoors, and came across a girl carrying a coal scuttle, who looked astonished at being accosted but showed her the way back to the entrance hall. Violette requested a cup of chocolate and some bread and butter to be brought to her, and she ran up the stairs and back to her room, exhilarated by her adventure, confused as to her feelings for Captain Death, and astonished at her own behaviour.

But not one of these things made such an impression upon her as that kiss. She touched her fingers to her bruised and swollen lips, and thought of it almost as a dream; and wished that it could happen again.

Being towards the tail end of March, and with the first stirrings of the London Season afoot once more, this was the last hunt of the season, so it was very well attended.

Violette was helped up into the saddle by John, who had groomed her new mare, named Flambeau for the white blaze upon her forehead which looked like a lighted torch, until her coat was gleaming satin, and she joined the rest of the meet outside the front of the house. Servants carrying silver trays of stirrup cup moved between the throng of excited hounds and the glossy, high-strung thoroughbreds stamping their hooves in their impatience to be at the gallop. It was a bright, clear morning with a high, pale sky and the feeling of spring in the air.

Violette had no need of a glass of stirrup cup to set her blood racing. She'd had no sleep at all, yet she felt as if her whole body was sparking with fire and fizzing with champagne.

Seated upon a great chestnut stallion, Lord Winterbourne was every inch the Nonesuch; freshly barbered, his cravat tied just so, his riding breeches spotless, his boots polished to a glorious shine. Upon sight of Violette, a fleeting expression of something

– surprise, perhaps – crossed his face. Violette could not think why. Her riding habit was correct in every detail, and she thought she looked well.

Lord Winterbourne tipped his hat to her. She had expected he would – it was only the courteous thing to do, and she'd spent a quarter hour before the looking glass, practising the merest hint of a frosty smile to offer in return. But yet again he wrong-footed her, turning his head away immediately to speak to his brother. It left her smiling at the back of his head, and turned frost to fury.

She was joined by Lady Clara, mounted upon a pretty roan mare. Clara was all admiration for her riding habit, and curious as to her horse. "I declare this is just like a mare we once had here in the stables." She called her brother across. "Kit, does this mare not remind you of Tilly?"

The mare whinnied, as if in response to her name, but Kit Taverner was all scepticism. "Clarrie, you hardly know one end of a horse from another, they all look the same to you. Miss deVere, how well you look today – and you have an exceptional seat upon a horse, I must say."

Violette might not have got in a sting to Lord Winterbourne, but here was an easier target, and she was exhilarated almost to the point of madness by her sleepless night and her boldness in seeing off the Excise men. She turned upon him her most radiant smile. "I am not used to riding aside, for of course I was brought up in the country, and let free to gallop about as I pleased on the farm horses. I have heard myself described as quite the country hobbledehoy!"

Violette did not think it possible for a young man to look more stricken. He blushed a violent shade of crimson, and sweat stood upon his forehead. His discomfort was compounded when his sister spoke out, quite astonished at Violette's words. "Miss deVere – that is a most shocking expression! I beg of you, do not say it! I cannot believe that anyone would say anything so cruel. You must have misheard."

Violette beamed at her. "Perhaps I did. As you say – it is unimaginable that anyone of breeding would describe a lady in such terms."

'Your horrid brothers can be as rude to me and about me as they like,' she thought to herself. 'But I have been thoroughly kissed, and seen off the Excise men, and saved a man's life – and that of a dog! while you have been abed, and Lord Winterbourne agonising over his cravat and admiring himself in the looking glass, no doubt. So there!'

With that, the horn sounded and the hunt moved off, with Violette laughing to herself.

CHAPTER 9

It was no surprise to Violette that, immediately upon their return to Sumbourne, Major Jennings paid a call. He had been so very attentive to her aunt at the ball, and although they had danced only the acceptable two dances together, one had been the first dance and the other, the supper dance, the two most notable dances of the evening.

Throughout supper he had fetched her aunt all manner of good things. "I see they have a delicious-looking dish of eggs in a parsley cream, allow me to bring you a spoonful, my dear; and there is a pineapple – I shall fetch you a slice if I have to stand guard over it with sabre drawn!" When supper was concluded, they had taken up residence upon a sofa, so engaged in conversation that Violette smiled at the notion of her aunt chaperoning her, and thought that it was more the other way round. Their heads could hardly have got closer without Major Jennings' lips pressing themselves upon Miss Felicia's cheek, and her hand had at all times been in imminent danger of being captured by his.

The Major arrived at eleven, the earliest hour for a call to be acceptable, and Miss Felicia sent the maid to bring Violette from her dancing lesson, where she had prevailed upon the dancing master to show her the waltz. He'd agreed, but with the very greatest reluctance, and upon her strict promise to never dance it in a public assembly, and never to breathe a word as to the identity of the person who had shown it her. "The young ladies might like to know it," he explained, "but it is their fathers who pay my fee, so I am sure you understand the need for discretion."

Violette waltzed her way into the morning room, to find Major Jennings and Miss Felica seated quite side-by-side upon the sofa, and Miss Felica flushed and rosy. Major Jennings rose to his feet when Violette entered the room, but before she had even time to make her curtsy to him, her aunt had rushed across the room and thrown her arms around Violette, and said in a strangled half-gasp, "Major Jennings has proposed to me and I have said yes, and I suppose I should have asked you, my dear, but I couldn't help myself!"

"Why ever should you ask me? Oh, Aunt! Major Jennings! I am so very happy for you both!" Violette meant it, every word. She rang the bell for Giles and sent him for champagne to toast the happy couple, and admired the ring that Major Jennings had the forethought to bring with him, and which now reposed in sparkling splendour upon Miss Felicia's hand.

"It belonged to my dear mamma. Once upon a time I thought to see it upon this very hand but when that did not happen, I carried it with me always as a fond remembrance – and even, perhaps, in hope, though it seemed most unlikely to ever be realised. But now here it is in its rightful place, and I could not be more honoured to see it." Major Jennings mopped at his brow with a great white handkerchief, and then Miss Felicia borrowed it to dab at her eyes. They were as giddy as two children, and by comparison, Violette felt very grown up and sensible. But as the day wore on, she began to feel more sensible still, for some little doubts began to niggle at the back of her mind.

Major Jennings' house at Oare was comfortable enough, and certainly quaint, with its vegetable gardens and views of the marshes, and his boat nearby for sailing up and down the Estuary. But did this mean that Major Jennings spent a considerable amount of time in his garden, and off sailing on his boat, when he was home? And how often was that? By his own admission, he spent much of his time traveling the length and breadth of the county, and was often in London.

'My aunt has a good acquaintance in this part of the world, and although her life is somewhat quiet, it is sociable enough; callers now and then, and an evening party got up for cards and such from time-to-time, and visiting the shops. Will she be comfortable, so far away and in such isolation?' wondered Violette. She then remembered that of course her aunt would have companionship – that of

Miss Sally Jennings. 'Which might be worse than no companionship at all,' she said to herself, with a wry twist to her lips. 'Though perhaps Major Jennings thinks to make his home here at Sumbourne Manor.' This gave her cause for some reflection. 'I love my aunt most dearly, and this has been her home always, and I would miss her greatly if she were not here. If she leaves, I should have to have another companion with me for the sake of propriety and who knows who that would be? But I am not sure that I would feel altogether comfortable with Major Jennings living here. Oh dear; it's quite a muddle.'

And part of the muddle, and somewhat pressing, was the matter of Captain Death. She had lied for him to the Excise men, and Major Jennings was their head. Did this make her his enemy? Would his men have apprised him of their meeting? What would happen if her deception were uncovered? These thoughts haunted her all day; and she began to dread her next meeting with the Major, which was to be that same evening, when he was to dine with them.

Violette picked at her fish, and pushed her meat around her plate, but even Miss Felicia, usually so concerned for her niece's health, did not notice her loss of appetite, so taken up was she with the Major, and recounting stories of their first meeting, all those years previously. "At the Assembly Rooms in Ramsgate, where I was paying a visit to the Roberts family. You met my friend, Miss Charlotte Roberts, when we were in Bath. Mrs George she is, now. And the Major – Lieutenant as he was then – asked for an introduction. It turned out that his aunt and my friend's mama were acquainted; and so we spent some happy evenings in one another's company. I will never forget my first sight of him, so dashing in his regimentals!" Miss Felicia twinkled at her Major, and he lifted his glass to her in silent salute.

There was the discussion of when they should be married, and what they should eat at their wedding breakfast. "It was the eggs in parsley sauce that persuaded me, so thoughtful was the Major for my comfort, and so attentive to me. We must eat them again at our wedding, and perhaps, Lettie dear, you could send to Lady Clara's cook for the receipt." Mention was made of where they might go for their honeymoon. "The Lakes are said to be pretty, though neither the Major nor I are so very fond of views," and the Major, bluffly gallant, raised his glass again, saying, "I have the prettiest view in the world before my eyes already, and nothing could compare to it!"

These love-bird croonings continued through the meal, leaving Violette to do little other than to nod and smile, and wonder when she could introduce the topic that loomed larger and larger in her own mind as the evening wore on. By the time the baked apples and vanilla wafers were brought in, her apprehension was such that she felt she must speak.

She took a deep breath. "Major Jennings," she began. "It was so very nice to see you at the Winterbourne ball. Tell me, how are you acquainted with that family?"

"Ah yes. Lord Winterbourne is of course a JP, and I have had dealings with him in that regard."

"A JP? What is that?"

"A Justice of the Peace. A judge, if you will. He serves upon the Bench and I have had occasion to approach him for a warrant. He is a pleasant enough fellow, I daresay. Something foppish in his manner. He is what I think is referred to as an Exquisite." From the tone of his voice, marked with a faint disgust, Violette gained the impression that he thought little of Lord Winterbourne.

"Foppish, you say?"

He snorted. "He attends upon the Bench but rarely, and cries off with the excuse that he has an appointment in London with his tailor. I have no patience with such a mollycoddle sort of fellow. He has no conversation other than that of finding the perfect polish for his boots. He seems so generally lackadaisical that I wonder he has the ability to get out of his bed in the mornings!" He took a swallow of his wine, and lowered his voice. "There's a rumour that the fellow's in straights and on the lookout to snatch himself up a plump little prize of a wife. You are lucky, Miss Violette, that he has not taken a fancy to you and your fortune!"

This was a most uncomfortable observation, perhaps a little too reminiscent of Major Jennings' time in barracks, and Violette made no answer.

Miss Felicia broke in. "What sensible woman would take him escapes me. Why, at the ball I did not spy him standing up with a single lady, a most shocking want of manners! I knew his mother as a girl, and she was very proper indeed; he did not learn his rude ways from her!" Miss Felicia was quite heated. It was clear that Lord Winterbourne's snub in Bath still rankled.

"Not enough of a gentleman to join his fellows at the card table after supper, neither. No doubt he spilled sauce upon his cravat and had to spend an hour or two before the looking glass with his manservant, tying a new one!" Major Jennings let out a snort of disapproval.

Violette helped herself to a vanilla wafer. This was a most difficult conversation, and she wished to turn the point. "But he invited you to the ball?"

"I received an invitation, yes. Not by his lordship's hand, of course, but I assume it was he put my name forward. I confess I was somewhat surprised to be invited, and should have said no, but I could not refuse. It's as well, in my occupation, to keep an acquaintance with all, for who knows what good might come of it? And, of course, I knew I should see my dearest Felicia – I may call you that now, may I not, my sweet?" He paused to smile at his beloved, and took her hand and raised it to his lips, and she blushed and fluttered accordingly.

Violette returned him to the conversation. "You were not willing to attend?"

"We'd had an information laid. That we might apprehend a band of smugglers putting into shore with their illicit cargo on that same evening. And indeed, my men reported that they did catch sight of such, and gave chase to one of the fellows, but with no success. I vow I would have caught him – had I been there! But the opportunity will present itself to me, never fear!" He let out a great rich chuckle of satisfaction. "Are you not surprised that I am so easily here, when the Excise Office and my home are so far distant? It is not merely for the sake of Miss Felicia's sparkling eyes, but because I have reason to think that the infamous Captain Death and his rascally crew have their rogue's nest in this very part of the county! So I have taken rooms at The Dragon, for I am determined to flush him out – by hook or by crook!"

Violette's wafer turned to choking ash in her mouth. She took a gulp of her wine. In a faint voice she said, "I met them, I believe. Your men, I mean. I was thirsty and went looking for a drink, and took a wrong turn and ended up in the stable yard and they were going to shoot a dog and I saved him." Her words tumbled out of her mouth in a great rush; her wine slopped onto the table. She put down her glass, and hid her shaking hands in her lap.

Miss Felica's hands flew to her mouth. "Lettie, dear! I can hardly believe such a thing! What were you thinking?"

Major Jennings looked quite grim. "There was some nonsense spoke, about a young lady and a dog." He did not repeat what had been said of her; the most ribald and disparaging of comments about her appearance – wearing virtually nothing, or so it was reported. "I must say, as someone who thinks of himself – if you will allow me that honour – as becoming part of your family in the future, it was a most unwise course of action, to be wandering about in the middle of the night in that way. Who knows what might have happened to you!"

Violette forced out a gay laugh. It sounded hollow to her ears. "Well, it was very silly of me, and gave me quite a fright, so I have learned a lesson from it. And now I shall ring for Giles to bring you in the port. There is tobacco in the caddy, and snuff. Please help yourself Major Jennings, and join us when you are ready."

With that, Violette whisked her aunt out of the dining room and into the drawing room. Here, she prevailed upon her to play some airs upon the piano, and fell back in her chair to revive her spirits with several cups of scalding tea drunk in quick succession.

CHAPTER 10

'So it *was* their mare that I bought at Canterbury; the mare that Clara Taverner recognised; though Kit Taverner said it wasn't, and made her out a fool. Why would he do that?

'And when Lord Winterbourne saw me at the hunt, he *was* surprised – not at the sight of me, but of my horse! He was afraid that I would know him as being what John said – in dibs to the bank. So, Kit Taverner knows it. And Lady Clara doesn't!'

It was towards the end of April, and the news was out, that Miss Violette deVere's period of mourning was over, and she had attended a ball. She might not be in the first dewy flush of youth, but she was single and she was rich. Those that had not seen her called her a beauty, and those that had did not; but all were fascinated by the idea of her, and all society was agog to see her.

In the days following the Winterbourne ball, Violette had been inundated with invitations for the London Season, and could have spent every waking hour engaged upon calls and cards and balls and dinners and routs and outings of all kinds, had she so desired. Accordingly, she had engaged a London agent to find somewhere for her to rent for these few months, and the result was a little house on the corner of Fitzhardinge Street, recently redecorated and still smelling somewhat of paint. It looked over Manchester Square, one of the most fashionable areas of London; and now, Violette was sitting in the parlour window. Face down beside her was a novel, newly arrived from the bookseller and with a dish of candied cherries beside it, but Violette, enchanted with the novelties of London life, was watching the people passing in the street. She was waiting for Lady Clara's carriage, for they had arranged to go driving in the park at three o'clock.

Being idle, and the house being quiet with her aunt carried off to a luncheon party, Violette's thoughts had returned, once more, to their well-worn path. 'Lord Winterbourne cannot be in straights, surely? I cannot believe it for a second! Lady Clara's ball must have cost a pretty penny and they have their house here in a very fashionable part of town, and Winterbourne Hall is enormous. Everything about that family is the very pinnacle of fashionable extravagance with no expense spared.

'Though I suppose I wonder a little at Mr Kit Taverner's choice of the Navy as a career. It's an unusual choice of profession for a gentleman of aristocratic birth, I should have thought, and dangerous, perhaps, in these uncertain times.

'His sister says he wishes to see the world, but a great many young gentlemen travel abroad without needing to earn a living by joining the Navy to do so. Is his choice one of financial necessity? Or is it simply that he is seized with a roistering, piratical spirit of adventure? Unlike his buttoned-up brother!"

This train of thought led her, inexorably, back to the vexing subject of Lord Winterbourne. 'It is no secret that a single man in possession of great debt must be in want of a rich wife. And if this is the case, why would Winterbourne be so very determined that he would not consider me for my fortune, when his brother is so very adamant that he should? His excuse is a poor one, indeed. What sensible man would give up the chance of a fortune merely for the sake of a pair of eyes prettier than mine?

'Oh, none of it makes any sense at all!'

She bit into a cherry, and picked up her novel again, but the story of a castle surrounded by cliffs and crags, echoing with inexplicable screams in the night and with a heroine seemingly incapable of rational thought was no match for the very real mystery that was occupying Violette's mind. She laid down the book with an exasperated sigh, and turned her gaze back to the window, her thoughts whirling themselves round in a circle yet again.

'Clara told me that Lord Winterbourne spends a deal of his time in the country but Major Jennings says he is hardly to be seen, for he is always in Town. He is said to be foppish, and he certainly appears a veritable Dandy, and Major Jennings considers him a fool, and lackadaisical – but he sounded none of those things when I overheard his argument with his brother. Why was he so adamant that he would make no play for me? Or indeed, for any woman, for he has no reputation as a flirt.

"Oh!' Violette shot upright on the window seat, seized by an astonishing thought. 'Foppish and a Dandy dresser, lackadaisical and not interested in marriage at any price, and his whereabouts a mystery much of the time. Perhaps – there are men, I have heard of, who do not – who do not wish for the company of ladies. Maybe Lord Winterbourne is one of those particular types; *not the marrying kind,* as I have heard it called. Or,' she was seized by another idea, 'perhaps all his money has been spent in the – the opium dens! This would account for his money troubles and his world-weary demeanour and his lack of interest in anything!'

These startling ideas might be said to have been generated by the over-consumption of novels from the subscription library, and were, no-doubt, the reason that so many parents frowned upon their presence in the hands of young ladies of a hitherto innocent disposition. But Violette's upbringing had been a great deal less conventional than that of her sheltered English counterparts.

Violette had spent the early years of her youth in Paris, where her parents had a wide circle or acquaintance; actors and dancers, and artists with their models and mistresses – raffish, déclassé, and none of them as stuffily respectable as they might have been. Rubbing shoulders with these in her parent's *salon* of an evening could also be found fervent young men and women fired up by the revolutionary writings of Sieyes and Lafayette, and grizzled intellectuals with a taste for philosophising. With his undiluted disdain for what he saw as the shallow preoccupations of the English *ton*, her father had even dipped a toe into the dangerous world of French politics with his attendance at meetings of the anti-royalist Jacobin club. But lively theorising over a good supper about the removal of the monarchy and the rebirth of France as a place where all citizens were treated equally and fairly was a long way removed from the reality of mob rule and anarchy, and before long it seemed expedient for Sir Charles deVere to move his family as far from Paris as possible. He and his friends found refuge in St Cloud sur Mer, a tiny town tucked away in the furthest reaches of the South, cheek by jowl with the Italian province of Nice. With no strategic significance to recommend it other than a tiny port where the fishing boats landed their early morning catch as the sun rose, life in St Cloud was peaceful, escaping the worst of the political upheavals that consumed the north to such a degree.

As the beneficiary of her father's radical views on the education of children – that they should learn by exploration and experience without having their heads stuffed full of unnecessary conversations about history and mathematics and the like – Violette was left much to her own devices. She spent her days with the village children, wading in streams and riding the donkeys used to transport goods up and down the steep hillsides, and at harvest time helping to bring in the crops; lilacs in May and lavender in August to be transported the twenty miles or so to the *parfumeries* of Grasse. She could climb trees and row a boat and tie a sailor's knot as well as any boy; and it was this, perhaps, which had dissuaded any of the young men of the village from courtship, even had her father allowed it.

Sir Charles deVere might have chosen love for his wife over what his father saw as his duty to his family and the class into which he was born, but at the same time he was strongly conscious of his dignity. Just as Sir William deVere had kept his unmarried daughter close, so his son did the same. Sir Charles would have come down very hard on any young man bold enough to court Violette, even if there had been a young man of suitable birth and breeding to make such a thing possible. There was not; and that was the end of the matter.

And just as St Cloud sur Mer had one foot in Italy and the other in France and was ignored by both, so Violette grew up with no real sense of where she belonged and what was expected of her. Left largely to her own devices, she read voraciously, day-dreamed continually, and, seated beneath the piano in her parents' drawing room at night, listened to conversations that taught her a great deal more about the ways of the world than most of her new acquaintance could comprehend. So the thought of Lord Winterbourne being of *a certain persuasion* was not as outlandish an idea to her as it might be to others, and fuelled by her passion for novels with their melodramatic settings and the astonishing predicaments in which their heroines found themselves, the thought of opium dens seemed not so very far-fetched, either.

'I do believe this is the answer – or something very like. He is concealing a dark and dreadful secret, and the last vestiges of his honour prevent him from marrying and subjecting his poor wife to his depraved lifestyle!' Her conclusions did not make her happy, 'but at least I can stop thinking about it,' she said, firmly, to herself. 'And as for his lordship – I am sorry for him, if opium dens are the reason for his downfall, but I suppose he may go and visit as many as he likes; I shall not waste another thought upon him!'

With that, she spied an elegant yellow-painted barouche turn the corner, with Clara seated prettily in it and her sour-faced companion across from her. Violette sprang to her feet, and ran for her bonnet and gloves.

CHAPTER 11

No sooner had this puzzle resolved itself to Violette's satisfaction, than another presented itself. 'Oh really!' she thought, irritably. 'Just as fast as one difficulty is dealt with, so two more spring up in its place!'

The Season by now was half-way through. A silver salver sat upon the hall table in Fitzhardinge Street, and each morning at breakfast, Giles would bring it in quite overflowing with invitations. Violette was enjoying herself immensely, in no small part because of her growing friendship with Clara Taverner. There was a difference of some years between them, but Violette had come to look upon Lady Clara as something of a younger sister, and had begun to suspect that she was lonely.

With both parents dead, her twin away in Portsmouth or on his ship a great deal of the time, and Lord Winterbourne apparently much occupied, there seemed no-one to keep her company but her cousin, Miss Flint – most aptly named for both her visage and her disposition. And Clara Taverner was not a girl content with her own company. She could find no amusement in putting her nose into a novel, or spending a quiet hour over embroidery or cutting paper shapes for an album.

One rainy afternoon, when the maid announced Violette into the drawing room of the Taverner's elegant townhouse in Cavendish Square, it was to find a game of cards in progress. The room was darkened by the overcast skies, and the candles lit, though it was not much after three o'clock. Lady Clara had her head close to that of a young man, and the two were deep in whispered conversation. Although for the purposes of propriety, Miss Flint was at the other end of the room, it was clear she had been asleep. At Violette's entrance she startled herself awake with a loud snore, which made Clara giggle.

"Violette! Come and meet my friend Mr Philip Marwood! Last night at the Frasers I trounced Mr Marwood at the card table, and he has come today to exact his revenge. Mr Marwood, Miss deVere."

Mr Marwood was a sharp-featured young man, with a wide smile which displayed a great many teeth. He made his bow. "The beautiful Miss deVere. I count it a singular honour to be introduced to someone whom all society is agog to meet! Clarrie has told me what a good friend you are to her. I have to thank you for it!"

Violette was somewhat irked at Mr Marwood's clumsy compliments and taken aback to hear him speak of Lady Clara in so familiar a manner, but mention was made that he was a friend of Mr Kit Taverner and had known him at university. 'That may account for it,' thought Violette, 'but even so, my aunt spends a deal of time telling me that my behaviour is not suitable for a young lady. I dislike it intensely, but now I am turned into my aunt's echo, and repeating her word for word!' For something about the scene – Clara's familiarity with the young man, and Mr Marwood's proprietorial air – made Violette uneasy. She could not have put her finger on exactly what, but just the very next evening, at Lady Dorset's ball thrown to celebrate the engagement of one of her many daughters, Violette's suspicion of the young man hardened into something close to active dislike.

She was looking absently towards the new arrivals entering the ballroom, while listening with half an ear to her aunt, who had struck up an acquaintance with a matron sitting beside her upon a row of small gilt chairs, when she caught the eye of Mr Marwood. At almost the same time, her aunt stood, to take a turn about the room with her new-found friend. And the very second Miss Felicia had quitted her seat, Mr Philip Marwood materialised in her place.

With a perfunctory "May I join you?" he sat down, summoned the footman to bring him a glass of champagne, and drank it off in one. "I was hoping to see you here, Miss deVere," said he, "for I wish that we might know one another better, and that I might call you my friend!" This was delivered with a wide smile, and a confiding air. Violette edged imperceptibly away from him.

He continued, "I understand you are but recently arrived in Town, as am I, and have been lately in mourning for your dear father, as have I also! In mourning for my own dear father, I mean. His death was several years ago, but I still feel it as keenly as if it were yesterday. So we have much in common, do we not? I hope you will feel free to call upon me should you need assistance in any small thing, for I am familiar with the best circles of society. You may have heard of my godfather, Sir Harry Gray, a director of Cornishmen's Bank, you know. He relies heavily upon me for all things. I enjoy being of service to the old gentleman, and he has no-one else to take such care of him." This was all delivered in one steady stream, punctuated by nods of the head and sympathetic smiles, but all the time Mr Marwood kept his eyes fixed upon Violette with a gimlet stare of steely intensity.

"You are very kind, Mr Marwood," murmured Violette, "but do not concern yourself for my comfort, I pray you." She looked for her aunt, hoping to catch her eye, for her return would force Mr Marwood out of his seat, but she was some distance away and oblivious to Violette's discomfort. "So you are here from the country, you say?"

"From Cornwall, where I was heading up some business affairs for my godfather, Sir Harry Gray, as I mentioned; director of Cornishmen's Bank, as I said, and very well situated in Mayfair, where I also reside. So tell me, are you familiar with that part of the country?"

"Mayfair?" ventured Violette, wonderingly.

He let out a loud hoot of laughter, which caused heads to turn in their direction. "I declare, Miss deVere. You are a wit! No, no. Cornwall, of course. A beautiful landscape, if you are interested in the Romantic, and I think you must be, for you have compelling eyes, Miss Violette – may I call you that? They speak of a passionate and soulful nature, indeed."

Violette hardly knew how to answer. She cast about for the safest topic to turn the conversation away from her passionate and soulful eyes. "So, your father … I am sorry to hear… that is, it must be pleasant to be employed in such a responsible role, and banking must be a most interesting occupation."

"You hesitate. I understand it. You are perturbed that a humble clerk with ink-stained fingers might be invited into the beautiful home of such as Lady Dorset!"

Violette was thinking no such thing, and blushed hotly at this slur upon her character.

He carried on, "Her ladyship is cousin by marriage to Viscount Marwood, and I, too, am related to the Viscount, for our grandfathers were brothers. Indeed, Miss deVere, you will be intrigued to know that I can trace my own ancestry to connections with many of the finest families in the land and have employed an historian to do just that. At home I have a framed chart showing those connections in beautiful manuscript, all set out in coloured inks." He paused, as if waiting for a reply.

"How – how fascinating and – and lovely, Mr Marwood," said Violette, faintly.

"But whereas that gentleman, Viscount Marwood, is the happy possessor of land and fortune, my own family – my mother, in fact – was ruined at the gaming tables by someone known for such underhand dealings. And so it is that you see me, a gentleman by birth and breeding, earning a humble crust by the charity of my godfather." He leaned towards her, confidingly. "I have expectations in that direction. Though perhaps I should not speak of them."

"No indeed! I wish you would not!"

"My mother was foolish, and my father deceived, and it is I who pay the price for such treachery. But I do it, I hope, with the utmost grace." He dropped his eyes modestly, and smiled a little self-deprecatingly, before leaning towards her once again. "Believe me when I say, with the most sincerest of hearts, Miss deVere, that I have great ambition. When I marry and come into fortune, through that marriage, or through my other expectations, I will prove to be just the equal of any of my connections. I intend to have the finest of everything. My wife will know what it is to be at the very heart and pinnacle of society!" He sat back with a very satisfied air about him, and nodded at her meaningfully.

At that moment Miss Felicia returned, and he was obliged to give up his seat. Violette was left wondering if he had been making a declaration to her, and what exactly that declaration was intended to be.

'I hope to see no more of that young man,' she thought. 'To make his family known in such a way – his mother ruined – his father broken by it – to a perfect stranger! It was quite shocking, and I cannot think what he meant by it!'

Mr Marwood was not the only new addition to Violette's social circle. Through the weeks that she had been in London, Miss Felicia and her gallant Major had been in daily correspondence. One morning in June she came to her niece in a state of apprehension, with a letter in her hand.

"The Major says he will be in London for a fortnight on business, and proposes to bring his sister with him, for he says she wishes to know us better. He says that they will put up at an inn. But I cannot help but think, Lettie dear, that this is not appropriate for Miss Jennings, who will soon be my sister, also. Perhaps we could invite her to stay with us, here at Fitzhardinge Street. What do you think?"

Miss Felicia did not look overly thrilled at the prospect of having her soon-to-be-sister paying a sustained visit, and Violette quite sympathised, but said, "Of course! We can hardly do otherwise. And although Miss Jennings was a little overcome by her nerves, perhaps, when we met her at Oare, it would be delightful to have the chance to be better acquainted. Write back directly, Aunt, and invite her most cordially. She could stay with us for the remainder of our sojourn here in London and travel back into Kent with us in three weeks. And we will entertain her most royally while she is here!"

Miss Jennings was to take up residence in a second-floor bedroom. This was, in fact, Miss Felicia's own room, in which she had delighted all these past weeks.

This room was papered in a sumptuous Chinese design of blue peacocks on a yellow ground and, facing east, it caught the early morning sun. It was a daily delight to Miss Felicia to wake into a room filled, as she put it, with the most vibrant sunshine, and she found the paper so exceedingly charming that she had enquired of the land agent as to where the same might be purchased, with a view to having it in a room in her new married home, wherever that might be.

The view from this room was of Manchester Square's central garden, a pretty planting of flowering trees and shrubs. And it was Miss Felicia's particular delight to observe the life of the garden. When she was making her morning toilette, there would be a parade of nursemaids with their charges; children with their hoops and balls and babies in their wheeled carriages. Putting on her bonnet and gloves ready to sally forth to a luncheon, she might see a small boy with his chubby fists clutching hold of the reins of his first pony and accompanied by a groom. And in the afternoons when she was resting with a copy of *The Ladies' Journal* on her lap and her feet up on the footstool, the young ladies of the schoolroom would arrive with their governesses, to sketch leaves in the botanical style or to promenade and exchange pleasantries with their contemporaries.

Miss Felicia's enjoyment of her bedroom was so complete that Violette begged her to reconsider. "Don't give up your room to Miss Jennings, Aunt! You take such a delight in it! I am sure she would be just as happy on the other side of the house, which looks out into the mews, with all the comings and goings of the carriages and so on. That room is painted in a pretty enough shade. With an arrangement of flowers upon the dresser it would do very well and we could order new window shades and bed furnishings if you like."

But Miss Felicia would not be gainsaid. "I knew Miss Jennings when she and I were girls together, many years ago. She was just as lively as you could wish, and I am sorry to see her reduced to such a sour state.

"My life has quite turned around, Lettie dear, since you came to live with me, and I met Major Jennings again. I cannot tell you what a delight it is for me to be able – through your own sweet generosity – to enjoy a life of society and gaiety that I thought lost to me forever. I wish nothing more than to share my happiness with Miss Sally Jennings and to be her good friend when I am married to her brother, and it means a great deal to me to give her the nicest room in the house, if it is in my power!"

Violette bowed to her aunt's wishes, though she felt it would take more than peacock wallpaper, a view of some baby carriages and a dose of strong sunlight to de-sour Miss Jennings. And she was quite right in her assessment of Miss Jennings' character.

Miss Jennings was made welcome upon her arrival at Fitzhardinge Street, and was greeted with the tea tray while the footman took her bags to her room. She watched Miss Felicia unlock the caddy and measure three spoonsful of her favourite Orange Pekoe into the teapot.

"That is so very wasteful! Two spoons would be quite sufficient. Such a flowery-tasting brew it makes, that I wonder at your serving it to your guests," and, frowning at the charming little cakes that accompanied it, "I dislike sponge cake excessively, far too rich for anyone's digestion and very disadvantageous to the waistline. A plain water-biscuit would serve you far better, my dear."

Upon being shown to her room, she felt compelled to mention that she considered yellow to be a most vulgar shade. "I vow I find it quite bilious, and the design of this paper is enough to give anybody the headache, to be sure!" She sighed heavily at the sound of a carriage passing by in the street – "What a rattle there is in these London streets!" and examined the window dressings with a critical eye. "Very thin, my dear, and hardly conducive to a good night's sleep. I daresay the sun streaming through them in the mornings is well-nigh intolerable!"

Miss Felicia could not help but spring to the room's defence. "But do look, Miss Jennings, I beg you, at the charming scene from the window! This is a most comfortable chair, and a footstool as you see. The trees are not so very large, so we are afforded an unspoiled view of Hertford House. It has such a sweeping drive that although the carriages stop quite discreetly inside the portico, it's possible to catch the occasional glimpse of their visitors. They entertain the most *bohemian* of guests – they are quite famous for it – and his lordship is in receipt of quite seventy thousand a year, or so they say! And I have seen his Royal Highness alighting from his carriage more than once!"

She would have carried on to impart the thrilling news that, reposing upon the fireplace mantel in the drawing room was a stiff white card with an engraved invitation to the Hertford's ball to be held in a week's time, considered to be the event of the season; but something about Miss Jennings' expression made her hesitate.

That lady drew herself up most stiff, and looked quite down her nose at Miss Felicia. "I wonder at you, my dear, for being so impressed by fortune, and so intrigued as to the comings and goings of someone of such loose morals. And as for sitting here and spying upon your neighbours, you may be certain I shall do no such thing!"

In short, it became instantly clear that Miss Jennings took offence most easily, and commented upon every single thing, and cast a critical eye over every arrangement made for her comfort and happiness. And rather than be uplifted and inspired by Miss Felicia's happiness, she seemed determined to undermine it at every turn, and to reduce that poor lady to her own level of unremitting misery.

CHAPTER 12

Towards the end of the week, Lady Clara arrived at Fitzhardinge Street in a state of high excitement, to invite Violette and her aunt, "And of course, your guest, Miss Jennings!" to accompany her and a group of friends to Vauxhall Gardens that evening.

"There is to be a display of fireworks from a hot-air balloon, and an orchestra to accompany the sight! I can't wait to see it!"

Miss Jennings had not been asked for her opinion, but gave it anyway. "Vauxhall Gardens? A ridiculous notion! Everyone knows that pickpockets and villains of all kinds haunt the shaded walks, and that no lady's reputation is safe! Miss Violette and Miss deVere will most certainly decline this ill-thought-out scheme, and you, Miss, should be guided by your elders and think better of it yourself!" She nodded her head most forcibly, to make her point plain.

Clara Taverner was far too well-mannered to say what her face expressed, which was that she very much disliked being addressed in that peremptory manner as *Miss*, and that Miss Jennings would do well to keep her unsolicited opinions to herself. Instead, she contented herself with saying, meekly, "We shall be in a good party, with gentlemen to protect us and I am sure none of us would dream of promenading in the shaded walks, Miss Jennings! Oh, Violette, *do* come. Mr Marwood has taken great pains to procure tickets and he is to be accompanied by a friend of his from the military, and Miss Flint as well, so it will be very proper, I can assure you!"

As if on cue, the door opened and the maid announced Mr Philip Marwood, who came bounding into the room. "Ah!" he cried, feigning astonishment to find Lady Clara there, 'I saw your carriage outside as I was passing, and thought I should find you here, so pleasantly occupied with our delightful friend Miss deVere!"

Clara blushed, and laughed, and Violette thought once again that she must find the opportunity to speak to her about her relationship with Mr Marwood, for it seemed that caution and discretion were in danger of being thrown to the winds. 'But it should not be my responsibility!' she said to herself in some annoyance, 'It is for Lord Winterbourne to look to his sister!' She wondered at him leaving his sister protected from her own youthful foolishness by nothing more than the ineffectual glowerings of Miss Flint; and she did not miss the fleeting glance exchanged between that lady and Mr Marwood.

"I was just explaining your plan for the outing to Vauxhall," said Lady Clara. Turning back to the room, she said in a wistful voice, "It's reputed to be very beautiful, and I have never been there, and wish more than anything that I might go! And you will love it, Violette, I *know* you will!"

"I don't believe I know much about it at all. I do like a pretty garden, but why would we wish to view a garden at night?"

Mr Marwood gave out one of his braying laughs. "Another of Miss Violette deVere's famous witticisms! I declare, I say to a number of my friends, until you have heard Miss Violette deVere speak, you have not heard wit!

Violette gritted her teeth. How dare this insufferable young man discuss her with his friends – it really was too much!

"Oh no, it's not gardens like that. Not plantings and such like. No, it's an entertainment! Mr Marwood has shown me this pamphlet. Listen!" she proceeded to skim through it, relating various titbits to her audience in a rapid monologue.

"There are avenues of trees with gilded statues here and there – and something about a view over a rustic landscape with hayricks and milkmaids and cows or some such, how odd … anyway, there is a big square in the middle with refreshments and music, and it is all lit by lamps made to look like stars and moons, and strings of Chinese lanterns too, they sound pretty, do they not? Oh, and there is a Pavilion for dancing and a building called a Rotunda, which has a ceiling painted with flowers and the walls all mosaic with great gilded mirrors and chandeliers and sconces, so that you can see yourself reflected in all these mirrors at once, which I think sounds charming! The chandeliers are made to look like baskets of flowers. Oh, it does sound so lovely!" She glanced up, just in time to catch Miss Jennings opening her mouth to venture her opinion once more, and quickly added, "It says here, *The Charm and Innocence of the Entertainments have made them the Delight of all Persons of Reputation and Taste; so that even Bishops have been seen here without injuring their Character.*"

Mention of Bishops seemed to quiet Miss Jennings' fears, and in any event, Violette thought it would be rather exciting to see the avenues of trees all lit up by lanterns, and to walk out at night in the dark seemed quite daring, and to listen to music and to eat at a table in the open air seemed a most enticing idea.

As well as that, she was swayed by three considerations. The first, that if Miss Flint could not effectively chaperone her charge in her own drawing room, then she certainly could not be trusted to chaperone her in a public garden at night, and perhaps Violette should ensure that her friend came to no harm. The second was the reaction of her aunt, who clapped her hands with delight at the thought of such an interesting adventure. And the third was that Miss Jennings was so very set against it, which made Violette want to do precisely the opposite.

"I should love to go and see a hot-air balloon," she said, firmly.

CHAPTER 13

Violette's first impression of Vauxhall Gardens was one of pure enchantment.

The carriages pulled up at the gates, and the company alighted in the highest of spirits, Violette and her aunt and the Major and his sister in one party, and Lady Clara and Miss Flint in the other. Waiting for them were Mr Marwood and his friend. Sergeant Jones was a stout fellow in his scarlet and black, which was complemented by a lumpen red nose that spoke of a liking for port, and an elaborate black moustache that perhaps owed something to the dye-pot.

As they entered the gardens and progressed along the first long *allée* of tall trees, it seemed everything Mr Marwood's pamphlet had promised and more. Dusk was falling, and the lanterns strung along the pathway glowed softly in the growing darkness. Suspended from the branches of the trees were pretty gilded bird cages filled with cascading flowers that perfumed the air, and beneath them was planted a hedge of box, cleverly clipped into an array of amusing shapes; spirals and pyramids and hearts.

In the distance could be heard a string quartet playing a lively air, and Violette and her friends joined the crowd heading in that direction. There were groups of friends chatting and laughing in low voices and although Violette could spy no Bishops, she did see a Reverend personage in his black with a most respectable-looking lady upon his arm, and hoped it was enough to put Miss Jennings' mind at rest.

There were families walking together, with children hopping from foot to foot with excitement. Lady Clara hopped from foot to foot herself and caught hold of Violette's hand. "Isn't it just what I said it would be? Oh, Violette, don't you love it?"

Violette laughed at her friend's enthusiasm, but she shared it. "I do love it! It reminds me a little of my home in France. My parents once took me to see a circus, and it has that same feeling of magic in the air!"

With that, she caught sight of one tall gentleman who divested himself of his beaver hat in order to scoop his smallest daughter onto his shoulders. He handed the hat to his son, a lad of ten years or so. The lad pulled off his cap and placed his father's hat proudly upon his own head, whereupon it instantly fell down across his nose giving rise to much merriment from his sisters. Violette smiled at the scene, although her smile was tinged with melancholy.

Something about the set of the man's shoulders, and the tenderness with which he engaged with his children caused her say to herself, 'This was the family I imagined I would have myself, one day, but time has passed me by. Although,' catching sight of her aunt with her arm tucked through that of her Major, 'perhaps life has just as much of a surprise in store for me. We none of us know what lies around the corner.' And her thoughts flew once again to Captain Death, and his arms holding her as they slept.

They reached the end of the walk. Here was situated a gilded statue of dolphins with fountains playing around it; and they turned a corner to find themselves in a great square lined with shops and galleries.

Everywhere they looked they saw flower beds and hanging baskets, and vines trailing down from upstairs balconies and archways of roses. It was quite as if they had been magically transported to some distant place far removed from the noise and smells of the city; with cloistered walks and colonnades and terraces, and here and there an alleyway opening onto some enticing vista. Miss Jennings was so taken with a depiction of cobblestones and ancient walls leading, as it were, to a sunlit garden in the distance, that she plunged towards it, only to be pulled up short – for these views were the most cunning of deceptions, no more than painted canvases intended to deceive the eye. This led to shouts of laughter from her companions, and blustering, embarrassed fury from the lady herself.

All along the walkways, chandeliers reflected their light in gilded mirrors, so that the whole scene glittered and sparkled. At every corner was an amusement of some kind – jugglers and fire-eaters and a conjuror who could produce a string of coloured silks from his mouth and make a bird appear from his hat.

They took their seats at a table, and ordered their supper of chicken and ham and salads of all kinds, and there were oysters and ices and syllabub.

Mr Marwood ordered a bowl of arrack punch to be brought to the table. "It's absolutely the thing here!" he declared. "I can't let you ladies leave without a mouthful, at least!" The punch came, and the ladies dutifully tried it. It was quite as delicious as he had promised, with spices and lemons, and the exotic flavour of cocoa-nut from the far-off islands of the Caribbean. All-in-all, it was a most lively party, and Violette was glad that she had come, whatever her reasons might have been.

But her gaiety was not to last for very long.

Major Jennings had struck up a great and instant friendship with Mr Marwood's companion, Sergeant Jones. Over supper, the pair of them imbibed freely of the arrack punch, and finished a bottle of wine between them and ordered another. As the ladies were finishing their ices they ordered a second bowl of the punch, "An' a brandy or two, for a li'l – a li'l – kick!" added Major Jennings, with a loud hiccup.

These brandies slid down easily, and a couple more were ordered. Relaxed and expansive, Major Jennings fell to reminiscing about his army career. His stories were long and somewhat rambling, and illustrated by the movement of spoons and glasses across the table to illustrate points of warfare, which made for dull conversation indeed. Miss Felicia tried her best to steer the conversation in a different direction, and Violette attempted to engage the ladies in a more diverting topic, but it was a thankless task.

One more glass of brandy was ordered and drunk, and it proved one glass too many. It led inexorably to the Sergeant and the Major guffawing over army stories of a most lurid kind, more suited to the smoking room of the barracks than the company of ladies.

Miss Felicia rose to her feet and moved round the table to her betrothed, and begged him in a low voice to desist. Whereupon he raised himself to his feet, swaying quite alarmingly, and pinched and patted her in a most familiar way that caused her to turn quite scarlet with shame. To top it all, he called out to Sergeant Jones in a booming voice, "Ain't I just the lucky fellow, to have brought down this plump li'l bird?"

Sergeant Jones leaned back in his chair and eyed her in a most offensive way, and agreed, adding, "and I bet she was a little beauty, once!" Miss Felicia knew not where to look, and tears of mortification sprang to her eyes.

Violette jumped to her feet. "Aunt! Excuse me! I believe the fireworks are about to start, and I suggest that we leave these … these gentlemen, here. Mr Marwood, perhaps you would summon the waiter and order a pot of strong coffee for the Major and his companion. And when that has been drunk, we shall meet you at the hot air balloon."

With that, she ushered the ladies away, Miss Felicia most distressed, and Violette furiously angry; Miss Flint, who had perhaps enjoyed the arrack punch more than was wise, a little unsteady on her feet and muttering in an undertone that this was not at all what she had expected when she agreed to come; and Miss Sally Jennings subdued for once, for even she could not find it within her to excuse her brother. She contented herself instead with making fearful comments in a low voice about the foolishness of setting out on their own, "For I think at least Mr Marwood should have come with us, and it is highly indecorous for a group of ladies alone to be at the mercy of these crowds!"

Violette agreed with her. They were put into a most difficult situation. "Perhaps we should leave," she said. Lady Clara gave a wail of anguish. "But we are here now, and no doubt Philip – Mr Marwood, I mean – will catch up with us in a while; and look, there is the hot-air balloon and here is the orchestra tuning up, and we have come all this way and I cannot bear to go without seeing it!"

They found a corner to stand in with a good view. The orchestra started up. With a great creaking of ropes, and roaring bursts of fire from the little stove contained in the basket and shouts from the balloon captain and cheers from the crowd, the anchors were detached from the ground and the balloon rose into the air. It was full dark now, and the balloon glowed pearly pink as it floated serenely upwards. Eventually it was high above their heads and with a crash of chords and a great roll of the drums, the fireworks display began.

All concerns about being ladies alone and devoid of gentlemanly protection were forgotten in the sheer rapture of the spectacle. The ladies joined the rest of the crowd ooh-ing and aah-ing with delight as gold and silver starbursts and multi-coloured whirligigs went sparkling and spinning into the night sky.

At last, the display came to an end, and the admiring cries of the crowd came to an end, and to great applause the balloon was lowered to the ground. But of Major Jennings and his friend there was no sign, nor any sign of Mr Marwood. With no gentleman to escort them, Violette determined that there was no help but for the ladies to make their way through the crowds on their own, and tight-lipped with fury, she gathered her companions to her.

Only to discover, much to her horror, that of Clara Taverner there was no sign, either.

CHAPTER 14

"Where can she be – oh, where can she have gone?"
Miss Felicia was beside herself, wringing her hands
with fear. Violette turned to Miss Flint. "Surely you
were at her side? She can't have just vanished!" Miss
Flint shrugged a little, and made the reply that Lady
Clara was young and foolish and known to be wilful;
which Violette thought a most unhelpful answer.

Miss Jennings was of no comfort. "Didn't I say
that it was a ridiculous notion to come here? No-one
would listen to me! Oh, it is all very well to see some
fireworks – though I declare I have seen better, for of
course my dear brother has escorted me to some
wonderful routs and military celebrations during his
career – but that silly young woman has put herself
in harm's way, that much is very clear. I shouldn't
be surprised if she is found murdered by the wayside
for the sake of her diamond earrings, for she should
have had more sense than to wear such jewels to a
place that is an absolute den of iniquity, populated
by thieves and – and kidnappers!" Miss Jennings'
voice rose to a wail.

Violette stared round her in horrified dismay. The end of the fireworks display marked the end of the evening for many of the revellers, and the crowd had turned direction with people intent on making their way back to the gates. Standing still, the ladies were jostled and pushed in the throng. "Come on, darlin'. Mind out the way, now!" – this good-natured enough, but delivered in the rough tones of a costermonger or some such.

Miss Jennings clutched her reticule to her. Her voice was shrill in her panic. "Be on your guard, I beg of you! Miss deVere, this is when the pickpockets do their work, in a busy crowd, and we are at their mercy, alone and unprotected as we are!"

"Oh, do hold your tongue!" Violette muttered under her breath. It was dreadfully impolite, but, really, Miss Jennings seemed determined to make matters worse. "We shall stand to the side, and wait until the crowd is gone. It's entirely possible that Lady Clara merely moved away from us, caught up in the crowd, and cannot see us. When the crowd has thinned a little, I'm sure she will arrive back safe and sound!" But the crowd dispersed, and she did not come.

Violette clenched her jaw. 'I will not cry, and have the hysterics. Something dreadful has happened to my friend, I know it – and there is no-one to help her but me, and I shall do it!' She took a deep breath, and in a steady voice, she said, "We shall go back to the supper room. I daresay Major Jennings and Mr Marwood and Sergeant Jones are still there.

"Aunt, you and Miss Jennings and Miss Flint can stay there with one of the gentlemen and the others can escort me to look for Lady Clara. There must be a manager or some such who can be of assistance. I am sure people get separated from their friends all the time. They must have some way of finding them."

It was not the ideal solution. Vauxhall Gardens was vast, acre upon acre of maze-like walks. Violette imagined Clara distraught, running from place to place in the dark, searching for her companions to no avail and herself, doing the same. 'We could be looking for one another for hours,' she thought.

They arrived back at the supper rooms to find the Major asleep in a corner, snoring fit to wake the dead, and no sign of Mr Marwood or his friend. The place was as busy as before, but the families who had dined there earlier had left, and it was a different atmosphere altogether. The women – 'I could not call them ladies,' thought Violette – were far from modest in their gaudy fashions, many of them with rouged lips and cheeks, and the men were louder. There were oaths, and shouting from one table to another and bursts of coarse laughter.

Miss Jennings, Miss Felicia and Miss Flint huddled around Violette like ducklings around their mother. Violette accosted a waiter. "I am looking for a missing young lady in a pink striped dress and matching pelisse, has she been here?"

He shook his head, impatiently. "Not seen no-one like that, Miss, sorry." Violette grasped his sleeve. "Could you at least go and waken that gentleman in the corner for me?"

The waiter went over and shook the Major by the sleeve, but to no avail. "'E's out for the count, Miss. Won't be no waking 'im 'til the morning, now!" With that, he whisked off to deliver his tray of drinks.

Violette stood irresolute, looking helplessly about her. "There's nothing for it but to go ourselves and find the carriages."

Miss Jennings let out a little scream of fear. "No, surely not – for I declare, we shall be swept along with the mayhem of the crowd and put out onto the street right into the melee of carriages and horses. We will be knocked to the ground and trampled, and at the mercy of any common knave or ragamuffin lurking at the gates who wishes to do us harm. We must stay here and wait for help to come to us!"

"What help would come, Miss Jennings? There is no help!" Violette turned to her aunt who, though quite pale with fright, at least seemed the most sensible of her three companions. "Aunt, we shall find the coaches. Lady Clara's coachman shall deliver you and Miss Jennings to Fitzhardinge Street and then take Miss Flint home. And John Hill shall come with me, and we shall search for Lady Clara." Violette spoke calmly enough, but there was a rising note of panic in her voice. "I am sure no harm has come to her and she is merely lost, for these long *allées* all look the same. Or she may have found some other amusement and not thought of the time.

"No doubt the other two gentlemen are with her – Mr Marwood and Sergeant Jones. And they will be looking for us, just as we are looking for them." This mention of Mr Marwood and the Sergeant seemed to reassure the other ladies. Though it did not reassure Violette in the least.

CHAPTER 15

... and we found our way back to the gates, and such a crowd there was, so that it seemed impossible to locate our carriages; and Miss Flint was quite beside herself, declaring that she would lose her place and be sent home, though why she should feel that she was to blame for Lady Clara's disappearance I cannot fathom; but she did seem a deal more concerned for herself than her charge, and worrying about going back to her cottage in Scotland, which surprised me, for I would not say she had a Scotch accent at all, but her cottage did sound very poor, and I felt sorry for her to exist upon a diet of porridge, which I believe they eat excessively, north of the border.

Miss Jennings was complaining all the while, and Violette quite white with fear for her friend. I was trying as hard as may be to support to the dear child, and keep my countenance cheerful, but I could not help but think that something dreadful had happened to poor Lady Clara, for one hears such stories!

I cannot tell you my thoughts on the Major, whose behaviour was quite the disgrace, and I cannot tell you how relieved I was when our carriage came in view and I saw John, pushing through the crowds towards us. I declare I quite clutched hold of his sleeve, so glad I was to see that dear familiar face!

Miss Felicia paused a moment; then she scratched out the last sentence. She was a little surprised at herself for having written it, and blushed at the rereading of it. For the truth was that upon seeing him she had positively burst into tears, and he had taken her hand in his own, and patted it, and said to her, "There, Miss Felicia, no need to cry now, whatever is the matter?" and she had gasped out, "Lady Clara is missing, and we are so very fearful for her!" which went nowhere near expressing her thoughts, which were that upon seeing John she would have gladly flung herself into his arms.

It was gone three o'clock before poor Lettie arrived back at Fitzhardinge Street, and I waiting for her with a good fire lit, for although it is the summer, I think a good fire has something comforting to it, and the tea tray was at hand, but I had passed a dreadful time as the clock ticked round, thinking the darkest thoughts about the safety of Lady Clara and my own dear Lettie, both. Though it was such a comfort to know that John was with her, for a more dependable fellow there could not be. She told me that they'd found the poor girl just as Lettie had suspected, that she had got herself separated from us in the crowd and taken a wrong turn somewhere, no more than that.

She was taken home to Cavendish Square and the doctor summoned, but apart from a fright the dear girl was unharmed. It was quite dawn before I got to my bed and I am still abed as I write this, for I am tired to death after such an adventure as our trip to Vauxhall Gardens turned out, and it is Lady Hertford's ball tonight!

Miss Felicia concluded her letter to her friend with a long description of the gown she was to wear to the ball, and then fell back against her pillows and slept, to relive in her dreams the surprising moment when John had clasped her hand in his, and she had been tempted – for one fleeting second – to lay her head upon his shoulder.

CHAPTER 16

Violette had not told her aunt the entire truth of finding Lady Clara.

She and John had traced their footsteps back to the place she was last seen, the launch site for the hot-air balloon. It was situated at the end of one of the walks planted with low hedges in the Italianate style. At the far end of the walk was a pavilion with tables and chairs set out in a terrace tiled in mosaic-work and pillars wreathed in ivy, as if located in the ancient ruins of Pompeii; and some lively airs were being played upon a violin by a fellow dressed in a toga, who might be supposed to represent Nero.

At first glance the scene appeared innocuous enough. But after a moment, Violette began to notice that each table was occupied by card players, and whatever games were in progress seemed pretty deep in play. There was no light chatter or laughter, but rather an intense concentration, with little speech other than to summon the waiter or to lay cards down upon the table with an oath. There was no sign of Clara here, and Violette made for the doors into the pavilion, only to find her route barred by a large fellow dressed in black.

"Miss, excuse me, but here are set up the gaming tables, and ladies are only allowed in this establishment if accompanied by a gentleman," he said, pleasantly enough, but quite firm.

"But I am accompanied –."

"Servants are not permitted into the gaming rooms, Miss," the burly fellow responded, looking John up and down in an insolent manner.

"But I don't wish to play. I am merely looking for my companion who is lost!" replied Violette. At that moment the door beside them swung open and two fellows came out, to the accompaniment of a burst of raucous laughter and a cloud of smoke redolent of pipes and cigars. As the two men passed by, she heard one say to the other, "That's a pretty pigeon being plucked in there!"

The other replied, laughing, "Plucked and roasted, my man, plucked and roasted!" and at that moment Violette heard an unmistakeable braying laugh.

"Mr Marwood!" She darted through the open door, followed closely by John, to find a great crowd of men, intently focused on something she could not see. There was a sudden chorus of whoops and howls.

"Someone's winning or losing heavy, Miss!" said John.

Violette pushed her way forward to find a green baize table, laid out with cards, and seated before it, Lady Clara, with Mr Marwood at her shoulder. She had a pile of coins in front of her; not many, but the unmistakeable glint of gold guineas. She picked up the coins with shaking fingers, and the room fell silent as she hesitated over the cards in front of her. She put the coins down, and picked them up again.

"C'mon, darlin! Make yer mind up, sweet'eart!" came a shout from somewhere in the crowd, and another voice called back, "One gets you five she goes for the ten!" and was answered by a chorus of replies, which quickly died away. For a moment there was silence; then Clara placed the stack of coins on the Queen of Spades, and a roar went up from the crowd.

"Painted Lady! Ten to one on the Painted Lady!" yelled the man beside Violette, "A guinea gets you ten on the Painted Lady!" Money changed hands. All around the room the men were taking bets on Lady Clara's choice of the Queen of Spades.

Seated opposite Lady Clara was a veritable Macaroni, white-faced and rouged, with a patch at his eyebrow. His hair was dressed high and powdered in the old style, his coat of old-fashioned cut in scarlet brocade, and he wore a ruby in one ear. At first glimpse, he might have looked a figure of fun, so very flamboyant was his dress, but then he looked up and Violette saw his eyes. They were cold as the grave.

He sat back in his chair, folded his fingers together and flexed them so that his knuckles cracked. In front of him was a great pile of money – and, saw Violette with a terrible start – a pair of pearl earrings set with pink diamonds.

162

The room fell silent once more. He drew a card from the pack beside him. There was no flourish, no ceremony. He was expressionless as he laid it face up on the table before him. The crowd erupted; "Helen! The Helen!"

Violette turned to John. "What do they mean?"

"Helen of Troy, Miss – the Queen of Hearts."

The man beside them turned gleefully towards them. "Easy pickings to be sure; the lady don't see that the bank's turned against her, but I do. It's a good night's work for me!"

Violette looked back at the table in time to catch sight of Lady Clara's dazed face and slumped shoulders, looking on as the coins on her card were swept up to join their fellows – and her diamond earrings – in the Macaroni's pocket. He stood, bowed to her, and left the room.

It was not until Violette shook her quite violently by the shoulder that Lady Clara looked up. Then it seemed she came somewhat to her senses, and looked about her quite bewildered. She appeared incapable of speech. Of Mr Marwood there was no sign, and no sign either of his friend, Sergeant Jones.

"My dear, you must come away, this instant!" whispered Violette. She took her friend's hand and pulled her to her feet to lead her away, but Lady Clara staggered, and one of the men grabbed at her in a most familiar manner. "Take your hands off her!" Violette snapped, outraged.

He turned a laughing face in her direction. "Just trying to help, Miss!" He affected an air of wounded virtue, and grinned round at his cronies. "Though I doubt an Amazon giant like yourself needs the help of any man. But I wouldn't mind giving it a go. If someone fetched me a ladder!"

There was a roar at this, and some slapping on the back. "What d'ye say, Miss? Want to take me on?" He winked lasciviously at her, and Violette burned with a ghastly mix of shame and fury.

John squared up his shoulders and stepped forward, fists clenched at his sides. Violette said, in a low, choking voice, "Come away John, and leave these horrible men be, I beg you." He gave a jerky nod of his head, though a pulse throbbed at his temple; and with his jaw set, he scooped Lady Clara up in his arms and hurried her out of the building, followed by Violette, and accompanied by catcalls and jeers from the crowd.

The birds were singing in the trees before Violette slept and then it was to dream of Lord Winterbourne. She was wearing her champagne gown, the fabric cold and sensuous against her skin, and his eyes were fixed upon hers as if he could not tear them away. They were dancing, but then he turned aside and said, in his unmistakeable languid drawl, "I would not look at this face over breakfast for all the money in the world. Even though I am in your debt… ."

She jerked awake. 'He is not in my debt,' she thought, confusedly. "Only, perhaps, for saving his sister." She sank back down into the depths of sleep once more, and into her dream stepped the man at the gaming tables at Vauxhall, with his crude comments about her height, and the coarse laughter of his friends. He was joined by Kit Taverner in his midshipman's uniform, and her mother, too. "Too tall! Too plain!" Their voiced mocked her; and in her dream, Lord Winterbourne turned his back on her, and walked away.

She woke to find her pillow wet with tears. 'I have endured this,' she thought miserably, 'for the sake of my friend, Clara. But I should never have had to, if her dreadful wretch of a brother had any care at all for the poor girl!"

CHAPTER 17

That evening was the occasion of Lady Hertford's ball. From dawn, carts had rumbled through Manchester Square and round to the back of Hertford House bringing deliveries of flowers and fruit, and there was a fish-wagon and a butcher's cart. As the afternoon wore on, the carts and wagons ceased, and then as the sun dipped towards the horizon these utilitarian vehicles were replaced with carriages as the guests began to arrive; first for the private dinner of not more than thirty guests, where, it was rumoured, the Prince of Wales would be in attendance, and then five times that for the dancing.

Having given over her room to Miss Jennings, who kept her window blind pulled very firmly down, Miss Felicia had to content herself with observing the thrilling events from the parlour window. She was as giddy as a schoolgirl, and could hardly contain her excitement, but at last it was time to dress. Violette had taken her to Mrs Bell's establishment, with strict instructions to that lady to steer Miss Felicia very firmly towards soft colours and simple styles, and now Hill helped her into her forget-me-not silk with something approaching reverence.

"Oh, Miss Felicia, you do look a picture! I remember dressing you, Miss, for your first ball ever, and you look just the same now as you did then!" And it was true that the soft blue brought out the colour of Miss deVere's eyes wonderfully, and set off her complexion quite beautifully.

There was a gentle tap at the door and Violette came in, dressed in gold tissue, and carrying a small leather box. She handed it to her aunt. It contained a set of sapphires in the richest and darkest of blues, set with their paler-coloured cousins, aquamarines. "On the staircase at Sumbourne is a portrait of *grand-mère* – your mama – and she has just your colouring, and is dressed in blue and wearing these jewels. I feel quite certain that they should be yours by right, and I cannot feel comfortable about keeping them – and in any event they would not become me as they do you!"

Miss Felicia opened her mouth to protest, but she could not speak, for she thought that if she did she would cry instead. She contented herself with putting her arms around her niece, and raising herself on tip toe to kiss her cheek with the greatest tenderness.

It was but a hundred yards from their front door to the pillared portico of Hertford House, and Violette was all set to walk the distance. "The weather is fine, and not yet dusk; the road is clean, and it's ridiculous to call the carriage round from the mews, to drive no distance at all! I see no reason to put the servants to such trouble!"

"Putting the servants to trouble is not something a lady would concern herself with!" said Miss Jennings, sharply.

Violette opened her mouth to make a retort, only to be stopped in her tracks by her aunt, who was equally decided in her opinion. "Lettie, dear, we cannot *possibly* arrive at Lady Hertford's door on foot! Even were I willing to risk my silk and sapphires on the public highway – which I most assuredly am not!"

Violette was something taken aback to hear her aunt speak so vehemently, and subsided into silence. Privately, she reflected that within a very short space of time the square would be such a mishmash of carriages and horses that they might step into their carriage at their front door but would travel no more than ten yards before being forced to step out again and continue on foot if they had any chance of arriving before the final dance of the night. 'But,' she reflected, 'this is the way that things are arranged. I must be guided by my aunt, who is the very soul of propriety, and I must leave my country manners back in the country where they belong.'

Her aunt was right to be concerned about the dangers of walking along the street – albeit only a hundred yards. When the footman opened the front door and they stepped out into Manchester Square it was to find everything noise and confusion. There were brushboys sweeping the road clear of horse droppings, and flower girls with their baskets, calling out their wares, "Buy yer girl a posy, milor', a tussy-mussie for the pretty lady, sir!" There were boys offering to hold horses for a ha'penny, and ragged children begging for farthings. And there was already a stately procession of carriages moving slowly round the Square, pausing to drop their occupants at the entrance to Hertford House before moving on.

'No wonder Aunt was so discomfited at the idea of walking along the street,' thought Violette. 'We would arrive with mud and muck splashed all over our skirts, and our hair disarranged by the wind; we would have been at the mercy of any desperate person who would snatch at our jewels, and have a band of ragged little children clamouring at our skirts. And we should have walked past all these carriages, one after the other, with everyone staring out of their carriage windows and commenting on our appearance, quite as if we were on the stage at the playhouse. No wonder my poor aunt was so horrified by the notion!' Not for the first time since leaving her home in France, she sighed inwardly at her own behaviour. 'I may have a very great deal of money and come from a family of standing,' she said to herself, 'but I seem not to be a lady and I wonder that I shall ever understand how to be one.'

She turned to the footman who was waiting to hand them into their carriage. "Go and ask Mr Giles for a handful of pennies or some sweetmeats from the kitchen, and give them out to these little children," she instructed. She caught sight of his horrified expression. "And when I come home, I shall check with Mr Giles that you did so!"

'Even the footman knows more about London manners than I do,' she reflected, sadly.

The first person Violette saw upon entering the ballroom was Lord Winterbourne, as splendidly attired and haughty-mannered as ever. He acknowledged her with the slightest nod of the head, and instantly turned away – but not before Violette thought she detected a smile lurking in the corner of his mouth. 'For heaven's sake!' she scolded herself. 'What does it matter if he smiles at me or not? Oh!' She ground her teeth in fury. 'I would do *anything* to stop thinking about that awful man!'

Violette and her aunt, accompanied by Miss Jennings, found a sofa with a good view of the dancing. A footman brought them champagne, and the ladies settled down to examining the gowns of the dancers, and to look about them to identify various of their acquaintance.

After a few minutes, Miss Felicia nodded towards a window embrasure, given a certain sense of privacy by elaborately swagged and looped curtains. Here was seated a young man, his head turned towards his companion. Both faces were concealed by the shadow, but a stray flicker of candlelight revealed a small foot in a silver slipper, and the hem of a gown in white and silver brocade.

"I do dislike to say it, Violette dear, but those young people are behaving quite indiscreetly. What can the young lady be thinking? Where is her chaperone?" It was but a moment before Miss Felicia saw things in a different light altogether. "Perhaps they are affianced! A love match would explain their behaviour. Foolish, certainly, but understandable."

"You are so much in the way of being engaged yourself, Aunt, you wish everyone else to be the same!" Violette was surprised to see a shadow cross her aunt's face at this bright comment but she did not linger upon it, for something about the couple had certainly caught her own attention. In that moment, the young man shifted in his seat, and the light shone full upon his features. It was Mr Philip Marwood. And with a ripple of disquiet, Violette recognised the white and silver gown as that of Clara Taverner.

Violette and her aunt had been speaking in low voices, but even so Miss Jennings had caught the gist of their conversation. She had no such delicacy of feeling, no lowered voice for her. "Is that not your friend, Lady Clara Taverner? And surely that is the young man who quite abandoned us at Vauxhall Gardens last evening?" To Violette's horror, Miss Jennings turned to her next-neighbour and proceeded to recount the tale of Mr Marwood's disappearance and that of Clara Taverner. There could be no mistaking her conclusion, that they had slipped away together for a love tryst. "We were most agitated with fear for the young lady, for it was quite dawn before she was discovered!" she concluded, with a vigorous nodding of her head.

"Upon my word, Miss Jennings, you are most dreadfully mistaken!" said Violette hotly, and loudly enough to be heard by their immediate neighbours. "Poor Lady Clara was caught up in the crowd, is all, and as soon as I went back with our groom – when the crowds had died away a little – there she was, and very glad to see us both, for she had quite a fright to find herself lost in such a way!

"And as for Mr Marwood, I believe he stayed with your brother, the Major, who was outside an entire bottle of brandy at the least and enjoying himself excessively, as was witnessed by us all!" This was a rebuke and a half, by no mistake. Miss Jennings opened her mouth wide, no doubt to make some tart reply, only to think the better of it, and close her jaws with a snap.

'Like the crocodile at the zoological gardens,' thought Violette, 'and I would wish myself in any other company!' Her wish was immediately granted. Miss Jennings rose to her feet with a deal of wounded dignity, and, quite turning her back on Violette, begged her new acquaintance to join her in a promenade of the room. With this, she excused herself from the company.

Violette turned to her aunt with a stinging comment about Miss Jennings ready upon her lips, but she had got no further than, "Oh, Aunt!" when Miss Felicia shook her head vehemently, raised her eyebrows and fairly screeched, "Why Lord Winterbourne, how delightful!" Violette turned her head to find him at her shoulder.

"Ah. Miss deVere –," he started, drawlingly, and Violette was so flustered that she simply said, "Yes, I will," and jumped to her feet. She caught his raised eyebrow, and immediately regretted that she had appeared so eager. To make up for it, she stalked ahead, stiff-backed, to join the next set of dancers and they took their positions in the set.

His countenance was its usual inscrutable mask. He bowed his head a fraction. "I'm obliged to you for standing up with me, Miss deVere, though I'm afraid you mistook my intent, which was merely to thank you for your interest in my sister; she mentioned to me that that had been some little confusion at Vauxhall with the crowds."

Violette wanted to sink through the floor. 'He wasn't going to ask me to dance, and I positively flung myself out of my chair!'

She thought her sense of humiliation could be no worse, but then a pretty girl with fair ringlets was handed into the set by her partner, who took his position beside Lord Winterbourne. It was Mr Marwood. He smiled at Violette, showing all his teeth. "Miss deVere, it seems that happy chance brings me to your side once more!" He stood very still, looking meaningfully from Violette to Lord Winterbourne and back.

She had no choice but to make the introduction. "Lord Winterbourne, may I introduce Mr Philip Marwood, lately arrived from Cornwall. And – and his partner."

Mr Marwood made no effort to introduce his companion, and without waiting for Lord Winterbourne to speak, immediately addressed him in just the same overly-familiar style he had employed with Violette. "I feel, sir, that we are already acquainted! Not only by my friendship with your brother, whom I knew briefly at Cambridge before we parted to go our separate ways, he to the Naval Academy at Portsmouth, and I to join Cornishmen's Bank under the patronage of my godfather, Sir Harry Gray, the director of that establishment, and also through my acquaintance with your sister, so delightful, whom I hope to know better, but also because your father and mine were the very best of friends in their youth, and my father spoke often of their roistering days together!" He said all this without drawing breath and with that same unwavering intensity of gaze fixed upon Lord Winterbourne's face that had so discomfited Violette.

Lord Winterbourne's countenance darkened at this dreadful impertinence. He cast a brief, scathing glance in Philip Marwood's direction, and looked away.

Violette raged silently at Mr Marwood. 'He reminds me of a fox,' she thought to herself, 'always looking about him for some opportunity for malice. As if I were not embarrassed enough; whatever will Lord Winterbourne think of me, for having such an acquaintance?'

At that moment the music struck up. Lord Winterbourne made his bow and Violette sank into her curtsey.

It was just as before. Their companions in the dance exchanged smiles, and remarks were made which led to brief spurts of laughter. But whenever the demands of the dance brought them together,

Violette and Lord Winterbourne met in excruciating silence. If she caught his eye, he looked away. If she looked away, she could feel his gaze burning into her. After the second set of steps and turnabout, Violette felt that she must speak, and with a great effort of will she forced her mind to the topics that the dancing master had suggested.

"I think we must speak, sir. We cannot spend the whole set in silence, surely?"

It was as if this was the cue he had been waiting for. "Indeed, Miss deVere. So tell me, what do you think of the weather?"

"Pleasantly warm, sir." Violette congratulated herself, this was a very ladylike response. They were separated by the dance once more, and when they came back together it was her turn to reply with a question for him. "And what do you think … I mean, where…?" Her mind went quite blank, and she opened and shut her mouth like a goldfish, searching desperately for something to say.

Seeming to take pity upon her, Lord Winterbourne continued, "And the floral arrangements? Do they meet with your approval?"

"Very striking. Though hothouse flowers are not really to my taste."

"You prefer wild flowers, no doubt. In a meadow, or some such. What is it that one does in a meadow? Cavorting? Frolicking, perhaps."

"Good heavens – well, I wouldn't say –" but once more they were separated by the dance. His next question was as to the quality of the music, and from that point on, he subjected her to a stream of conversation of the most dull and innocuous kind, wondering if it would rain the next day or be warm, whether the room could be considered fractionally too hot or too cool, and other such nonsense; each of these rapid observations falling from his lips as lightly and inconsequentially as snowflakes.

At first, Violette gazed upon him with some astonishment, waiting for him to pause for long enough to allow her an answer, or hoping that his next pronouncement might be something of interest, but such a topic was never forthcoming. She rapidly came to regret her desire for conversation, but was brought up short when she glanced up at him of a sudden and surprised a broad smile upon his face, and was struck by the realisation that he was teasing her, and enjoying her discomfort immensely.

Just at that moment, the pattern of the dance called upon them to promenade down the line with their hands clasped. Lord Winterbourne reached out and took Violette's hand in his.

Lord Winterbourne abruptly stopped his nonsensical chatter. Violette was suddenly acutely aware of the nearness of his body; his arm encased in its velvet sleeve, his hand in its white glove, his fingers gripping her own. She could not raise her eyes to meet his; the moment seemed to last and last as they stood there, hands clasped, each of them silent. There came to her the memory of Captain Death; his breath, hot upon her neck; the commanding way he had pulled her to him and how she had swooned in his embrace. And now she was all heat. A blush suffused her from head to foot, and she was seized by an all-encompassing wave of desire; but her desire was not for Captain Death, not at all! No, it was Richard Taverner she wanted; for him to lift her in his arms, and stalk out of the ballroom with her, and take her – where, she knew not, and to do what, she knew even less.

"Oh!' she thought to herself, confusedly, 'Oh, how I want …. I wish …' and she raised her head to find him gazing at her with some inexplicable, desperate intensity, and she could not look away.

And at this moment, the music ceased.

He did not let go of her hand. His eyes did not leave hers. There were some snatches of conversation in the room and laughter, but faint, as if sounded from a long distance away. There was a brief pause, and a hush, and then the musicians struck up again.

Violette placed her hand upon Lord Winterbourne's velvet-clad shoulder. Beneath her fingertips, the rich pile of the cloth moved from dark to light as she brushed her fingers back and forth, resistant one way and yielding the other. She moved deeper into his embrace, aware of the strength of his body through the thin stuff of her gown. It would take but a turn of her head for their lips to meet.

For a moment they were still, clasped in one another's arms. Then he moved, and she with him. Round and round they went. The music seized her. The blood sang in her veins; his hand upon her back was firm, compelling her to follow where he led. She pressed herself against him, and closed her eyes, oblivious to everything around them; and her treacherous body flamed once more with the remembrance of lips pressed commandingly upon hers and her eager acceptance of the kiss.

The music stopped. There was a brief smattering of applause. And then a profound and deeply unsettling silence.

Violette opened her eyes. All around the dance floor were clustered groups and knots of people, staring.

She saw Miss Jennings with her grim smile in place, and her aunt, wide-eyed and open-mouthed with shock.

A handful of couples only had joined them in the dance, Violette noted. Lord and Lady Willoughby; the Earl and Countess of Grantchester. Miss Pritchard and her fiancé and Dorothea von Lieven and her husband.

'It was a waltz!' Violette realised, belatedly; and then, 'Everyone who danced it is engaged or married. Everyone but us! Good God – what have we done?'

Lord Winterbourne stepped away from her with the slightest of bows. His mouth was set in a grim line, but other than that he showed the same coolness of expression, the same chilly formality and arrogant lift of the head that she had known before. He offered her his arm to escort her back to her seat, his gaze distant and dismissive. She gasped, as if doused in cold water, and took one stumbling step away from him, turning her head to hide the tears that started in her eyes.

And she caught sight of Philip Marwood.

All heads were still turned towards the dance floor, so only Violette could see that he had his arm around Lady Clara's shoulders, urging her faltering steps through the double doors that led to the gaming tables set out in the next room. Lady Clara made as if to turn away. Mr Marwood cast a quick and furtive glance behind him and then grasped her wrist and pulled her out of the ballroom. As the doors opened, Violette caught a glimpse of a puff of white hair, and a white face, patched and powdered.

Dread fear for her friend caught Violette in its grip. "Lord Winterbourne! I must speak with you – on a matter of some urgency!" The floor was filling up around them as couples assembled themselves into sets for the next dance, and the musicians were taking some brief refreshment and sorting out their music sheets before striking up again.

"I cannot think we have anything to discuss, Miss deVere. It was a pleasant dance, but I'm afraid I'm engaged for the next. Come, let me escort you to your companion." Lord Winterbourne averted his eyes, and stepped back another pace.

Violette crossed the space between them in two furious strides. She grasped his sleeve with both hands. "Lord Winterbourne! I *insist* you hear me!" Her voice was shrill with temper.

There was an indrawn breath from those around them and a moment's horrified silence. In the sudden hush, Violette heard a shocked whisper.

"Winterbourne's made a fool of that girl, look, and she's after him for it!"

Lord Winterbourne took her wrist in a bruising grip and marched her off the dance floor, the crowd parting silently before them and closing behind in a flurry of excited conversation. He took her to her aunt, and left her with a single curt nod.

Miss Felicia took one look at her niece's white face and rose to the occasion. With her head held high, she announced to no-one in particular that her niece was overcome with the heat, and swept – as much as her diminutive stature would allow her to sweep – out of the ballroom, Violette's hand clasped firmly in her own. She guided her down the stairs to a small anteroom, and sent the maid for their cloaks, and a footman to summon their coach.

There was a gentle tap upon the door. Opening it, Miss Felicia found a stranger before her. A tall gentleman of indeterminate years, beautifully tailored in a deep blue evening coat of impeccable cut, and wearing an expression of the utmost concern.

He bowed to Miss Felicia, and handed her his card. "I beg you to forgive me; we have not been introduced. I couldn't help but see that the young lady is in some distress and it appears you have no gentleman companion with you. I wonder if I might be of assistance? I do not mean to impose, and shall take my leave if you wish.

"I heard you send the footman for your carriage, but with such a crush in the street who knows how long it might take to arrive? I was on the verge of departing, myself, and my carriage is at the door and waiting for me this instant. I wish you would allow me to send you home in it, for I can but suppose that your friend would desire the comfort of her own fireside as soon as it can be arranged. The coach can return for me, I am in no great hurry to leave. Indeed, I have been pressed to join a game of hazard, and would be pleased to do so."

Miss Felicia cast a hasty look behind her at Violette, who was now quite openly weeping, and stepped out into the hallway, pulling the door to behind her.

"It is most kind of you, sir," she said. "I pray you, do not concern yourself. My niece is merely overcome with the heat, and to sit quietly for a few moments while we wait for our coach is no matter, and will do her some good. Our house is but a step away, and we shall be home in an instant.

"But if you do wish to help – we have a companion, a Miss Jennings, left in the ballroom. If you could send someone to fetch her away, I would be indebted to you. She is wearing a very particular gown of apple green taffeta with a trim of mustard-colour gauze. I am sure a footman could find her out for us."

"I shall do it; it will be my pleasure." With this, the gentleman made his bow, and withdrew to accomplish his task.

Miss Felicia looked at the card in her hand.
Sir Harry Gray, it said.

CHAPTER 18

"...cannot think what came over either of them, they both behaved quite disgracefully and put themselves in the way of some dreadful malicious gossip.

That unpleasant Dorothea von Lieven was there. Married to the Prince straight from the schoolroom, and it has gone to her head; a mere chit of a girl – she clearly considered herself quite the guest of honour and called all the dances without a moment's regard for her hostess. I suppose being from one of the German countries she thought nothing of waltzing, so she quite insisted that the musicians strike up.

I'd have expected Isabella Hertford to protest, but she did not, but then that lady herself is known more for her liaison with the Prince of Wales than her common sense; I have spied his carriage coming and going from Hertford House at all hours of the day and night.

Lettie and Lord Winterbourne were on the floor, and quite absorbed in one another, by all accounts. They must have been unaware that the floor had cleared, for of course as soon as the waltz was called, all the single young ladies returned to their chaperones, as was only proper. So the only other couples on the floor with them were married – and seeing a married couple dancing together is an unusual sight at a London ball, it must be said! – or affianced. It meant that there were not above a dozen couples on the floor waltzing and quite in the middle of the floor was his lordship with his arms quite wound about poor Lettie, and both of them oblivious to all around them! And if that wasn't bad enough, when the dance ended, she positively ran after his lordship and clutched hold of him in the boldest manner, and was quite shouting at him! With everyone looking on!

I dislike him intensely, of course I do. A ruder and more arrogant gentleman you could not find. No doubt he had said something to upset the child, and she had good reason to be cross. But her behaviour – she absolutely lost her head! What she was thinking from start to finish I cannot fathom.

The kindest interpretation is that it was a lover's tiff, and the worst is – well, I hardly know. I have heard talk that they were secretly betrothed and that he has let her down, and there are whispers of a suit for breach of promise! And that is not the worst of it. I leave you to imagine what else is said!

O, my dear friend, the damage to them both seems irrecoverable to me. Two reputations quite lost! The only remedy would be if he were to declare himself, and give credence to the idea of a lover's quarrel, which would turn disgust into delighted amusement; but when I mentioned this to Violette in the carriage coming home, she turned as white as a sheet and declared that she would not think of such a thing!

Luckily, Lady Hertford's ball is the last of the Season, and all will be departing Town in droves, and so our own flight will be of little import. We are to leave on the morrow, though we had thought to stay another week at least, but I hardly dare to think of going out of the door, and seeing people looking at us – or turning their heads away, whichever it might be! Hill is quite beside herself with trying to pack, and the cook has departed in high dudgeon. Our guest Miss Jennings is much distressed by this turn of events and cannot keep her opinions to herself, which adds to the general air of misery and chaos that surrounds us.

Miss Felicia paused, and blotted away a drop of ink which had fallen from her quill. It might as well have been a tear, so disappointed was she in the way events had manifested themselves. She concluded, *'So, my dear friend, your reply to this should be directed to Sumbourne Manor. We shall never dare show our heads in London again, and I daresay even Bath will be no good. We shall have to bury ourselves once more in the depths of the country in the utmost disgrace, and when I might have the delight of seeing you again, I cannot imagine.'*

Miss Felicia folded up her letter and traced the direction upon it and sealed it with the greatest care. With a heavy heart she went downstairs and placed it upon the silver salver beside the front door, ready for the footman to take it to the post.

This letter said hardly any of the things that Miss Felicia wished to confide to her friend, and she regretted with all her heart that she was not joining the general exodus to Bath. It would be such a comfort to her to sit over a glass of ratafia with Mrs George, and talk freely of her concerns; a letter felt too stiff and stilted for what she wished to say. For she could see, as maybe Violette could not, that her impetuous action had consequences with a wider reach than simply that of Lady Hertford's ballroom.

As carriages departed Town, so cards of invitation were left for amusements to continue in coast and country, where the soft breezes and pretty views were so much more pleasant than London in the sweltering heat of late summer. The last of the strawberries would be in season, and charming picnics would be planned, for ladies attired in sprigged muslins and country bonnets to roam at will amongst their host's strawberry beds, to the very great chagrin of the head gardener, and dispose themselves picturesquely upon the grass to eat their prizes with dishes of heavy cream. Expeditions were planned for coastal pursuits in Lyme or Weymouth; sea-baths for the adventurous, the study of fauna and flora for the scholarly and coastal walks and the admiring of views for all.

Others would remove to Bath or Tunbridge Wells to recuperate with a water-cure after these hectic months in Town, and for those of a more sporting bent, it was but a few weeks before the grouse moors would be busy once more. In short, in these last few days of the London Season, the fashionable streets would be filled with the carriages of those making a last round of calls before taking their leave, and footmen delivering notes of invitation to door after door.

Miss Felicia was still in her wrapper, having slept hardly a wink all night. It was not much past dawn but the sight of that silver salver, empty but for her own letter, was too much for her. For she knew that once her own letter was taken to the post, that silver salver would remain empty for day after dreadful day. There would be no visiting cards left; no letters of invitation for boating parties or drives out to visit a picturesque ruin, and she would be left to moulder away back in Sumbourne once more. It was with a heavy heart that she returned to her room.

"I suppose it is a good opportunity to arrange for my wedding," she said to herself. But somehow that thought was no consolation at all.

CHAPTER 19

Violette came down to breakfast heavy-eyed and heavy-hearted. Her aunt was keeping to her room, and presumably Miss Jennings also, so Violette sipped her chocolate in solitary – and miserable – contemplation of the events of the night before.

It was scarce nine o'clock, and she was startled to hear the rattle of the knocker at such a ridiculously early hour. She started to her feet. Her slice of toasted bread fell from her suddenly nerveless fingers and landed, buttered side down, on the Turkey rug.

'It must be Lord Winterbourne come to declare himself, as my aunt thought he must. I cannot accept him, I cannot! Oh, what shall I say to him?'

But it was not his lordship. Instead, the door to the breakfast parlour flew open to admit Clara Taverner and behind her, Giles' flustered face. "Miss deVere, I beg pardon. Your ladyship – if I might show you to the morning room –."

Clara ignored him and fairly flung herself upon Violette where she plunged instantly into a veritable storm of weeping. Violette nodded to Giles over her friend's shoulder, and he departed, his sense of decorum sorely offended.

"My dear! Whatever are you about? Let me pour you some chocolate. Or I can ring for a glass of lemon cordial, for the weather is so stifling and you look so heated! I pray you, *do* sit down and tell me what's wrong!" Clara subsided into a chair, sniffing, and while she composed herself, Violette bent down and picked up her slice of toasted bread and examined it. It had acquired an unappetising layer of red and blue fluff, and she laid it back upon her plate and pushed it away from her.

"I shall have some chocolate, if I may, though I am quite too distracted to drink it!" Clara untied her bonnet and laid it upon a chair. Dark shadows lay beneath her eyes, which were red with weeping. She lifted her cup of chocolate in shaking hands and took a sip. Then she put it down again, and looked across the table at Violette. "It's so very early, I know, but I haven't slept all night. I am so happy that you and Richard … that you are to become my sister!" Her words were gay enough, but her countenance was not. "I had not the faintest idea, and Richard is such a close sort of fellow, he never breathed a word."

"You are quite mistaken! There is no suggestion that Lord Winterbourne and I – that is, he has not – and even if he did –," but Clara was not listening.

"It means I can speak freely to you in a way I have wanted to for so long! I am in the most dreadful scrape, and have no-one to turn to, and durst not tell my brother. But you can help me, now we are to be sisters. You can help me, as no-one else can!" With that, she buried her face in her hands, sobbing most pitiably.

Violette ran round the table to sit beside her friend, snatching up a napkin to dab at her eyes, and taking her hand in her own. "Clara dearest, whatever is the matter? But come away from the table, I pray you! We really cannot sit here with the crumbs and dirty cups about us and my aunt will be down directly, not to mention Miss Jennings. It's shaded in the morning room, and cool. We'll sit in there and you shall tell me what's amiss. Come now, pick up your bonnet and dry your eyes, there's a dear."

The morning room window was open a little so that a breath of air moved the window blinds and fresh flowers were in the vases. Violette sat her friend in a comfortable chair. "Now – tell me all, and we shall make it better, between us. It cannot be so very dreadful, surely."

"I'm engaged to be married! To Mr Marwood, and I wish I wasn't!"

"Good God – that jackanapes? Oh, Clara, whatever possessed you?"

"Nothing possessed me! I had no choice! You do not know the half of it, of the events at Vauxhall Gardens. He says that Miss Flint will admit that we spent time alone together, quite unchaperoned; and if that was not enough – oh, Violette, he has the means to ruin me, and he will. Violette, you must go to Mr Marwood and tell him – *beg* him – to release me!"

Violette was aghast. She was horrified at her friend's foolishness, and hardly knew how to start to help her. "But I can do nothing! This is something for your brother, Clara! You must tell him, and as soon as may be!"

"I can't! I won't! I would rather marry Mr Marwood! I started to tell my brother of our visit to Vauxhall but I only got as far as the hot-air balloon and then told him some gammon about the crowds, for I couldn't face telling him the rest. I feel so ashamed of myself, and Richard would be so very angry! He will call Mr Marwood out, you can be sure of it, but Mr Marwood is a man devoid of any decency and honour. He will like nothing better than to shout the name of Clara Taverner round every coffee house and disreputable tavern in London. I shall be ruined if I do not marry him, and in the most utter despair if I do!"

"You must help me, Violette, you must! There is no-one else I can ask."

At this moment, Miss Jennings voice could be heard upon the stair. Violette seized Clara's bonnet and jammed it over her curls, hissing, "I will help you, I will! Let me think over how it may be achieved, but go now, I beg you. I hear Miss Jennings above. She must not suspect that anything is amiss, for she will worry over it like a dog with a bone."

She opened the door of the morning room and looked cautiously out into the hall. Giles materialised instantly, and Violette said, pleasantly enough but in a rapid, low voice, "See Lady Clara out, Giles, if you please."

He crossed to the front door and held it open. Clara turned to Violette and clutched her hands in her own, speaking in a heartfelt whisper, "Oh, Violette. You are the kindest person I ever met, and I am so glad to have someone to tell my troubles to and to mend matters for me. It has all been weighing upon me most dreadfully but now I feel so very much better, for I know you will find a solution!" At that, she positively skipped out of the front door and into her carriage, as if she had not a care in the world, leaving her friend feeling quite the opposite, as if all the cares in the world had descended upon her own shoulders in one dreadful blow.

'I am in the most dreadful fix,' Violette said to herself. 'I wish with all my heart that Clara had not told me her troubles. I must help her, and I know not how to go about it, but have given her my word. I must collude with her to keep her secret from Lord Winterbourne, which I do not wish to do at all, and it means dealing in some measure with Mr Marwood, the prospect of which fills me with dread.

'What the foolish girl has done, and what hold Mr Marwood has over her, I do not know. And I am most dreadfully hungry, for I never ate my breakfast at all!'

Violette tottered back into the breakfast parlour, only to find the table cleared and a fresh cloth laid. 'Oh, how vexing! And I must eat something, for I feel positively faint.' She rang the bell for the maid to bring her some strong coffee and some soft rolls and butter, but no sooner had she taken the first welcome mouthful than the door knocker rattled once more and she heard Lord Winterbourne's voice in the hall.

'Good heavens! I cannot face him with my stomach positively rumbling! Giles will put him into the morning room and he can cool his heels for a moment. I must finish my breakfast, at least!' She crammed the rest of her roll into her mouth. But it seemed that, like his sister, Lord Winterbourne had little care for early morning courtesies. Yet again the door to the breakfast parlour flew open, and in he burst.

He was in a furious temper, that much was evident. He pulled off his driving gloves of yellow kid, and flung them at a nearby chair. His beaver hat followed, and his driving cape went flying after them. "Well, Miss deVere! I know not what you might have to say for yourself, but I tell you now, I have thought of nothing but your monstrous behaviour towards me last night. You force me into making a declaration I had no intention of making!" He let out a laugh quite shocking in its bitterness. "Cleverly done, Miss deVere! You have me pinned! We shall announce our engagement forthwith, and I can hardly tell you how much I dislike to do it!"

Violette had started to her feet upon his entrance, but with her mouth full of bread and butter she could do nothing but stare at him, chewing frantically; and he stared back.

At last – it seemed an age – she swallowed. "Well, I do not wish in the slightest to marry you, sir, you may be sure of it! And – and I most assuredly will not." She sat down and took up her coffee cup and smiled brilliantly at him over its rim.

He stopped in his tracks. The wind was quite taken from his sails. "You will not? But you must! We must!"

"Do sit down. Perhaps you would like some coffee? Or something stronger. A glass of brandy? Perhaps you would be so kind, since you are near to the door, to poke your head out into the hall and ask Giles for one. I am certain you will find him loitering quite close.

"Poke my head -? 'pon my soul, Miss deVere, you most certainly are a cool customer!" Lord Winterbourne was forced into an unwilling smile. He drew out a chair and sat down, and Violette poured him a cup of coffee.

"Milk – hot or cold? Perhaps you would prefer cream. Sugar? Let me pass you the bowl, sir, and here are the sugar tongs. And let me butter you a roll, they really are quite delicious.

"Delightfully domestic, are we not? Is this how you envisage our mornings when we are married? Breakfast together, and then you to do – well, whatever it is that you like to do with yourself during the day. Opium dens, perhaps? Or gambling hells or the Gentleman's Bathhouse in Drury Lane?"

Violette had the same sensation she'd experienced after seeing off the Excise men when they'd thought to shoot Captain Death's dog. A kind of mad, fizzing excitement seized her, making her blood run hot and her brain run cool, the delicious sensation of speaking frankly and boldly without a care for the other person's feelings, and the desire above all to laugh at the expression on Lord Winterbourne's face as he struggled to understand her. Bafflement, certainly, and astonishment at being addressed so.

"Opium dens? What the *devil* – and the Gentleman's Bathhouse in Drury Lane?" Much to Violette's bemusement, he let out a shout of laughter. "You have an unnerving ability to wrong-foot me, Miss deVere. I am utterly mortified to discover that a gently-bred woman would know of such things." He raised his coffee cup to his lips, and remarked, "You have butter upon your chin, my dear."

What little amusement Violette had found in their situation vanished upon the instant. How was it that Richard Taverner could so easily infuriate her and to such an extent? "You should be ashamed of your behaviour, sir! To come bursting into my house at this hour, and make a mock of me – it is insupportable!"

"It is insupportable that you would for one moment consider my presence in opium dens and the like!" His temper rose to match her own. He banged his coffee cup back onto its saucer. "I cannot think where you might draw such a conclusion. Were you a man, I would call you out for such an insult!"

He could not sit still but jumped to his feet and took a few impatient steps about the room. After a moment, he got himself under control. "I apologise. I recollect your upbringing. You are not acquainted with the ways of polite society, of course. Your father's disdain for his family's ancient lineage and his position in society." His drawling tones dripped icy contempt. "Your mother's *theatrical* connections."

"How dare you throw my family at my head!" Violette was rigid with fury. "It's true that I am not well acquainted with the ways of London society. My father turned his back on it and if you are its representative, I can see why! You are the very epitome of everything that my father despised! I was brought up to believe that the mark of a true gentleman was a deal more than the cut of his coat or the arrangement of his necktie. I have known peasants working in the fields and fisherman at their catch who had more tenderness for the feelings of others in their little finger than you have in the whole of your being!

"Where are your true feelings, sir? Where is your kindness? You leave your sister exposed to her own folly by the negligent ministrations of Miss Flint, who has not your sister's best interests at heart –." At this, Violette bit her lip, for she'd not intended to divulge anything of the conversation she'd had with her friend. With a great deal of will, she clamped her lips shut and took a long breath.

Lord Winterbourne could only stare at her. The rigid set of his shoulders, and the sight of his face, as white as his shirt points and with a spot of colour burning high upon his cheekbones made Violette feel almost sorry for him. She'd had enough of this jabbing to-and-fro; now she sat forward with her elbows upon the table. Her voice was almost kind.

"Please sit down. Do not fear. Whatever it is that makes you neglect your duties and your family – for neglect them cruelly, it seems to me, you do – but whatever that secret, you are in no danger of my finding it out. For I tell you now, Richard Taverner, I am in love with someone else, and have not the slightest intention of marrying you. And you may tell any of your acquaintance that the reluctance was on my part, and that you behaved with absolute propriety."

"In love with someone else? But how can you – that is, I do not understand the half of this!" Lord Winterbourne sank back into his chair. Reaching for his coffee cup once more, he raised it to his lips. A single drip of coffee landed upon his necktie, but he appeared not to notice it. The cup rattled in its saucer as he replaced it.

When at last he spoke, his voice was surprisingly gentle. "My dear, we *must* be married whether we wish it or no. You may care nothing for your own reputation, and you clearly care nothing for mine, but that is not the point. The damage is already done. The scandal is already established. After you left the ballroom, my next partner refused me entirely!

"It is not just our reputations that are in danger, here. Your aunt is soon to be married to a most respectable gentleman with a career in the law. I have a young sister in the marriage market, and a brother needing to make his way in the Navy who will be dependent upon the goodwill of men of standing to advance his career. You are very much mistaken if you think I neglect them, for I have greater care for them that you can know – but no matter; the point is that we cannot see others punished for our own mistakes and shortcomings.

"The waltz was bad enough. What came over me I cannot say, and I apologise unreservedly for my part in our mutual undoing; but your screeching at me in front of all was the nail in the coffin. The consequence is that an engagement is forced upon us to safeguard the reputations of those we love. We have no say in the matter. I am as sorry for it as you may be, Miss deVere."

"But I refuse to marry for convenience or for reputation! I shall marry for no reason other than love," Violette was determined to speak plainly and calmly, but despite herself, her voice shook, "and if I am not loved for myself, then I shall not marry at all." She paused, and then, despite her best intentions, she couldn't help herself but add, acidly, "And look where we find ourselves, my lord. Sitting together in this way, when I am very well aware that you would rather not see my face across the breakfast table in the mornings – I think it a matter of not enough guineas in the bank, am I right?"

Lord Winterbourne started horribly at that, and sprang to his feet once more; he clamped his lips tight together and paced back and forth a moment, clearly struggling with some great emotion. Finally, he spoke. Gone was his distinctive, drawling delivery; gone was his self-righteous fury; gone was his tight-lipped control. He spoke with a sincere and passionate intensity. "Miss deVere, enough, I implore you! You misjudge me cruelly! And let me tell you, wishing to marry for love is not the province merely of foolish young ladies in novels! My father married my mother for her fortune alone, and I would not wish that fate upon anyone, man or woman alike!"

Violette stared at him in some amazement. She rose to her own feet. Her voice was as passionate and outraged as his own. "I misjudge you? Indeed, sir, I believe I understand you very well! You make it abundantly clear that you have no desire to marry me for any reason!

"You will not lower yourself to marry me for my fortune and do not wish for my love, and all you have ever said to me or about me has been wounding and unkind!" It was quite the novelty to see the arrogant Lord Winterbourne at a loss for words, and she smiled, a cold, tight smile.

When she spoke again, her voice was as icy as his. "This unexpected visit of yours at a less than convenient time has been most entertaining. I thank you for it. I take your point. I see that, for the sake of those we love, we have no choice but to go through the motions of being engaged. And we shall stay engaged for as long as it takes; until such time as your sister is married, and Mr Kit Taverner takes his lieutenant's examination and starts to make his own way in his career, and my aunt has left my side and embarked upon her new married life away from my sphere.

"But then, sir, you will do me the honour of allowing me to break our engagement for some unspecified reason, although you will do the gentlemanly thing and let it be known that it is due to some fault of your own; and we shall proceed with our lives as if this whole sorry episode never happened."

Violette rang the bell for Giles, who entered so rapidly that it had to be as Violette supposed, that he'd had his ear pressed against the door all this time.

"Lord Winterbourne, I bid you good day! Giles, assist Lord Winterbourne with his gloves – I think one of them flew under the table – and show him out."

He left. Violette rang for a glass of brandy, and drank it off in one.

Her aunt did not appear until late in the morning, to survey the empty silver platter by the front door with the most mournful of expressions, and was soon joined by Miss Jennings, all ready to fly with her bandbox packed and her luggage ready for the coach.

Violette came into the parlour to find her aunt sitting silently by the window, looking out onto the square with so dejected a countenance, that Violette's heart quite smote her. She affected a gaiety of tone that she did not feel. "Well, Aunt, you will be pleased to know that we do not have to scurry away in quite the underhand manner you might have envisaged. Lord Winterbourne arrived at a most unlikely hour this morning and we are engaged to be married, and so respectability is restored all round!"

Miss Sally Jennings nodded her head. "Just as I thought! I was telling your aunt that I thought I heard him arrive, when I was coming down to take my breakfast; but I am so very discreet, you know, that I retired back to my room and rang for the maid to bring me up a morsel to sustain me, instead, and asked if it was his lordship downstairs, and she told me it was. And then I asked if Lady Clara had come earlier on, for I quite thought I heard her voice as well, though it was unconscionable early so I found it difficult to believe, and she said that it was. And then I said I was very glad to hear it; 'for poor Miss Violette has been badly treated,' I said to her, 'quite distraught she was, last night! But however it's come about, Miss Violette brought him up to scratch, and that's the main thing!'"

"You discussed my situation with the servants?" said Violette faintly.

Miss Jennings nodded violently, and continued, "It was quite the talk of the ballroom after you ran away in such a panic last night! And I was dismayed to be summonsed away by that gentleman, whoever he was, that you sent after me. It was most officious of him to presume, for we had not been introduced at all, you know!"

"A gentleman, by the name of Sir Harry Gray," murmured Miss Felicia, at Violette's raised eyebrow, "he offered his help, and was so very kind."

" I was occupied in going round to as many people as I could, for I felt it a matter of honour to stand up for your good name, so I said, to as many people as would listen, 'A number of gentlemen have danced attendance upon Miss deVere over the past weeks, which is hardly surprising given her fortune, but I do not think she likes above two or three of them. Others might call her a flirt, but I suppose I would not. And Lord Winterbourne is a very particular sort of gentleman, so he may not like her being so direct and easy in her manner, but she has not the advantage of a respectable upbringing, as we are all well aware. I am sure his Lordship is not a jilt, and no doubt the mystery of such a public display will be found out soon enough.' And I am proved right, am I not? And you do not need to thank me, at all!"

Violette had no idea what reply to make to this, but merely nodded at Miss Jennings, with her lips compressed, and withdrew rapidly, to be followed a moment later by her aunt.

"My dear." She laid a hand upon Violette's arm. "Take no notice of that silly woman. But tell me, are you happy with this outcome? For I did not think you fond of Lord Winterbourne at all, nor he of you! Do not marry him if it will be for reasons other than love – if it is merely to conform to the demands of society. Better to be an independent old maid than a miserable wife!

"I have enjoyed myself so very much these last weeks, but if you wish to refuse Lord Winterbourne and go quietly back to Sumbourne, we shall depart forthwith, and no more said about it. I would not blame you, and I care not one jot what society or the Miss Jennings of this world might say!"

Violette could make no reply, so overcome was she by such kindness. She ran up the stairs to her room, where she flung herself on her bed and burst into tears.

CHAPTER 20

When she was recovered enough, she bathed her hands and face and changed her gown, and went downstairs, only to find Mr Marwood seated in the parlour and being entertained, with some degree of difficulty, by her aunt.

He rose to his feet when she entered, and made her his bow. She dropped him the slightest of curtsies, and silently wished him at the devil, but said, in a cool voice, "Mr Marwood. How do you do, sir?"

"I am well, very well, Miss deVere, and hope to find you the same, though I do not expect it after your rapid departure from Lady Hertford's ball last night, for word has it that you were most distressed. So I was come to see if I can be of any use to you. Dame Rumour is abroad, and I hear that your engagement to Lord Winterbourne is shortly to be announced, is that not the case?"

"It is, sir." Violette remained standing, which put Mr Marwood in a quandary. He could not sit while his hostess stood, and could not reach his glass of sherry, which was upon a small side table. He manoeuvred himself so that he stood with his back to her aunt, and raised his eyebrows and widened his eyes meaningfully, by which Violette deduced that he wished to speak to her in private, and wanted Miss Felicia from the room.

"Aunt. I wonder if you would be so kind as to step out and, ah, have a word with cook, for I believe she was looking for you most particular with regard to a – a Tipsy Pudding."

"A Tipsy Pudding? But I can't think why … oh! Yes, my dear, a Tipsy Pudding, now I recollect!" With that, Miss Felicia hastened from the room, and Violette followed her to ensure that the door was shut tight. She quite leaned against it, but although her legs might be shaking, her voice was steady enough. Mr Marwood. This morning I received a visit from Lady Clara Taverner. She was most agitated, and informed me that due to a misunderstanding she had agreed to become affianced to you.

"I am glad to see you here, and I am sure we can resolve this difficulty. I believe you to be fond of Lady Clara, and I know you cannot mean to cause her distress." Violette paused, thinking that Mr Marwood would wish to make some observation, but he remained silent, smiling at her in that intense way he had, with his head cocked to one side.

"Tell me, Mr Marwood, is it true? That you and she are engaged to be married?"

"Well," he said, consideringly, "It is – and it isn't. It's true that I've suggested marriage, and really, she is in no position to disagree. Clarrie Taverner has the damnedest luck at the card table. She really is an absolute lamb to the slaughter when it comes to sharping."

"Is that what you are – a sharp?"

"Me? Good God, no!" There was a pretty little burr walnut table to one side of the room, and upon it a lacquered tray containing the decanter of sherry and some glasses. He poured some into a glass, and held it up to the light to examine its contents, and gestured Violette to a chair. "I really do insist. You look, if you will excuse the observation, quite done in, and I wish you would be comfortable, for this might be a long conversation." He placed the glass beside her, and settled himself back into his own chair with every sign of comfortable ease, crossing his legs and flicking a speck of dust from his sleeve.

"To answer your question. No, Miss deVere. I am not a card sharp. I am more of … an introducer, let us say."

"And you introduced Lady Clara to a person at Vauxhall who – to carry on your imagery – fleeced her, am I correct?"

"Fleeced? Sheared to the bone! And my acquaintance now has in his possession a number of notes of hand from that young lady. He wishes them redeemed, but she hasn't the blunt to do it. Now, some little while ago, I happened to discover that upon her marriage she receives a nice little sum from her mother's side of the family. Hah! It appears that her thieving father could not get his hands on that, at least! And it put such a notion into my head!"

"To run her into debt, and then offer her a way out by marrying you?"

He let out his usual whoop of laughter. "On the head, Miss deVere, absolutely on the noggin! I say you are one of the smartest women I ever knew! We marry. She receives her sum and hands it to me, for of course a wife's settlement becomes her husband's property, and I redeem those unfortunate notes of hand and no-more said about it."

"And pocket a nice sum for yourself, in the process. A most unpleasant scheme and I daresay a long while in the planning!"

"Miss deVere, I cannot tell you what a joy it is to converse with an intelligent woman who understands the workings of a man's mind and does not wish to discuss bonnets and sonnets all the livelong day! You are quite right. I have been playing a hand that was dealt me a very long time ago, by none other than old Winterbourne himself. Let me tell you a story." He leaned towards her. His eyes were unnaturally bright, and he smiled at her again, that peculiarly wolfish grin that showed his teeth.

"My grandfather was Viscount Marwood's second son. Of course, the estate was entailed, so his older brother inherited, and his son after him, and his son in turn, my cousin Marwood. He has it all; title and wealth, the property and land. My own father inherited a substantial sum from his mother, who was an heiress in her own right, with connections to the Gray family, and he married a girl straight from the schoolroom with nothing to recommend her but a pair of pretty eyes. She came with very little, Miss deVere. A few hundred a year at most." He paused, and took a sip of wine. "I would not be such a fool as to marry a woman for nothing more than a pair of pretty eyes, you may be sure of it. Though your own eyes, Miss deVere, are something compelling, I will admit."

Violette's fingers twitched upon her own glass. She would have liked nothing better than to have thrown the contents of it full in his face.

He continued. "My mama had a fondness for the card table, and fell into bad company, and lost what there was of my father's fortune. My father died in debt and by his own hand." He swallowed, convulsively. "You may like to read of such things in those novels you ladies so much enjoy, Miss deVere, but let me assure you, seeing a man dead – be it of a broken heart or a shot to the head – is not such a pretty sight as all that.

"Upon my father's death we were cast adrift and would have been homeless, but for the charitable hand of the Grays. Sir Harry Gray is my godfather, you know; one of the richest men in the City. And from his boundless wealth, he provides my mama with a cottage upon his estates in Cornwall. Kind of him." He spoke with the most bitter and coldest of tones, chilling in its bleakness. "I was sent to university for an education, with the expectation of earning my living at the bank, grubbing about with ink-stained fingers in the mire of other people's money, and with none of my own. While my godfather possesses such wealth as cannot be imagined, and my cousin Marwood enjoys the very finest things in life and the son of the man who ruined my family struts about the town with his quizzing glass to his eye."

He paused, breathing heavily, struggling to control his white-lipped passion. He picked up his glass once again, but he couldn't contain himself, and he burst out, "Do you know who this man is, Miss deVere? Can you guess? None other than Winterbourne, of course!" His glass broke in his hand; he was oblivious to it.

"Lord Winterbourne?"

"Yes, yes! His father – a rake and a gambler of the first order – had my mama quite under his spell, and took her for every penny and more besides. Oh, you may admire the gleaming white edifice of Winterbourne Hall, Miss deVere, but it is my own inheritance - yes, *mine!* Which paid for it! And I am vowed to take possession of what is rightfully mine, and if I cannot, then I shall see every stone of that monstrous building tumbled to the ground before I am through!" He fell back in his chair and dashed his hand across his eyes. There was a moment's silence.

"Mr Marwood." Violette's voice was gentle. "You have cut your hand, sir. I think that you should have it dressed. Please let me send for a physician, or allow my carriage to take you back to Mayfair, at least." Her initial fear of him had given way to a kind of – not sympathy, but compassion. She could see that he had been done a terrible wrong, but it was by his foolish mother, and his father who had not the courage to stay in this world and care for his family in the face of ruination. Richard Taverner was to blame for none of it and his sister should not be the one to pay the price.

Philip Marwood was calm, now. Blood was seeping between his fingers; he looked at his hand with some astonishment. He laughed. it was a chilling sound. "You see what I am come to. Driven to it, Miss deVere. I shall take my leave presently, you will be rid of me, I vow. But I have not set out the point of my visit. I shall finish my story and then you may take what action you will."

His voice, when he continued, was calmness itself. "I concluded that it would be a sweet revenge upon that family to take their most prized possessions from them – the daughter of the house and the house itself."

"The house? How?"

"Winterbourne puts a good face on it but it's whispered that he's pretty much under the hatches. A quiet sale of some jewels or a portrait or two is all very well, but it won't do, you know. The property in Grosvenor Square is mortgaged to the bank One bill too many unpaid to his tailor; one bill too many unpaid to the fishmonger. All it would take is a gentle word in the right ear for that one tailor, that one fishmonger, to place his bill in the Chancery court. It would be Winterbourne's undoing. His creditors would be upon him like a flock of black-hearted crows and his properties sold from under him.

"As for Clarrie Taverner? She is little more than a simpering ninny, and winning her has been all too easy. A little gift here, a small sum of money there, and Miss Flint looks the other way as I flatter and wheedle my way into Clara Taverner's heart and bring her – oh, so easily – to the point of ruination!

"I had it in my power to do it, and I cannot tell you the joy it brought me to think on it. But then, why, you chanced to enter the game, Miss deVere! By engaging yourself to Winterbourne, you have saved him from his creditors. They would not take him to the courts now. They will think him close to riches once more, and will stay their hands, d'ye see."

He laughed. It was a sound of joy. "I like you excessively, Miss deVere. A woman who can spar with words just as a man can feint and parry with a rapier; a worthy adversary, indeed! It is a delight to be so open with you and set my problem before you – for a problem I have, and you are both the cause and the solution.

"You have befriended Lady Clara, and she has come running to you and blackened my character, and I wish she had not. She should come to understand that a wife's loyalty is to her husband; it can be a hard-won lesson that takes some time to learn." He flexed his fingers. They were long and smooth and pale and his knuckles white beneath the blood smeared across them.

Violette took a deep, shuddering breath. "I think I understand your point. Lady Clara might be spared the – the necessity of marriage. Or perhaps you will refrain from this damnable scheme altogether, if the notes of hand are paid off by someone else. I shall pay them. How much, Mr Marwood, will it take to save my friend? What is the sum that Lady Clara owes?"

He smiled at her. "I believe I shall not tell you, Miss deVere. It is not quite that simple. Not merely a mathematical equation, for it comes all at a price. Clara Taverner, spoiled and petted and foolish as she is, with her brother and their debts on the one side. And you, Miss deVere, on the other!

"What care I for Clara Taverner's paltry little sum of money? It's nothing, compared to *your* fortune! You have only to say one word, and I will abandon Clara Taverner. You may pay off her debts if you choose, or not. It is nothing to me. I will abandon my schemes for Winterbourne. I give you my word on it – for I am a man of my word, as a gentleman should be – to leave that fishmonger be, and that tailor, and not to whisper to them of the Chancery court.

"Why Winterbourne has not married some money and saved himself before now I do not know, but depend upon it, he has come to it now. He knows that without your fortune his days are numbered. Why would you choose to save him, Miss deVere? What is he to you? It is most certainly no love match and the whole world knows it. Break off your engagement to Winterbourne, and marry me instead!"

"Indeed, I shall not! Lord Winterbourne should know of your dealings with his sister, and I propose to tell him! And then it will be Lincoln's Inn Fields at dawn, Mr Marwood!"

Philip Marwood abandoned all efforts at gentility, and fell back in his chair, laughing so much that he had to pull a handkerchief from his pocket to mop at his streaming eyes. "Winterbourne call me out? He won't stir sticks to do it, you can be sure! I wouldn't put your trust in that deceitful devil, Miss deVere! Announcing his engagement to the richest prize on the marriage market will keep his creditors at bay for a while, but until he has you safely wedded and bedded and those golden guineas have passed from your hand to his, he dare not risk it being put abroad that he cannot drum up the readies to settle his sister's debt.

"Oh, my darling Miss deVere! You think I am a sharp, but believe me, there is none so sharp as Winterbourne. I would hazard that he sought you out from the word go, and has played you for a fool. Why, I would wager that you find yourself engaged to him with hardly an inkling of how he's done it!"

His keen, assessing glance told him that his words had hit home, and he let out another crow of laughter. "I'm right! Ha! You think I play a long game? I am *nothing* compared to Winterbourne! He weighs up the odds, Miss deVere. He would stand by and see his sister reduced, and living a life of fear under my rule, rather than chance that you and your fortune might slip from his fingers!"

Violette had determined to be strong and stand her ground against Philip Marwood, but this was too much for her. His words pierced her to the very heart. She sank back into her chair, her hand over her eyes. 'Can it be true? I thought I was clever to work out that Lord Winterbourne is something other than what he presents to the world, but not clever enough, it seems!

'When I overheard him say to his brother that he would never marry me – did he know I was there? Did he say it to bluff me? But then, I more or less forced our engagement upon him, and it was quite against his own will. Or was it? Was that all a part of his plan as well?'

Violette forced her mind away from this dizzying conundrum, and turned her attention back to Mr Marwood. He was gazing at her with, she thought, some element of sympathy, a little crease of concern between his dark brows. He stood, and put her glass into her shaking hand, and encouraged her to take a sip or two and crossed the room to stand looking out of the window, giving her time to recover.

After a moment or two, he turned back to her, and spoke in a low voice. There was no hint of the half-mocking tone, and gone was the glinting smile. "It's a shock to discover the truth about the man you are intending to marry. Truly, I am sorry to do it. It worries me that you will not be strong enough to withstand the lure of marriage to Richard Taverner and only then will you see how he laughs up his sleeve at the pair of us.

"I have come to have great respect for you, Miss deVere, and think you deserve better than to be deceived in such a manner. I offer you the chance to join your lot with mine. Believe me when I say that it is poverty that forces my hand. I would not have told you of my dear mother, who spends her days quite devoid of the companionship and suitable society as befits her upbringing; nor of my godfather who holds the whip hand over me and forces me into schemes that I would despise, were it not that I am driven to it by despair.

"If I were rich I would be free. I would be the most generous, faithful and kind of husbands, I can assure you. I was once the happiest of children, and wish nothing more than to be a good father to children of my own, and to see my mother restored to her rightful place in the world. You have the means to bring all of this about. And think on this, Miss deVere. You will never know for sure why Winterbourne wishes to marry you, and will always wonder if it is a sham, and he only ever wanted you for your fortune alone. But I have been utterly sincere with you, and have shown you truly what I am.

"You think me a villain, but I can assure you that my heart is that of a gentleman; whereas Winterbourne behaves like a gentleman, but at heart is something quite different and I think you know it. Which would you rather – a villain you can trust, or a gentleman that you cannot?"

"I take my leave. I'm sure that you wish to think this over for a day or so. I shall await your answer – though I hope it is not too long in coming. I give you good day, Miss deVere."

He bowed and went out, leaving Violette fuming – and frightened – behind him.

'Two proposals in the same day, each of them as abhorrent to me as the other! I do not know what to think. Much of what Mr Marwood said to me had the ring of truth about it, but how can I trust his words when they are motivated by such spite and bitterness?

'Has Lord Winterbourne played me for a fool all this time? I have come to understand how fast scandal and gossip can fly through London society. Did he know who I was from the very start, and when we met at Madame Audabon's, did he see me – rich, and so very unprepossessing, and nervous – an easy target? Can it be as Mr Marwood says, part of some game that I do not understand? Have I played straight into his hands?

'Oh, I wish the whole pack of them at the bottom of the ocean; Mr Marwood and Clara and her brother, too, for putting me in such a fix!'

CHAPTER 21

The day following this pair of unwelcome proposals, a plain carriage bearing two heavily veiled ladies – Miss Violette deVere and Lady Clara Taverner – made its halting progress along Fleet Street.

This part of London was a long way removed from the tranquil boulevards and elegant new buildings of Marylebone and Manchester Square. Despite the disquieting and potentially unpleasant nature of her errand, Violette could not help but be intrigued, for this was a London which was all bustle and business.

The narrow thoroughfare was a chaos of carriages and horses, making progress slow, and it was hemmed in upon each side by ancient black and white buildings leaning drunkenly this way and that. Leading off were little cobbled streets and alleyways opening into unexpected courtyards, with names suggesting an older London altogether. There was Fetter Lane, with its suggestion of blacksmiths' forges turning out manacles and leg irons and chains, and Shoe Lane and Butter Alley, reminiscent of long-lost industries and markets, replaced now by taverns and pie shops and coffee houses.

Here was the ancient church built by the crusading order of the Knights Templar, back when Richard, known as the Lionheart, was on the throne. Surrounding it were the Inns of Court and the Inns of Chancery; buildings which had been constructed centuries ago by the Plantagenets and the Tudors after them. This was the home of the law, and the lawyers, black gowns flapping, could be seen making their way towards the courts at Bow Street or the Old Bailey, followed by their scurrying clerks, arms filled with law books and bundles of red-beribboned pleadings.

Darting between them were boys bearing stacks of newspapers, for this was the home, too, of the *Morning Post* and the *Chronicle*; and these newspaper establishments were cheek by jowl with the clattering print rooms, turning out music sheets, books and plays, religious tracts and scandal sheets with their scurrilous cartoons lampooning leading figures of the day. No-one was safe from their jibes, and Violette shuddered at the thought that if a breath of her business were to be discovered, Lady Clara's name and her own would be set out in all their folly for the whole of London society to laugh over.

A new type of prosperity was in the area, too, marked out by construction on every corner. Buildings on the Strand were being demolished to make way for the construction of a grand new court building, the Royal Courts of Justice, and groaning into being were the great stone edifices of the banking world. Many of them dealt with wealth engendered in the very furthest parts of the country; the industrial north with its wool and cotton mills, and the rural south with its mines for tin and copper and the arsenic quarries, and those for chalk and granite.

It was outside one of these establishments, an imposing building of pale stone, with the name, Cornishmen's, carved above the lintel and repeated on a shining brass plaque by the front door, that the carriage halted.

Clad in a plain but well-cut driving coat of brown broadcloth, John alighted from his seat beside the coachman to waylay a footman who had stepped forward to open the carriage door. They conversed briefly; the footman held open the door to the building for him, and resumed his position on the broad, shallow step that led onto the street. After a moment or two John reappeared, and handed Violette and Lady Clara out of the carriage – both ladies dressed as inconspicuously as may be with hooded travelling cloaks of dull poplin hiding their dress.

John spoke in a low voice. "If you would step inside, Miss Vi – beg pardon – Miss Smith – a footman will escort you to his Lordship's office. But I wish you would allow me to accompany you. I do not like to think of you and her ladyship - that is, er, your companion, Miss – not quite knowing what's to happen."

Violette was touched by this display of concern. "We shall be perfectly safe. I have never met Sir Harry Gray, but I am assured he is quite the gentleman. Wait here for us. I am sure we shall be in safe enough hands, and probably not long about our business."

With that, she took a deep breath, and linked her arm firmly through that of her friend and they followed the footman into the building and up a flight of shallow steps of a richly veined red marble, which reminded Violette of a side of raw beef, and made her feel slightly nauseous.

"I seem to spend a lot of time scolding myself to be brave," she thought, "and there really is no need for it. The first time I met Mr Marwood he went to great lengths to tell me that his godfather was elderly and inform, and Miss Jennings described him at the ball as officious, and so I imagine we are to deal with some irascible, gouty old gentleman. The worst that can happen is that he turns us away with a flea in my ear – or should that be, fleas in our ears – though I don't know what that means, exactly.

"And I have been in a bank before, and absolutely forced that poor Mr Chapman in Folkestone to talk to me about my money, though he disliked it so much. This building might be much smarter and a deal larger, but there is not really much difference in it!"

At that moment, they reached the top of the staircase. With a whimper of fear, Lady Clara reached out a trembling hand to her friend, and it was grasped in Violette's trembling own. The footman flung upon the big double doors ahead of them and announced, in a sepulchral voice, "Miss Smith and Miss Jones!"

Sir Harry Gray's office resembled nothing so much as a grand drawing room. It was richly panelled in some dark wood and with a deep-piled Turkey rug in jewelled shades of green and blue upon the floor. Sporting prints hung upon one wall, and on another, a splendid large portrait of a horse. And there was a dramatic study of a stormy sea, which immediately caught Violette's attention.

To one end of the room was a substantial fireplace with a heavily carved mantle and a gilded mirror above, the empty hearth hidden by a tapestry firescreen, and a pair of low sofas in green brocade before it. In the centre of the room facing the door was a large desk with a leather top, and coming to meet them, a splendid figure of a man.

He was in dark tailoring, with a perfect knot in his cravat, and an enamelled pin to hold it in place. His hair was a rich brown, with the merest thread of grey at the temples, and his breadth of shoulder, splendid turn of calf and ruddy complexion spoke of a man who enjoyed a hearty outdoors life. This was in no way the pallid shade of illness and old age that Violette had been envisaging.

"Miss Smith and Miss – er, Jones? Your man sent up my card, so I believe we must have met before; but I have to confess I am at loss to recollect the occasion. You must forgive me."

"Sir Harry Gray?" Violette could not help her surprise, but hurried on, "I beg your pardon, sir; we have not met. It was not to me that you presented your card, but to my aunt at Lady Hertford's ball recently. I hope you don't mind the presumption. My name is Violette deVere." With that, Violette put back her veil.

"Miss deVere! What a pleasure it is to meet you." There was a moment's awkward silence. Sir Harry looked from Violette to Clara and back again while Violette waited for Clara to speak, and she did not. She was trembling so much that Violette was alarmed for her, and reached out a hand to steady her.

Sir Harry looked at Lady Clara with some concern. "Dear lady – I pray you be seated. Allow me to help you." He saw them both to a pair of upright chairs before his desk before returning to his own seat.

"Now then, how may I be of service? His voice was low and smooth with a slight country burr to it.

"I am – that is, we are – sorry to come in such a measure of disguise and secrecy, and to your place of business, too. But a difficulty means that calling at your house in Mayfair is impossible, and I could not write a note nor send in my card, for to do so would give away my identity, and then by association that of my friend, whose problem this is ..." Violette tailed off.

"And until you had the measure of me – you could not trust me and lay your problem before me. Is that the truth of it?"

Violette nodded. There was another long and awkward silence, while Violette waited once more for Clara to speak, and once more she did not.

Sir Harry stepped in. "Miss deVere, I noticed you admiring my paintings. That one is by Stubbs. Have you an interest in horses? I daresay it's thought odd to have a portrait of a horse, but I purchased him as an untried foal, and he turns out to be a good lad, and has won me a farthing or two at Newmarket. I must confess to being proud of him."

"I know very little of horseflesh, sir, but he seems a splendid animal. But it was the other painting that caught my attention. I rather think it to be by Mr William Turner, am I right?"

"It is indeed, Miss deVere! You have quite the eye!" Sir Harry jumped from his chair and ushered Violette over to the painting and they stood before it for a moment, while Sir Harry pointed out this feature and that. "He is a young artist still, and not well-known when I purchased this, but I am something of a collector and this caught my eye. You say Mr William Turner as if you have an acquaintance with the artist?"

"I do, sir! I know him well! This is the view of the bay seen from Ferme de St Cloud, where I grew up. My father, you know, fancied himself a patron of the arts and Will Turner spent some time with us some years ago. We are of an age, and he was the most bad-tempered of young men!"

Sir Harry laughed at this. "I think him a genius, destined for great things! Should we not forgive a genius his poor manners, Miss deVere?"

This exchange served to break the ice between them, and perhaps having the attention away from her a little restored Lady Clara into a sense of equilibrium, for when they went back and resumed their places at the desk, she seemed a great deal calmer.

Sir Harry was all business, now. He leaned forward, his elbows upon the table and his fingers steepled beneath his chin. "So, tell me, Miss deVere, how I can be of assistance. You do not bank with Cornishmen's, I know that, and, if you will excuse me from saying – it is well known that you are a very wealthy young lady. So I cannot think this problem is something financial."

"My friend here is fallen into debt. It is hardly by her own fault but by foolishness and by trusting the wrong gentleman. I would help her, but I do not wish to apply directly to the gentleman in question, so I don't quite know how to proceed."

It was enough for Clara. "Hardly a gentleman – do not call him that, Violette! Someone less of a gentleman there could not be!" She threw back her veil, and turned a stricken countenance upon Sir Harry. "My name, sir, is Clara Taverner, and it is Mr Philip Marwood, your own godson, who has taken advantage of me most underhandedly and there is no one who can help me but you, and oh, I wish you would!" Clara's voice faltered at this. She bowed her head, swallowing back the tears that threatened to overwhelm her.

Sir Harry half-rose from his seat, as if he could not help himself. Violette had the fleeting impression that he intended to walk around his desk, and quite gather Clara into his arms. Instead, he crossed to a Chinese cabinet. Upon its ebony surface was a silver tray with glasses and a decanter.

He poured a small amount of wine into a glass, and brought it across to Clara. "Take this, my dear. It's brandy, but a very fine one indeed, as smooth as silk. A few sips only, and you will feel quite restored." Clara dabbed at her eyes, and sipped obediently. A little colour came back into her cheeks.

Sir Harry smiled at her. "Come, we are not gentlemen of business, but friends – I hope I may say – solving a difficulty, are we not? We shall find more comfortable seats, and I shall ring for chocolate. Miss deVere, you would prefer coffee, or tea, perhaps? or can I offer you a glass of ratafia? And you shall tell me all your concerns Cla - Lady Clara, is it not? And I shall solve them for you. Take my arm, I beg you; a few steps only."

He ushered Clara across the room, and saw her into a comfortable chair with a cushion behind her back. Violette followed on, seemingly forgotten, and found her own seat, unable to resist a smile as she watched him move a side table closer to her friend, and place the brandy glass upon it.

Helped a great deal by Violette, and considerably restored by the combination of a cup of chocolate and the glass of brandy, Clara managed to stammer out the situation with Mr Marwood.

"He claimed acquaintance with my brother, and we became friends, I thought, and played cards one evening, and then another. At first it seemed I could not lose. I won some small sums of money from him, and he was so very nice to me over it, and it was the greatest fun. But then – but then –." She bowed her head, overcome with shame.

"I know it; an old trick, to lure in some unsuspecting victim through making them win, and then making them lose. Each time they win a little less and lose a little more. Is this what happened, my dear?" Sir Harry spoke in the mildest and kindest of tones, but even this was enough to produce a fresh bout of weeping. He passed her his pocket-handkerchief, and she buried her face in it.

"We went to Vauxhall. I was so excited to go, but I did not understand that it was all a sham and designed to catch me out. When the fireworks began, Mr Marwood and his friend spirited me away to the faro rooms. And there was a man –." Her face quite blanched with horror at the recollection, and her voice faltered.

Violette took up the tale, and recounted the scene she and John had witnessed. "He was a sharp of the first order. What Mr Marwood was thinking to take Lady Clara into such a gambling hell and leave her to face such a villain … and then I saw him again at Lady Hertford's ball, I think; though it was but a glimpse."

"It *was* the same man at Lady Hertford's ball! He spoke to me in the most horrid way, and said he was ready to denounce me to the whole room if I did not give him the money I owed him, there and then. I was brave at first, and said my brother would not believe him, and would call him out if he did so. But then he smiled and showed me what he carried in his pocket. My mother's earrings that she gave me upon her deathbed. My mother's earrings – that I gambled away!"

She sobbed into the handkerchief, and Violette continued the story. "Apparently, this man had financed Lady Clara's game with the security of her jewellery and upon her note of hand, but now he demands payment of the note in full, and has told her that every week that passes will make the debt increase."

"It's because of something called interest, which I do not understand, for it wasn't a bit interesting, and I was very frightened!" Clara had no tears left. She leaned back in her chair, white and shaking, and her voice was a mere wisp of sound as she completed her tale. "Mr Marwood says that the only way I can pay the debt will be upon our wedding day, for I had been so foolish as to tell him that I had a – a settlement."

"A settlement that would come to you upon your marriage? Oh, my poor girl." Sir Harry did not speak for a moment or two, and took a turn about the room.

"You have done the very best thing, to come to me. All shall be resolved, with the greatest of discretion, and your brother shall know nothing of it, you have my word upon it. Now, I shall send you home in my carriage, for I must needs speak with Miss deVere, and between us we shall find out a way to deliver you from this scrape." He was standing, his hand resting upon the back of Clara's chair, and she turned a little in her seat and raised her eyes to his.

Such very blue eyes they were, with tears sparkling upon such very long lashes, it was no wonder that he was something discomposed by the sight; more, when she reached up to clasp his hand, and lay her cheek upon it and say, in a faltering whisper, "Why sir, you are so kind to me. I cannot thank you enough. And I vow you are not so very old as Mr Marwood made you out to be, at all!"

Sir Harry could not help himself at this. He let out a shout of laughter. "The villain – made me out to be a dodderer, did he? Now that is something I will not forgive!" With that, Lady Clara was seen into his carriage and sent home, and he settled down to have a serious conversation with Violette.

CHAPTER 22

"I do not know, Miss deVere, how much you are aware of my godson's situation. I shall apprise you of it, and you will understand better what he is about. It closely relates to Lady Clara's family. I would not speak of it, except I gather that you and Lord Winterbourne are … are well acquainted."

He spoke with some delicacy, of which Violette approved whole-heartedly. 'He is as much a gentleman as his godson isn't,' she reflected, 'and he may come from humble beginnings, and be in commerce, which some consider distasteful, but I see before me a man who is trustworthy and kind-hearted as well as clever. I like him very much!'

She answered him, "I am close to that family, sir. I think of Lady Clara as quite my sister, and I tell you in confidence, for it is not yet widely known – but my sister she will be in name as well as thought, very shortly."

Violette spoke quite without thinking, and then blushed at the falsehood. 'She will never be my sister in name, for the idea of my marrying her brother is nothing more than a sham. So this is what it will be like for all the months to come, speaking of my marriage and knowing it will never take place. How shall can I bear it? To lie to everyone, not just strangers – though oddly, Sir Harry Gray does not feel like a stranger at all, but a good friend already. But to all those dear to me. My aunt for one.' She felt like crying but composed herself, for Sir Harry was speaking.

"Ah. Well then, I shall be a little more open with you than I might otherwise have been, for it is a matter requiring some discretion, as you will understand.

"I am related to Mr Marwood by the bonds of marriage. His mother and my dear late wife were cousins and close friends. Philip was much in our company as a child, and a sweet boy he was then – a sensitive child, bright and eager, and kindness itself. I thought him to have great potential for a successful and happy life.

"Lord Winterbourne's father and Mr Marwood's father moved in the same circles; acquaintances rather than close friends, you understand. Mr Peter Marwood was as upright and solid a gentleman as you could find, but I am sorry to say that Anthony Taverner was a gambler and a rake of the first order. There was not a woman in London safe from his attentions, and it was no secret that he married his wife for her fortune, having run through his own.

He was known to treat her and his children with the most absolute contempt. He denounced his own wife for an adulteress when their son was born with such unusual colouring; although his pale hair is that of his grandfather – no more than a quirk that runs in that family – skipping over some children and landing on others for some unaccountable reason. Indeed, I believe he tried to set aside the boy as his heir; but the property was entailed and he had no proof of his wife's so-called infidelity. Mother and child both paid a high price for his unfounded suspicions. But I shall say no more on that.

"He was a man determined to possess the very best of everything, and he cared not how he achieved it. He became obsessed with showing his wealth to the world. He tore down the house that had been in his family's keeping for generations, and built new from scratch. It might be called Winterbourne Hall, but Winterbourne's Folly is how it came to be known. It was founded upon the miseries and losses of others, for just as he spared no woman his attentions, so he spared no man – nor woman, for that matter – at the gaming table. He had already run through his own fortune and that of his wife, and all the money set aside for his children. When he died he left his family upon the point of complete destitution. One step from the poorhouse, Miss deVere, not more than a single step!"

He hesitated a little. "Forgive me, Miss deVere – I would not cause you pain."

"Tell me all, Sir Harry, I beg you. Do not think to spare my blushes – they are nothing, compared to Lady Clara's happiness."

'And my own,' she reflected. 'I will not divulge Mr Marwood's schemes as they relate to me. I suspect that if Sir Harry knew of them, he would not hesitate to tell Lord Winterbourne and I would not have that for anything. Until I get at the truth of Lord Winterbourne's behaviour, I needs must keep my concerns to myself for a while.'

Sir Harry continued. "So we come to Mr Marwood's mother. She was married from the schoolroom, and knew nothing of the ways of the world. A sweeter, more trusting girl you would not wish to meet. She fell under Sir Anthony's spell, and was ruined. Her husband could not face the disgrace. Bankrupted. I shall not tell you how he died, Miss deVere, but you might be able to guess.

"I know something of it. Mr Marwood spoke of it a little. I confess it touched me to see how keenly he felt his father's loss. I fear he did not think it – that is, some might consider it –." She couldn't finish her thought.

"Some might consider it a gentleman's choice, I think is what you mean. Philip took it very much to heart. He was very young, and felt …. betrayed, perhaps." Sir Harry stopped at this, and took a moment to collect himself.

'He is a man of great understanding,' said Violette to herself, 'and despite myself, I cannot help but feel some sympathy for Mr Marwood. I think Sir Harry will deal fairly with him.'

When Sir Harry spoke again, his voice was brisk and business-like. "Well, it seems that my foolish godson has carried quite the grudge against that family since then, and time has served to strengthen his resolve to be revenged upon them. I do not condone it, but I can understand it. In his eyes, the Winterbournes have gained at his expense. It would appear that they have lost nothing, and he has lost all.

"He expected to be a gentleman and live a gentleman's life, and instead he has to take a clerk's employment, which chafes upon him something bitter. And he sees his mother beholden to my charity – as he considers it. I do not see the situation through the same eyes.. I am proud to help her, and happy to know that she lives a pleasant life free from care – albeit it one away from society and the lure of the gaming tables. And I am very fond of my godson, and if I can make my life from nothing – for I joined my father and brothers in the Cornish tin mines when I was but a little lad, Miss deVere – but if I can make my life from nothing, then so can he.

"I paid his way through Cambridge, and had hoped to see him advance through the bank and achieve a position of great respectability in time. I am grieved more than I can say to see that this plain and worthy route through life is not to his taste. But all shall be mended, Miss deVere, I can assure you. I shall settle Lady Clara's debt, and give my godson such a dressing down that he will not forget in the longest time!"

Violette had to stop him. "Sir – forgive me. We did not come to ask you for money. Indeed, Lady Clara cannot possibly move from being in debt to one – one gentleman, we shall call him, although he is no such thing – to being in debt to another. And you are a stranger to the lady. You cannot make her a gift of the money, for tongues will wag! I shall pay her debt. For we shall be – that is, it will be still a family matter."

Yet again the words stuck in Violette's throat. 'I will *not* be her family. Another lie!' Aloud, though, she said, "But I do not wish to be involved in the transaction itself. And so I ask you to be a go-between, for this is gentlemen's business alone. I thought you could persuade your godson to do the right thing; pay off his associate, and have done with all this business and remove himself from Lady Clara's circle of acquaintance."

'And from mine,' she added to herself.

"Ah. Yes. You are right, Miss deVere. It shall be as you wish. Although I trust that such a sordid transaction of money as this is, will not affect what I hope will be a friendship between us. I have the very greatest admiration for Lord Winterbourne. I know him a little, and would hope to know him more. He has some interest in mining properties that are on leases held by the bank in Truro, and serves on the board of a charity in that part of the world, to provide schooling for bright boys from mining families – something dear to my heart, as I suppose you can understand.

"I see, as perhaps others do not, that he has turned his family's fortunes around since he inherited the title. How he's done it I cannot conceive. He was but fifteen years of age when his father died, and his mother then an invalid, his sister and brother babes in the nursery and creditors queuing at the gates."

"You think highly of that gentleman, it seems. You would not consider him to be … untrustworthy, in any sense?" Violette fiddled with her reticule, unable to meet Sir Harry's searching gaze. 'It is not through hard work alone that Sir Harry has made his way upwards to such success,' she reflected, 'but by something else; he cannot be deceived, and I think he understands more than I am willing to tell him.'

When he spoke again, his voice was gentle. "He is a proud gentleman, Miss deVere, but in the dealings we have had together he has struck me to be as upright and honourable as they come, and determined at all costs to avoid any breath of the sort of scandal that dogged his father's footsteps."

This view of Lord Winterbourne was a revelation to Violette. 'I have been thinking him the most determined fop without a thought in his head, and yet he is admired by Sir Harry Gray for his diligence and honour. I would not for a minute have thought him interested in charitable works! And yet I take Sir Harry to be astute in his opinions. This adds greatly to the mystery of Richard Taverner.

'Perhaps I have been mistaken in my assessment of him. When I think on it, he was as eager to enter into our engagement as I was – meaning, not at all – but although I said I would not, and gave him the chance to make me out to be the villain, he would not do it. He was as careful of my reputation as his own, and that of my aunt as much as those of his own brother and sister. Perhaps he was kinder to me that I deserved, and I was too angry at the time to see it.' This was a sobering reflection.

Sir Harry was not finished. "I remember Philip as a child, you see – and his mother still lives. For my own dear wife's sake, I would not cause Mrs Marwood more anguish. But this is a serious matter. I shall have to think how best to deal with it, but be assured, Miss deVere, dealt with it shall be!"

Violette stood to take her leave. "I do not know how to repay you for your kindness," she said. He smiled. "You could invite me to call, perhaps … at a time when your charming friend will be with you."

CHAPTER 23

One of the drawbacks to living in London, felt Violette, was the lack of opportunity for a good long walk. There *was* walking, of course; the carriage would come round from the mews and she would step into it with her aunt, and they would be borne away to Piccadilly, where they would dawdle along the streets, nodding to their acquaintance here and there or stopping to exchange the time of day every hundred yards or so. They might purchase some little gift or other treat from Fortnum and Mason, browse the shelves at Hatchards book shop, or sniff the fragrances at Floris, but this hardly constituted the sort of brisk exercise which Violette enjoyed. So when, the day after the visit to Fleet Street, a messenger arrived from Sir Harry Gray bearing a small parcel containing Clara Taverner's diamond earrings and her notes of hand, Violette slipped out of the house unnoticed, and set out upon a brisk walk to Cavendish Square to deliver them to her friend in person.

Her thoughts turned once more to Lord Winterbourne, and she wondered if he might be at home, and if she would encounter him. The strange thing was that, having been so very frank with his lordship – having told him exactly what she thought of his behaviour, and possessing, as she saw it, the upper hand throughout their conversation, and very effectively wrong-footing him throughout, Violette had discovered that her animosity towards him was quite gone.

Perhaps it was the comical vision of them glaring at one another as she frantically chewed her bread and butter. Maybe it was the knowledge that he had spoken to her as if to his equal in understanding. It might have been the strength of his concern for the others around them, in which he'd come across as sincere, and genuinely troubled at the situation in which they found themselves, or possibly it was Sir Harry Gray's considered regard for the gentleman, but Violette had begun to very much regret some of the things she had said.

'Opium dens and the Gentleman's Bathhouse! Whatever was I thinking?' she scolded herself. But she couldn't help laughing when she thought of the look on his lordship's face. 'It may have been wrong of me,' she said to herself, 'oh, but it was so immensely satisfying to see Richard Taverner quite lost for words, and that inscrutable countenance of his darken with real emotion!'

Lady Clara was pleased to see her and took possession of her earrings with great relief but she he asked Violette to take the notes of hand away. "I cannot bear to see the dreadful things! They should be burned, but I can hardly call for a fire to be lit in the morning room in the middle of summer and I cannot throw them on the kitchen range. I have never set foot in the kitchens in all my life and can't start now. Cook would be most put out and I would be beset by maids and footmen trying to assist me. Do you take them away with you and burn them for me, I beg you."

It being the time of day when calls were paid, and with London society agog at the events of Lady Hertford's ball, Lady Clara's drawing room was a lively scene with quite a crush of visitors. Violette's arrival was a source of marvellous interest to all; she was quizzed unmercifully, and congratulated on having landed his lordship.

"He's been the most eligible bachelor of the town for so many seasons, my dear, we were beginning to doubt he would ever be snapped up! Though I had my suspicions that something was afoot, for several of my acquaintance had seen him quite unmistakeably smiling at you in the dance! *That* was enough to set tongues wagging, you know. He has never been known to smile at any lady." The footman was hovering with the cake stand. Lady Andover hesitated over the delights of pink sponge cake flavoured with rose water and a cinnamon wafer sandwiched with orange cream.

Mrs Baxter-Lees was eager to add her own thoughts on the matter. "And of course, he positively swept you into his arms for the waltz! I have never seen the like – so vastly romantic! I said to my husband that I felt sorry for you, to have so many eyes upon you at the end, for of course there had been no formal announcement, so all were something taken aback. Nothing else was spoken of afterwards – every drawing room was quite abuzz! Why, it was only the day before yesterday, was it not?"

Lady Andover swallowed her mouthful of wafer and continued. "I heard the news of your betrothal from my maid this very morning. Are we the very first to share this happy news? I thought it must be true, for the servants know everything long before we do ourselves!" She finished with a trill of laughter.

Violette managed to escape at last, only to hesitate upon the doorstep. The blue skies had given way to grey, heralding the onset of a summer shower.

'Well,' she said to herself, 'I have two choices. I can return to the house to send for my carriage, which means putting myself back into that nest of vipers, or make a very brisk walk home and hope that the rain holds off for a while.' Accordingly, she set off at a rapid pace, only to be halted after a dozen steps by hearing her name. She turned, to see Lord Winterbourne striding towards her.

"I did not know you were calling upon my sister, for I should have joined you in the drawing room, though I much abhor being quizzed by company and leave it to my sister to engage in gossip and speculation."

"You were wise to avoid it! I have been subjected to a veritable Spanish Inquisition, which I certainly did not expect."

At this moment the first few drops of rain started to speckle the pavement. Violette attempted to open her umbrella. "I shall be caught in the rain, I think, but I have an umbrella and you do not; I pray you, do go home, for I wish you would not get wet as well!"

Lord Winterbourne took the umbrella from her grasp and shook it out for her. it was a pretty affair in green watered silk with a frill around the edge and a handle shaped like a parrot's head. It was a very feminine article indeed, but without embarrassment, Lord Winterbourne held it aloft over both their heads, and caught Violette's hand to tuck her arm into his own. "It's a shame to spoil that pretty bonnet, Miss deVere," he said with a smile.

"I would not have thought you a connoisseur of ladies' bonnets, Lord Winterbourne," she replied.

He laughed. 'I have been told by my sister that it is always a good plan to compliment a lady's bonnet!"

"Especially if you cannot compliment the face beneath it, I suppose," said Violette acidly, and then blushed furiously. She'd spoken more tartly than she had intended, being taken aback at his sudden appearance at her side, their proximity beneath the umbrella, and his astonishing good-humour.

He made no reply to this, other than a kind of slight shrug. After a moment or two, he said, slowly, "I understand that you overheard something of my conversation with my brother."

Knowing that his opinion of her was poor in the extreme, and that nothing she could say would make him dislike her more than he did already, there was nothing to be lost or gained by plain speaking. "Yes. It's true what they say, that eavesdroppers hear no good of themselves. You have no need to explain yourself to me. I understood your meaning perfectly."

"I doubt that you did; but no matter. I want to apologise. Please – allow me to accompany you. Where are you going?"

"Only back to Fitzhardinge Street. My aunt quite abhors the idea of my walking unaccompanied and would be most put out to discover it, but she was sequestered in her room with her correspondence and our guest Miss Jennings was waiting for her brother to call, so it seemed as good a chance as any to slip out unnoticed." She couldn't help herself but burst out, "My aunt is so very concerned with behaving correctly, and I miss the freedom of the countryside! To go where I please, without judgment or explanation, to walk in the woods and ride across the Downs. And I miss hearing the sound of the sea beating on the shore."

"You do not enjoy London?"

"London is unlike anything I have ever experienced before. I liked it exceedingly at first. But I have come to view London society as nothing more than a husband-hunt, and despite the peculiar circumstances of our engagement, you must believe that it was never my intention to trap you." Violette sighed. "I have had enough of this deception; it weighs upon me something heavy."

"Well. If there is one advantage to being engaged, my dear, it is that we may share an umbrella and shelter from the rain together," Lord Winterbourne replied, smiling, but then he continued in a more sombre tone, "I do understand your feelings. Like you, I often feel hemmed in by the demands and expectations of London society, and the constant constraints of having to behave with such absolute propriety!" Violette was astonished to hear him speak so freely, and made no reply.

The rain showed no sign of stopping, pattering upon the silk above their heads. Violette took a deep breath. "I love that smell; the freshness of the rain upon the dusty pavements. It has a particular fragrance all its own.

"Petrichor. That's the name of the smell."

Violette looked at him in astonishment. "How odd. I never knew there was a proper name for it. However do you know it?"

"I must have read it somewhere. Probably in the encyclopaedia." A muscle twitched at the corner of his mouth. Violette laughed; she couldn't help herself.

A carriage or two passed them by, splashing through the puddles, but other than that the streets they passed along were quite deserted. Being of a height, their steps matched easily, and they walked in a strangely companionable silence for another hundred yards or so.

Lord Winterbourne cleared his throat. "I wished to see you because I wanted you to have – to accept this small gift." He fished in the pocket of his coat and produced a slim book bound in cracked brown leather. The gilded lettering on the front was quite worn away; it was clearly much-read. "It belonged to my dear mamma, and she treasured it. I hope you will accept it in apology for the comments I made about your own mother, and forgive me." His voice cracked a little. "Though I am afraid that what I said – albeit in the heat of the moment – was unforgiveable."

Violette opened her mouth to protest, but he stopped her. "I beg of you – please take it! You said something to me which gave me much pause for thought … that I had been very harsh in my manner towards you. It has been a long time since anyone dared rebuke me so. Not since my mother died." He hesitated a little, and when he spoke again, his voice was low. "It was wrong of me, and I wish I could explain it, but I cannot. Though perhaps it was a lesson I needed to learn."

Violette tucked the little book into her reticule. "Thank you. I shall take very good care of it."

He cleared his throat again. "You also said…" but Violette interrupted him.

"Please, let's not go over what is done. We both said some dreadful things. Let's agree to forgive one another, and leave it at that."

"But I must ask you. You said you were in love with someone. So why are you not – do you not – surely you would wish to marry him?" Violette hesitated; but there was a strange intimacy to their situation. Walking side-by-side, their arms linked, heads close, but not looking into one another's faces and quite alone in the deserted streets, it was a situation that invited confidences, and Violette knew with absolute certainty that Lord Winterbourne would not betray her.

It was a relief to speak her thoughts aloud. "It sounds ridiculous, but I have met the gentleman only a very few times. Do you think it possible to have love at first sight? It sounds so foolish, the stuff of novels. But if I could hate – um, someone – at first sight, could I not love another at first sight, too?"

"Was the someone you hated at first sight, me?" For some reason, Lord Winterbourne seemed unfazed by her honesty, and a smile played around his lips.

"It was!" Violette laughed. "But I don't hate you now!" There was a moment's pause, before she continued. "But all the same … it's hardly possible that he would wish to marry me. And even were it to come about by some strange chance, I would be cut from society for ever.

"My father married for love entirely and threw up his friends and family to make a new life for himself. Perhaps I could do the same. Return to France, and make my life at St Cloud. The house is still there, standing empty." Violette sighed. "But it would mean leaving my aunt, and I have come to love her so dearly. And you and I are bound to the course we are set upon for many months yet. When my aunt is married, and you and I announce that our engagement is at an end, that might be scandal enough to force my return to France in any event. Maybe with – with the gentleman I speak of. Maybe not."

By now they had arrived in Fitzhardinge Street, and they halted outside Violette's house.

Lord Winterbourne 's voice was very gentle, and he placed his hand over Violette's as he spoke. "Violette, upon my oath I will not hold you to our engagement a moment longer than is necessary. And if you meet this gentleman again and find you truly love him, why, no-one would be happier than I."

Violette looked at his lordship in some amazement. She opened her mouth to make a reply, but was stopped by the shrill voice of Miss Jennings, who positively flung open the front door of Fitzhardinge Street and scolded Violette inside.

"Miss Violette! Whatever are you about? Your gown is sadly muddied and I cannot think what you are doing - to be loitering so in the street with a strange man! Oh - your lordship! I did not see it was you.

"I suppose you may come inside out of the wet if you must, though take care of the step, for I have had the maid whiten it twice, for a poor job she made of it to start with. In any event I am certain you wish to take yourself back to your valet, for your Hessians have quite lost their shine and I would expect you to be ashamed to bring them into the house of a respectable young lady."

With this most uninviting invitation, Miss Jennings turned her back upon the hapless couple, and left Lord Winterbourne to say, meekly, that he thought Miss Jennings was quite right, and he knew his place and would not sully Violette's doorstep with his unsuitable footwear. "My boots are indeed beyond redemption. With your permission, I shall avail myself of your umbrella to take myself home, but shall send it back forthwith." He laughed. "Let us pray that none of my acquaintance should see me, for do you doubt that it would become next week's fashion, for a gentleman of style to be seen with a green silk umbrella with a parrot handle?"

With that, he turned himself about and strode off, waving the umbrella high in the air like a flag.

Violette watched his retreating figure with astonished bemusement, before running up the stairs to her room, quite disregarding her wet shoes and the bedraggled state of her gown. She opened her reticule and pulled out the book Richard Taverner had insisted she accept. It was a battered copy of Shakespeare's sonnets, and inscribed, in a childish hand, *For you my dearest Mother upon yr birthday from yr son Richard d'Arthur Taverner aged 13.*

Violette read the inscription twice; and then she burst into tears. Though whether she cried for the young boy, whose father was to die not two years later and leave him to care for his invalid mother and two babes in arms and facing debt and ruination, or for the loss of her own mother when she was not much older; or whether it was for some other reason altogether, she could not tell

CHAPTER 24

Invitations to a masquerade ball to celebrate the betrothal of Miss Violette deVere and Richard Taverner, Lord Winterbourne, were sent out by the end of the week; the very last invitation of the London Season. They had the desired effect, turning speculation into indisputable fact, and transforming Violette's hoydenish behaviour on Lady Hertford's ballroom floor into that of any other lovestruck young lady; foolish but forgivable. And there was more than a little discussion between mammas, of how a plain lady of advanced years could succeed where their younger, prettier daughters had failed.

The ball was to take place at Winterbourne Hall on the first Saturday in November. This was somewhat outside the scandalous excitements of the London season or the more domestic comforts of Bath, but nonetheless promised to be a most splendid occasion. Every room in Winterbourne Hall would be thrown open, and fifty guests could be accommodated overnight, as could their valets and ladies' maids. Their coachmen would be found accommodation in the upper floors of the coach house and their grooms above the stables in which reposed not only the glossy carriage horses, but also the bold warriors of the hunt. For, just as guests at Lady Clara's birthday ball had undertaken the final hunt of the previous winter, so those celebrating her brother's engagement would enjoy the first hunt of the next.

The happy couple would open the dancing and much would be made of them, and they would spend the evening saying often how very happy they were, and being quizzed about where they first met, and what were their first thoughts of one another, and was it love at first glance, and all the other sentimental claptrap that accompanied these events.

Violette dreaded it.

The questions and the conversations, a whole evening of falsehoods and artifice, and to spend another night in that chilly mausoleum of a house; to wake the next morning and face it all again. And this with the knowledge that it would continue unabated for months to come, in Bath through the winter, and in London again in the spring, and through yet another autumn in the country; only to end when she announced that the betrothal was over, and would face down yet another wave of gossip and speculation. Violette grew paler and thinner by the day, so that her aunt became increasingly concerned for her, and was content when at last they quit the pretty house in Fitzhardinge Street, and returned home to Kent.

In an effort to stop herself going over and over the dilemma in which she found herself regarding her engagement, Violette threw herself into her scheme of gardening. She announced her plans one evening over dinner, " ... for the gardens here are neat enough, but very dull with their flat gravelled walks and box hedges."

"They've probably been the same ever since the house was first built! My father disliked change, and was not given to the vagaries of fashion, nor one for spending money where he did not need, so the passion for razing gardens to the ground and turning them over to lakes and landscapes seems to have passed us by. But you will be moving to Winterbourne Hall upon your marriage and you will be able to make of those gardens what you please, I daresay." Miss Felicia could hardly help a wistful note from creeping into her voice, for she was beginning to think that she would miss her niece's company something considerable.

Violette was saved from any reply by Miss Jennings, who had travelled back with them from London. With the Major once more ensconced at The Dragon, she showed no sign of returning to her own home. "No doubt, brother, when you are master of the house here, you will have your own plans for the gardens. I myself have had a conversation about this very subject with the gardener, a most grudging sort of man who could scarce spare me two words. The kitchen gardens are useful enough, I daresay; but very small."

The Major nodded his agreement, and swallowed his mouthful of roast beef. "They are small, and I have been thinking of a scheme for cabbages. Need a lot of ground for cabbages."

"You could enlarge the gardens greatly if you were to pull up the trees that line the shaded walk. The walk would not be missed; it has a very ugly aspect."

This was a most uncomfortable conversation. Violette had wondered, in passing, if the Major might think of taking up residence at Sumbourne, though it had not occurred to her that he would consider himself head of the household, nor that Miss Sally would accompany him. And it certainly hadn't crossed her mind that they would take it upon themselves to pull the house and gardens about as they pleased. "So ... you think to make your lives here at Sumbourne Manor? But what would you do with your property at Oare?"

"Let it out to tenants." Miss Jennings' reply came pretty quick, and Violette looked to her aunt for a comment on this, but Miss Felicia kept her head lowered over her plate, and did not look up.

Violette tried to keep her tone pleasant. "Well. I do not know how long it will be before I marry. Our engagement may last a year or more. And at the moment Lord Winterbourne and I have made no plans as to where our future home might be."

'That, at least, is true,' she thought, 'and Miss Jennings may quiz my gardener and make plans for getting a tenant for the house at Oare as much as she likes, but she will find herself back there within the week, and there is no doubt about it!'

"In the meantime," she spoke very firmly, "I shall be continuing here, in my own home! Shaded walk and small kitchen gardens notwithstanding!" Violette smiled brilliantly at Miss Jennings. And I would like a pretty garden with flowers, so I have a fancy for tulips, though I doubt I have ever held one in my hand, if you can imagine that."

"How do you know that you would like them, then?" Miss Jennings retorted.

"I have seen them in paintings. Of the Dutch school. There was a positive mania for them at one time, for they grow in the most wonderful variety of colours and shapes. Sometimes you plant a bulb and what flowers is something you did not expect at all!"

"I have a violent dislike of surprises," said Miss Jennings, quite heated, "and a garden filled with them sounds a foolish idea to me."

Violette bit back her own retort, and tried to smooth over the waters by changing the subject slightly. "Well, I have spoken to the gardener and he thinks it a scheme plagued by difficulties. He tells me that they are quite out of fashion and he doubts he could obtain the bulbs from a plant dealer here, so they would have to be brought from the Low Countries, and with all the trouble brewing once more on the Continent, this is impossible."

Miss Felicia looked up, glad, thought Violette, to move the subject away from the question of Miss Jennings living at the Manor. "It was bad enough when the French were fighting amongst themselves, and then along came Mr Bonaparte and things settled down for a while. But he seems to have gained the taste for power. Now he turns his attention to every other country in Europe and seems set to fight everyone!"

"I saw just such the point made in a cartoon sheet a day or two ago where the artist had made a most amusing caricature of him as a snarling dog with a bone – you see the wordplay here, Miss Violette? Bone-apart, very clever, very clever!" The Major harrumphed, and helped himself to third glass of wine, spilling a little on the cloth.

Behind his back, Miss Felicia gestured for the footman to remove the decanter. "Lord Winterbourne must worry about his brother, Mr Kit Taverner, away at sea."

"I daresay he does," replied Violette, "though Kit is only on patrol in the Channel to watch out for threats to the English coast, and even that is only for a few weeks at a time. It's not as if we are at war with the French just now, after all. Most of his time is spent at the Academy at his studies. He's in no more danger than the rest of us."

"He'll be more interested in catching a few smugglers than keeping those frog-eaters at bay, I daresay. Though I hope he saves that rascally Captain Death for me!" Major Jennings finished his wine, and looked round for the missing decanter in a slightly befuddled way.

"I don't really understand how smuggling works, Major Jennings." Violette was glad the subject had moved away from her garden and house, with its associated topic of who was to live where and when, to the much safer ground of smuggling. The Major could be guaranteed to hold forth at length, thus sparing any of the ladies from contributing to the conversation other than to urge him onwards. 'Which is a shame,' thought Violette, 'for when we were alone, Aunt and I used to laugh immoderately at any silly thing, and always had plans afoot to do something interesting. Those days seem to have vanished with the intrusion of the Major and his sister into our lives – and our home. I worry about my aunt. I wonder if life with Major Jennings will be quite what she expected when she accepted his proposal. But she is too loyal to speak badly of him to me. And if she loves him, then I must learn to love him as well!'

"So Major, tell me – surely it takes hours and hours to sail to France, and then hours to sail back. So how can English sailors get to Calais and back all under cover of darkness? Indeed, how can they manage any of this without the French trying to shoot them for spies?"

"Ah! An excellent question, Miss Violette! The French sailors – not the Navy sailors, you understand, but the merchant ships and the merchants themselves on shore – why should they turn down a healthy trade with the English just because their political masters tell them to? They are just as unscrupulous! French boats will put out into the Channel and be met midway by their English counterparts and the cargo transferred, so the English smugglers can leave the Kent coast at midnight and be back at dawn and no-one the wiser! And as for the English navy – why, there have been reports that even the Navy ships have met up with their French fellows out at sea, and helped themselves to a keg or two of brandy!

"If we were at The Dragon, I could show you, for I have quite the war office there. Why, you have inspired me! I shall invite you to take your dinner with me, Felicia my dear, and yourself, Miss Violette. My sister shall be hostess, and you shall see all my maps and charts and you will understand all!"

With that, the evening drew to a close, and after he had drunk his glass or two of port, and a cup or two of tea, and washed it down with a glass or two of brandy, the Major mounted his horse and rode, rather unsteadily, back to The Dragon, to put his scheme for a ladies' dinner into operation.

CHAPTER 25

This dinner was to occur at the end of the week. On Saturday morning, Miss Jennings departed to join her brother and check that the arrangements were in hand, and Violette and her aunt were in the little sitting parlour at the back of the house when Lord Winterbourne was announced with Lady Clara.

He strolled into the room with his hat in his hand and his quizzing glass to his eye, wonderfully attired as usual, his boots gleaming and his driving coat a perfect marvel of capes and buttoned pockets.

Violette stepped forward to greet him, and he bowed over her hand. "My dear." He turned his attention to her aunt. "Miss deVere. 'Pon my word, what a charming room! Such a vibrant design of wallpaper – your choice?"

Miss Felicia blushed and smiled and recounted the story of the peacock wallpaper. "It was in my – my sitting room," she could not bring herself to say the word bedroom aloud to a gentleman, "in our house in Fitzhardinge Street, and I said to my niece that I should find out the design and have it in my own house if I – I mean, when, of course, when I should marry the Major; though Miss Sally Jennings took against it quite vehemently.

"In any event, Violette insisted that this little parlour needed cheering up, for it is north-facing which makes it a trifle dark at times, but it has a very charming view over the gardens. And will be even nicer when the gardens are replanted, for Violette has quite the scheme afoot; and she said I should have what I liked, wallpaper not gardens that is, or I sit here more than she does!" Miss deVere finished in a rush, suddenly aware that she was gabbling, and in painful recollection of that other meeting with Lord Winterbourne at Madame Audabon's in Bath, when she had made such an absolute fool of herself. She added, faintly, "My niece is all concern for my comfort, for she is such a dear girl!"

"Indeed, Miss deVere, I see that she is very kind to you; and as for your paper, I like it a great deal." He held his quizzing glass to his eye, and surveyed the pattern. "Peacocks. A very pretty shade of blue."

'He could not have said anything to please my aunt more!' Violette smiled to herself. 'He has quite charmed her into forgetting the snub he administered the first day we met. I see you, Richard Taverner! You might be a leader of fashion, and as such assume the haughty disdain of the Ton, but I believe I start to get the measure of you at last! And when we are married I shall – oh! But we shall not be married. Of course, we shall not. What a fool you are, Violette deVere!' She turned away in some confusion, and crossed the room to join Lady Clara.

"I see you have your bonnet to hand and your pelisse. Are you expected somewhere, Violette?"

"We are walking to The Dragon. It is such lovely weather, and I feel that we should make the most of the sunshine, for winter will soon be upon us."

Lord Winterbourne joined in the conversation. "If you are walking, perhaps we might join you? I believe, Miss deVere, that Major Jennings of the Excise is putting up at the inn. We are acquainted, and I understand you and he are affianced. I should like to pay my respects to that gentleman."

So it was settled. Violette put on her bonnet, and Lord Winterbourne offered Miss Felicia his arm. Lady Clara linked hers with Violette, and their little party set off down the lane towards Sumbourne Cove.

Major Jennings was surprised and perhaps a little put out to find Lord Winterbourne and his sister accompanying his guests, but was instantly reconciled to their presence when Lord Winterbourne introduced the subject of his war-room. "I understand from Miss deVere that you have a whole room devoted entirely to the smuggling trade. It would be so very useful for me to hear a man of your experience and expertise explaining your research; for of course I sit on the Bench as a Justice of the Peace from time to time. In fact, Major Jennings, I think you have appeared before me to prosecute a case or two, have you not?"

"I have indeed!" came the eager reply. "And you sent Jem Clements, a wicked sort of fellow, for transportation – which was better than he deserved, for the Bloody Code is not repealed, as I pointed out to the Bench. A good hanging sends a powerful message to the men who embark upon the smuggling trade, and a warning that there will be no mercy shown!"

"I believe that a journey of several months chained by the neck and across a rough sea, and leaving behind those you love and all that is familiar is already a punishment of particular severity. And I admit to having some sympathy for men forced into the smuggling trade by their desire to do better for their families, Major, and would not see them transported, let alone hanged, for wanting bread to feed their children." Lord Winterbourne's tone was mild enough, but there was a hint of iron beneath as he continued, "Jem Clements was a smuggler, that's true enough; but as well, he beat his wife and children and starved his animals. He was no loss to anyone, and transportation can be a great force for good, in that it can offer the opportunity for a man to make something better of his life. Perhaps Jem Clements was one such. But some of my fellows on the Bench are more minded to your point of view, Major."

"They are! And begging your pardon, your lordship, but I hope they prevail upon you when I finally lay my hands on Captain Death. I should like to see him do a merry dance upon the gallows to pay him back for the merry dance he's led me! The number of times I've had him within finger's reach – but it seems he can wriggle himself out of any situation. Transportation is too good for the likes of him!"

"He's the very coolest of customers, I hear. I believe there is a generous bounty on the fellow's head."

"There is! And I mean to have it, too! It will set up my cellar very nicely indeed; in fact, the landlord here is holding a case of port for me, an excellent vintage, and cost me not more than three shillings the bottle, which I think a very reasonable sum. If you and Lady Clara would care to join our party for luncheon, then I would be honoured if you would take a glass or two with me and give your opinion."

"I should be delighted to do so, Major," came the reply; and without further ado the Major ushered him into the back parlour of the inn, which he had appropriated for his war-room, and left the ladies to follow as they chose.

Violette remembered perfectly well the Major's objections to Lord Winterbourne as foppish and a Dandy and his disgust at his lordship's avowed lack of interest in any sort of judicial proceedings, 'but somehow, just as he charmed my aunt, so he charms the Major. He appears a different man altogether!'

Her thoughts were echoed by her aunt. She drew Violette aside to whisper, "I can hardly believe this the same gentleman who was so dismissive of us both in Bath when first we met. This must be your doing, my dear. You have redeemed his character with your love, it seems!"

'But I have not!' thought Violette, in some confusion. 'We cannot blame the redeeming power of love for this transformation, for he has made it very clear he does not love me at all. Yet again, Lord Winterbourne puts me on the back foot. He has astonished me with his cruelty, and now he confuses me with his kindness. Damn and blast the man!'

Major Jennings' war room was heavily panelled, with a curving window embrasure with leaded panes of old-fashioned bottle glass looking out to sea, and a narrow buttoned-leather seat constructed beneath it. This prompted Clara to say, "How very quaint this is – it's like being in a little ship! It reminds me of your own house, Violette, with its beams and low ceilings, and makes me think of the stories of priest holes and secret passages and the gallant Cavaliers hiding from those horrid Roundheads!"

Major Jennings seized upon her remark. "You have hit upon it, your ladyship, for I do indeed believe there to be a secret passage in this inn! I have suspected for some months that goods are landed in Sumbourne Cove in the dead of night, and I thought that in setting up here I would either catch them or at least stop them, for to get off the shore they have to pass this very window. But I can sit here all night long and see no lights, and open the window wide and hear no sound, and still walk down to the beach at dawn and discover a whole flotilla of boats landed there. How those fellows get the goods away remains quite the mystery, but solve it I shall!"

There was a long table littered with wind and tide tables and charts showing the rise and set of the full moon. Lord Winterbourne bent over these with his quizzing glass held to his eye, and seemed particularly interested in a large map of the coastline covering one wall, all set about with pins and strings leading from one sheet of paper to another.

"Ah – I see you are intrigued by my notes!" The Major stabbed at the map with a stubby forefinger. "These are the places where Captain Death has been sighted. I have informers who keep me abreast of events along the coast. He was here, you see, at Lyminge, with a cargo of brandy, and three nights later he was spotted at dawn at the King's Head over towards Sandgate, in conversation with the landlord. Here again, at the Whistling Man in Hythe. And there is mention of him in the West Country, with a veritable network of contraband runners working for him along the Cornish coast, though this seems a little far-fetched. I think he is to be found more in these waters."

It was a dull half-hour for Clara, Violette, and Miss Felicia, but they were relieved by the appearance of Miss Sally Jennings, flushed of face and with her gown enfolded in a voluminous apron, which she untied as she spoke, and cast into a corner.

"There's cold game pie and a rabbit stewed with plums, and there's tomatoes, and that girl in the kitchen cut herself with the knife when I came upon her, sudden like and quiet, for I wished to make sure that she was taking good care, which clearly she was not! The potatoes are good, though scarcely enough for two guests extra who were not invited as far as I am aware, and there is chicken in a herb sauce, which is to our dear mother's receipt, though it calls for dill, and there was not dill to be had, so parsley has had to do for it. I stood over the cook and watched her close so I think it should be edible enough. And a dish of apple fritters with cream.

"I would be surprised if the cream isn't something sour, for it has a most unappealing yellow tinge to it, but the landlady was quite heated at the suggestion, and says that it comes from her own brother's farm and he has the best cows in the county. Well, we shall see!"

With that, they repaired into the dining room, where the deVere ladies and Lord Winterbourne and his sister were greeted warmly by the landlord, and Major Jennings and his sister were not.

Over luncheon, the Major's talk turned, yet again, to the subject of Captain Death. "You would not believe, my lord, how many times I have been a hair's breadth from catching the fellow, only to have him elude me once again. And not just elude me, but make sport of me into the bargain! You have it right, sir, when you call it a game of cat-and-mouse.

"Why, take Miss Violette's desire for tulip bulbs! It would not surprise me, Miss Violette, if a bag of tulip bulbs was delivered to your door in a week or so, and it would be he, Captain Death, making mock of me, 'pon my soul it would!"

"But how would he know I wanted such a thing? I spoke of it at home in my own house, and there was no-one in the room but us, Major Jennings – you and me and my aunt and your sister!"

"And the servants, Miss Violette, don't forget your servants! No doubt as wily a collection of rascals as ever was. Why, it occurs to me that I should quiz them just as I have quizzed the servants here!"

"Really, Major! You can hardly think that I shall allow you to interrogate people who have served my aunt so faithfully for so many years!"

The Major had the grace to look shamefaced, and this seemed to Violette to be the perfect opportunity for the ladies to leave the table. She rose to her feet. "I should like to walk down into the cove. Miss Jennings, Aunt, Clara – would you care to join me? I'm sure that the gentlemen are keen to get back to the Major's war room."

This suggestion was greeted eagerly by Lady Clara. "I should love to go down to the water's edge. I vow I have asked my brother to take us to Ramsgate for the sea-bathing more than once, but he quite refuses! He has the most absolute horror of the water!"

All eyes turned towards Lord Winterbourne, who gave an exaggerated shudder. "The very thought of sea-bathing makes my blood run cold. Violette my dear, I beg of you, do not think of a sea-voyage for our honeymoon; the effects of the salt air upon one's velvets – begod, my valet would never forgive me!"

The Major could not help himself but let out a disbelieving 'harrumph!" and there was a moment's uncomfortable silence.

'How odd,' thought Violette. 'Lord Winterbourne knows that we will never embark upon a honeymoon at all, let alone by sea. So why does he say it, and in that distant, drawling voice that I had somehow quite forgot? I suppose it's all to carry on this dreadful deception in which we are engaged, but I cannot think Richard Taverner enjoys lying to his sister any more than I enjoy lying to my aunt.'

Lady Clara continued blithely, "Yes, so even though our house is but five miles from the coast – a half-hour journey, if that – I have never been as close to the sea as I am now. So do let us go and explore, Violette!"

The ladies made their cautious way down the steep steps cut into the cliff face to the curving half-moon of shore. The white cliffs topped with their fringe of rough sea grasses lay behind with clusters of pink-flowered sea-thrift growing in the crevices.

On the far side of the cove was a great fall of tumbled rocks with here and there shallow pools of water left by the outgoing tide. These reflected the cloudless blue sky of a golden autumn afternoon; and out towards the horizon the sea was a deep emerald green.

They crunched their way across the shingle to the water's edge, where Lady Clara was enchanted by the shallow waves foaming onto the shore. She poked at some seaweed with a stick and shrieked when a crab ran out from under it and scuttled down into the water, and saw a little fish swimming in a rock pool and collected a handful of cockleshells. "I shall give them to Miss Flint. She can decorate a box or some such, for she has a great passion for nonsense of that sort!" and then she pounced upon a small white stone with a hole through it.

"Look, Violette! Do you not think this as near a heart shape as you could wish, and they say a stone with a hole in it is for luck, and I shall give it to – I mean, I shall keep it." She caught herself with a guilty giggle, and cast a look over her shoulder to see Miss Jennings and Miss Felicia a distance away, before she whispered, "You may guess who I shall give it to! Sir Harry Gray, to wear upon his watch chain!

"Sir Harry arrived at Winterbourne Hall a few days ago, quite unexpected! He was in the area by chance, he said, and then recollected that he had some business with Richard. Richard said afterwards it was nonsense and did not necessitate that gentleman travelling all the way from Mayfair to do it, and could have been settled in a letter. It was all very odd." Lady Clara was very pink about the cheeks, and her eyes were sparkling with mischief.

"Sir Harry asked me if we would be leaving for Bath after your engagement ball – which I quite invited him to, for I was sure you would like to see him – or would we be returning to London for Christmas? He said that London at Christmas has a great charm of its own, and he would be pleased to escort me to the theatre at Drury Lane where he has a box. We should see the Pantomime, which is a story of Harlequin and Columbine, and has real magic and people flying across the stage! I should so love to see it! But just then Miss Flint *would* come bustling in, and started talking about the tea tray, and that was the end of the conversation and he took his leave. But he asked if he might write to me. And I said he may.

"He told me afterwards that he never had any business in Kent at all, but so positively desired to see me again that he acted like a fool!" She let out a cascade of giggles.

Violette was not as astonished at the idea of Sir Harry feeling the need to call upon Lady Clara as that lady was herself, and had to hide her smile behind her hand.

"I thought that Richard would laugh when I confessed that Sir Harry had made up the visit in order to see me – for of course I could not have a correspondence with a gentleman without Richard's blessing. I wouldn't wish to keep a secret from my brother again," a shadow passed across her face, "but he didn't see the funny side at all.

"He has been so peculiar since he informed me of your engagement. Extraordinarily cross at times, which is quite the opposite of what I would have expected, and he is normally very even-tempered. I wondered if you and he had a falling out? Though that cannot be the case. When the carriage was brought round and I told him that I was coming to pay a call upon you with Miss Flint, he quite ordered her out of the carriage and said that he would escort me himself.

"He positively beamed – and it could only be at the thought of seeing you, my dearest friend!"

CHAPTER 26

As the night of her engagement ball drew nearer, Violette came to dread it more and more. Her misery was compounded when, the day after the visit to The Dragon, a servant arrived from Winterbourne Hall with a parcel for her. It proved to contain a necklace, a triple row of matched pearls with an amethyst centrepiece, and was accompanied by a note.

Miss deVere. I hope you will accept this gift from me to mark our betrothal. It is customary upon such an occasion for the gentleman to give the lady a gift, and our guests at the ball will quiz us about it. Winterbourne.

'There could hardly be a more formal note,' reflected Violette. 'It's just what Lord Winterbourne would do; the right thing, the correct thing, the thing that all society would expect. And yet yesterday he was so very kind to my aunt; patient with Major Jennings, courteous to Miss Jennings and with great care for his sister. The difference is quite astonishing. It's as if he cannot decide which is the real person – chilly Lord Winterbourne or charming

Richard Taverner. I don't know what to make of him, and I begin to suspect I never shall.'

With not a single idea in her head for a masquerade costume, and heavy-hearted about the whole enterprise, Violette travelled to London to consult with Mrs Bell. Mrs Bell exclaimed over the necklace, and conferred with her assistant, and held up lengths of fabric, murmuring of autumnal hues and silk embroideries. Violette stood before the mirror as if carved from marble, with the choker clasped about her neck.

'This weight around my neck reminds me of the conversation between Lord Winterbourne and the Major, about criminals being transported. I, too, am preparing for a journey I never looked for, where nothing lies ahead but enduring desolation and misery and the ending is one of loneliness and solitude.

'My aunt shows me that life as an old maid is not such a hardship. I have the comfort of wealth and I should count my blessings, for they are many.' She swallowed the tears that prickled at the back of her throat 'Oh, but I do not *want* to have to count my blessings and be grateful for such small comfort! I wished for so much more – a house filled with children, and someone to love me with all his heart.'

She let her thoughts dwell for a moment on Captain Death and the familiar warmth flooded through her as she recalled the night she spent in his arms and the desolation she felt to wake in the morning and find herself alone. 'But even if I saw him again – even if I knew where to find him, which I do not – I cannot envisage a future with Captain Death. A man less fit for marriage and children and domestic concerns there could not be!

'Lord Winterbourne doesn't want me, and I can't have Captain Death. Perhaps I should accept Philip Marwood. Maybe he is, as he says, a man whose behaviour and attitude would be softened by wealth; such things do come to pass. Maybe I could learn to like him. I should at least have companionship, and the comfort of children around me.

'But I cannot pretend to believe that he is anything other than a villain, no matter what he might have said to persuade me otherwise!'

Philip Marwood had vanished from sight, but it did not reassure Violette that he was gone for good. 'I would not put it past him to still have some dreadful scheme up his sleeve for the ruination of the Taverner family. And if Mr Marwood has been held accountable by his godfather,' she thought, with some degree of dread, 'no matter how discreet and tactful Sir Harry might have been, there is no doubt in my mind that Mr Marwood would see my hand in this.'

CHAPTER 27

On the evening of the ball, Hill came in to help her dress. She shook out Violette's gown of a heavy coffee-coloured silk worn over a stiff petticoat that made it stand away from her body. Over the silk was a floating layer of dove-colour spangled gauze embroidered in silver thread and caught up with clusters of velvet violets tied with chocolate silk true-love knots. Violette had resisted this last, feeling it to be too girlish, but Mrs Bell would not be dissuaded. "There is nothing girlish here. You will look regal, a young and vibrant Elizabeth Tudor to the life, for Lord knows, Miss deVere, you have the colouring for it!"

The neckline was low, and trimmed at the back with a high starched collar or silver lace that framed Violette's head. Hill fastened Lord Winterbourne's necklace, brushed Violette's curls until they shone and placed the delicate headdress of silver and peals. She stood back to admire her handiwork. "Oh miss, you do pay for the dressing, as they say. The right clothes and jewels turn you into quite the beauty!

Such a difference in just a few months, since first you set out for Mrs Fitzallen's party in Bath. And the mystery of who sent you the beautiful gown you wore that night, which has never been resolved; why, perhaps it was Lord Winterbourne himself, who as soon as he laid eyes upon you wished to marry you. A more romantic story there could not be!"

Violette sighed. If only such a thing were true. Like all young girls, she had dreamed, once, of the thrill of a love match, and had wished for such a thing with all her heart. 'But this is not that thing. This is a business arrangement, come about through debt and deception. Lord Winterbourne is doing what is right, and not at all what he wishes.' She stared at herself in the looking glass. 'You have only yourself to blame for your hot-headed folly, Violette deVere. For the sake of trying to do the best thing, you have sentenced yourself to the worst.'

She went downstairs to be greeted by her aunt in the pretty flounced prints and puffs of a Versailles shepherdess, complete with ribbon-bedecked crook and a cotton sheep to match tucked beneath her arm. Miss Jennings had refused to dress up in a costume and instead was in a striped gown of tobin on a brilliant pink ground, colours which did little to help the sallow colour of her face. Miss Sally was in her usual form. "A brown dress for your engagement, dear? How very odd. And those pearls are sadly mismatched, I fear," she finished with a sniff.

Major Jennings, wearing his uniform and fidgeting about the room in a state of great agitation, burst out, "Miss Violette – at last, my dear, at last!"

Violette was quite taken aback. "My apologies, Major Jennings, if I have kept you waiting-," but he stopped her with a finger tapped to the side of his nose, and a meaningful look at the maid, who was exiting the room with the coal scuttle. As soon as she was gone and the door was shut, the Major continued, "Not waiting for you, not at all my dear, but you will never guess what that blackguard has done! A note left for me at the inn. I have it with me!" From his breast pocket he took a folded slip of paper, and read aloud, "*Apologies, Major, for the delay, but the tulip bulbs are on their way.*" Miss Felicia exclaimed, "What an odd little rhyme!" and Violette had to turn away to hide a smile.

"May he enjoy his joke, for it's the last time that gentleman bests me!" The Major's ruddy countenance was mottled purple with indignation. "An information is laid that goods from the Continent are to be landed in Sumbourne Cove this very night. No doubt the Captain supposes it to be the perfect opportunity, for your ball will have distracted every person of rank in the county. What a nasty surprise it will be for that gentleman when his unholy crew rows ashore under cover of darkness in the small hours of the morning, and my men are there to greet them!" He crowed with satisfaction. "I shall have Captain Death at last, and it will give me the greatest satisfaction to put a bullet in him!"

The coach made its way along the coastal path, with the coachman up on his box, the Major riding alongside and John following behind on his own horse and leading Flambeau. The slow sweep of the Downs rose up to the left and to their right was the gentle swell of the English Channel, with the setting sun tracing a long finger of sparkling red light across the water. It was a beautiful sunset, the sky the blue of a robin's egg, the few drifts of cloud edged in pink and gold; but Violette gazed out across the water, unseeing.

'On the other side of this water is France. Captain Death is out there somewhere with his crew, all unaware of what is waiting for them when they return. The Major is so seized with the desire for revenge at having been made a fool of all these months that he will see them all sent to the Assizes. It will be transportation at best, and hanging at worst, and I doubt Lord Winterbourne will be able to save them.

'I must spend my evening feigning delight in an engagement to one man while my heart breaks for another, and I don't know how I shall bear it.'

The coach drew up before Winterbourne House, and Violette passed between the imposing stone pillars of the entrance and into the reception hall. She observed the vast black marble floor and the gleaming statues in their alcoves, the grand sweep of the elaborate staircase and the high, echoing ceilings. 'I hate this house. There is nothing here of beauty or history, nothing warm or welcoming. These statues might be works of art, but it's art of the most sinister and ugly kind. This floor might be of the most expensive marble, but it comes from some far-off place where men slave in the baking heat of the sun. The creaking floorboards at Sumbourne, cut from the ancient oaks of my own parkland, and polished by the tread of my own family's feet for century after century, are more precious to me.

'All here is imposing, built for no reason other than to demonstrate wealth which, as Mr Marwood has told me with understandable bitterness, is built upon the misfortunes of others. I could never live here. After tonight I will never have to set my eyes upon it again, and I am glad of it.'

When Violette entered the ballroom, it was to see before her a fantastical array of characters. Robin Hood and Maid Marian, Antony and Cleopatra, Roman centurions and gladiators, and Julius Caesar in a bloodstained toga, perfectly lively despite the knife seemingly plunged into his heart. Lady Clara in trailing white silk, her hair loose and crowned with a wreath of flowers and herbs was Ophelia. There was a Queen of Spades dripping with jet beads, and a King of Hearts in scarlet satin, and here was Lady Hertford in silver as the moon and her husband all in cloth of gold and an awe-inspiring wig as Louis XlV, the Sun King.

Lady Andover was there with her friend Mrs Baxter-Lees, these two ladies enjoyably scandalised at the sight of Mary Abercrombie in black velvet as Mary Queen of Scots accompanied by her husband in a kilt that showed his legs. And all wore, or carried, elaborate masks of jewels and feathers.

Even the ballroom itself was in disguise. The white ceiling was covered with a painted cloth depicting a dark sky with stars and the moon. Trees planted in great pots and swathed with ivy reached up to these glittering constellations, artificial birds perched upon their branches, and where there would have been chairs were banks of mossy green velvet.

Lady Clara met Violette as she entered the ballroom. Violette gazed about her in astonishment. "Good heavens. How on earth –?" Clara took her hand. "It's not the best thing! Come with me!" She pulled her out onto the terrace. "There!" she said, "Do you not think me clever?"

The terrace was unrecognisable. It was become a mystical woodland glade, and Violette thought that if she were not familiar with the architecture of the house, she would never have known that the soft grass beneath her feet covered stone and tile, or that the lush plantings of trees and flowering shrubs had not been growing here for decades. Some clever scheme gave the illusion that the balustrades were little more than the tumbledown remains of an ancient building, overgrown with graceful swathes of ivy, and as Violette crossed the terrace to investigate, she was rewarded with a drift of rose petals and perfumed leaves falling upon her as if from the skies above.

"I have footmen stationed on the roof, and when they see anyone come out onto the terrace, they are to throw a handful of this pretty stuff over them!"

Lady Clara grasped Violette's hands and swung her round, unable to contain her delight. "I never knew I had so many clever ideas for a ball. I wish I could arrange another, for I had to leave aside as many ideas as I could put into practice!"

At this, Violette spied Sir Harry Gray, looking every inch the splendid Cavalier, making his way towards them with eyes for no-one but Lady Clara. Violette whispered in her friend's ear, "I think you will soon be arranging any number of marvellous entertainments, when you are one of society's leading hostesses!" Clara turned to Violette, her eyes shining, and replied, "It's true! Oh Violette, he has asked me, and I have promised him my answer in the morning. But you cannot doubt what it will be!"

When Violette re-entered the ballroom, it was to be greeted by Kit Taverner in a striking ensemble which he informed her was a 'Hastings fisherman' – a knitted sweater in blue and white stripes, with a jaunty spotted kerchief tied about his neck; knitted stockings and canvas britches, and a red cap pulled low over his forehead. "I'm on shore leave for a week and Clara wanted to go and see this exhibition of paintings. Richard prevailed upon me to escort her and I was glad to do it. He says we have neglected her, and perhaps he is correct; in any event he has dispatched our cousin Miss Flint back to Scotland. I never did like her, to be honest with you. Half-sprung much of the time, if you ask me," he mimed a glass being raised to his lips, "and Richard as good as hinted at some havey-cavey business or other.

Anyway, I saw this jolly fellow in a painting with his boat, and I rather liked the look of him."

"Your brother couldn't escort her himself?"

"Said he had some business." Kit looked suddenly shifty as he said this, and was evidently relieved to see Lord Winterbourne himself approaching them.

Violette had informed him of her Queen Elizabeth costume and thought he might complement it by coming as, say, Walter Raleigh or Francis Drake, but he was in a most striking outfit; a floor-length black cloak and a broad-brimmed hat, and hooked over his arm was a golden bird mask with a long curving beak He smiled faintly at Violette's look of astonishment. "I gave Clara *carte-blanche to* arrange things as she liked, although I told her I absolutely refused to wear a costume myself." He sighed. "It was a battle of wills, but my sister won – and you see me in the costume of a Venetian plague doctor, which is most apt, for it certainly plagues me to wear it! You, on the other hand, look delightful. What a beautiful costume. From Mrs Hill in London, is it not? Ah! The musicians are ready to strike up, it seems. It falls upon us to open the dancing."

With that, he extended his arm, and they moved away to the centre of the floor to a smattering of applause.

Violette smiled at the company, but her lips felt curiously stiff. As for his lordship, it seemed he could not meet her eye, and they danced the first in smiling, excruciating embarrassment, aware of all eyes upon them, and the second, too. Then Lord

Winterbourne – as scrupulously polite as it was possible to be – escorted her back to her aunt, and sought out his partner for the next.

Violette was engaged for one dance after another, but as the night wore on, her wretchedness mounted. 'I cannot bear another minute playing this charade. I would give anything for this night to be over.' Her wish was granted soon enough. The supper dance came to a close, the partygoers headed into the supper rooms, and the musicians laid down their instruments and found their way down to the kitchens for their own refreshments.

Violette watched Major Jennings as he helped her aunt to one dish after another, and made a hearty meal himself – all ease and eagerness, unlike Violette, who felt that even the smallest morsel would choke her. But at last the final ice was consumed, and the punch bowl emptied, and the remaining dish of honeyed figs plundered to its depths. Great excitement greeted the announcement that there was to be a display of fireworks before the dancing resumed, and the guests began to move outside onto the terrace, chattering and laughing, with the figure of Lord Winterbourne, unmistakeable in his long black coat and wearing his golden mask, leading the way.

But Violette caught sight of Major Jennings slipping out of the ballroom and she set out to follow him. For she knew what she had to do.

'I am going to Captain Death. I don't know how, but I must do something. Even if all I can do is scream a warning, at least I shall have tried! I can be there and back before dawn, and no-one will be any the wiser.'

She ran along the corridor that led to the stables, remembering how she had done so before, and what it had led to, but was brought up sharp, when a figure stepped out of the shadows. It was Philip Marwood, flushed, and unsteady in his gait. Drunk perhaps, though not enough to be befuddled. Grasping Violette's wrist, he pulled her into a little side room and shut the door behind them.

"I have waited to hear from you and have heard nothing! It is not at all the done thing to leave a proposal of marriage hanging in the air my dear; I really thought I would have had the courtesy of an answer before now!"

"Mr Marwood – excuse me! I'm sorry. I should have answered you, and you are right to be annoyed with me, but I beg you, might we talk about this in the morning?" Violette took a hurried step towards the door, but he forestalled her.

"We shall not! You will listen to me! I know what you did, Miss deVere! You went running to Sir Harry with tales of poor little Clarrie Taverner's misfortunes and for that, I was roundly abused and sent away with my tail between my legs.

"Let me tell you where I went. I was sent to cool my heels in the West Country yet again, that God-forsaken place. And do you know what I did there? Why, go through the mine-owners' books, a task to be undertaken by the very lowest of the bank employees. I was not even entertained by such gentry as inhabit those miserable acres, but put up in some hell-hole of an inn.

"It was designed to be a lesson for me and it was. It reminded me of why I wish to get out of the situation in which I find myself, beholden to rich men who scorn me for a poor one. Nothing to do, night after night, but to eat a dish of herrings for my supper and slum it by the fireside with a jug of the ghastly swill of cider that they serve in those parts, and plot my revenge!"

"And are you arrived from there – this instant?" faltered Violette. Mr Marwood's behaviour was very strange. He seemed not drunk after all, but mad.

He laughed. "Ah, you might wish that I was, but no! I have told you where I went, and now let me tell you what I did. I brooded. I brooded upon your coldness, Miss deVere. How I had been honest with you, and sincere in my proposal of marriage, and how you had betrayed me. And I came to think how strange it was that I knew so little about you, when my business has always been the pursuit of knowledge. Knowledge is power, you know, knowledge is power, but I had been remiss. My regard for you had blinded me to my ignorance of you.

"I decided to remedy this situation. So, a few mornings ago, I abandoned that make-work I had been set to, and boarded the stage and arrived here in Kent. I have heard it called the Garden of England and a fruitful harvest I have encountered here, with the people here willing, as they say, to be plucked for a shilling. I've found out your history, Miss deVere. Ah, indeed I have."

"My history? I don't think I understand you, sir." But Violette did understand him, very well. 'He knows,' she thought to herself; 'how much is unclear, but enough.'

She was right. His next words confirmed it. "A great black-beard rogue; his great black hound of a dog and you, Miss Violette deVere! A juicy tale, to be sure. Indeed, the landlord of the inn at Little Hougham was only too delighted to accept a sovereign for his recollection of a young lady found in a shepherd's hut, wrapped in nothing more than a blanket and her clothing quite torn to pieces."

He laughed, looking Violette up and down in an assessing manner. "I thought that Winterbourne's debt was the scandal here; but his bills are nothing compared to the shame of the woman he intends to marry. How did you think to get away with it, my dear? It is the best and jolliest joke of them all. You had me foxed, you know. But enough. To business, for unfinished business it is.

"I offered you marriage and I offer it again. But this time you have no choice but to accept my offer and its terms. I shall set it out as plain as maybe, in case you don't quite understand it.

"One the one side we have reputation. Not just yours, but that of your friend and your aunt, as well. Clarrie Taverner is on the marriage market, and prime untouched merchandise she is, to be sure. And I understand your aunt is to be congratulated on her own engagement to a most upstanding member of the community. But stay!" He posed theatrically, his finger in the air, and his face a ghastly parody of innocent surprise. "Can it be true, that these two irreproachably respectable ladies have spent all these months in the company of a woman who is – to use vulgar parlance – 'a game pullet', 'a light-skirt', a 'prime article'? In short, a woman of the easiest virtue with no reputation at all? A woman with whom no honest gentleman would wish to associate – at least not for the purposes of marriage!"

His voice lost its mocking tone, and descended into something approaching revulsion. "As for your aunt, why, she has resided in the very same house for all this time. Perhaps she, too, is a piece of prime bachelor-fare! Perhaps here we have a veritable nest of plump little game birds for the plucking!"

"Enough! I shan't listen to another word of this filth!" Violette turned once more towards the door, but Philip Marwood sprung at her, and grasped her wrist, twisting it behind her back. "You *will* listen! And I'll tell you what you are going to do!

"You will go to Lord Winterbourne this instant, and you will inform him that you will not marry him. It is an easy enough task to perform, and I can't wait to see the expression on Winterbourne's face when he finds himself jilted and shamed, and knows that ruin and retribution are hot on his heels! His creditors at the door, Miss deVere, his creditors at the door!" He let out an ugly high-pitched squeal of merriment. "I don't need to explain to you the consequences if you refuse. Your aunt's happiness, your friend's happiness, your own reputation – vanished between one word and the next!

"You went to visit my godfather at his place of business in Fleet Street. Did you notice, I wonder, the print shops for which the area is renowned? They trade in cartoon sheets, Miss deVere, making mock of those in society, to be laughed over across the length and breadth of the land, from country tavern to city coffee house, from brothel door to palace gate. Do you wish to experience the unutterable degradation of finding yourself the subject of their scurrilous humour?

"I thought you a clever woman but you are a simpleton indeed if you think you can spend the night with a ruffian and never be found out! You have played straight into my hands, and I thank you for it!" He released her, and stepped back, to study the results of his words.

Dread fear had Violette entirely in its grip. She was aware of her heart thundering in her chest, and as much as she would wish to flee, her feet felt as though they were nailed to the floor. She could not have moved so much as to blink an eyelid.

She spoke. Her voice was not above a whisper. I beg you. I implore you. It's not true. What you say of me. Nothing happened. I swear it – I have done nothing of which I am ashamed."

Philip Marwood shrugged. "So you say. Perhaps people will believe you. Oh, I *do* like a wager, Miss deVere. Are you of the gambling persuasion? Are you willing to risk everything upon the chance, the one remote chance, that society will believe the best of you?

"I shall give you a moment to compose yourself. Wipe your face. Tears will not save you. I shall be upstairs in the ballroom, nicely situated to see Winterbourne's face when you whisper your news in his ear!" The door banged behind him, and he was gone.

Violette sank to the floor, her face in her hands. All she could do was repeat, in a broken whisper, "What have I done? Oh, what have I done?"

'I have been the most wretched fool as ever there was. I told myself over and over that the night I spent with Captain Death was a dream, but deep down I always knew it to be true! And I wilfully turned my face away from the knowledge that I would be found out in the end!

'I've teased my aunt for her oh-so-prim concerns for the opinions of others; and I've been dismissive of society's expectation, thanks to my father, who had nothing but scorn for it all. But now I see the damage I've caused! By my own folly I've become involved with a dangerous smuggler; I've lied to the Excise, and eavesdropped on a private conversation so that I have heard horrible things about myself. I could not control my temper, and went running across the ballroom floor positively screaming at Lord Winterbourne, with the most utmost disdain for the situation into which I plunged us both.

'And the result is that, like something from a fable or a fairy tale, I have all the things I have ever wished for, but all twisted about and tainted.

'I wished for excitement and adventure, and positively embraced a most shockingly scandalous liaison with Captain Death, as if I were the heroine in a novel. I wished to marry a gentleman who had no desire for my fortune and for a brief moment I thought Lord Winterbourne to be that gentleman; but now I doubt everything about him, and we find ourselves betrothed in the most wretched circumstances and with no prospect of a wedding at all. And I wished I could meet a man who was completely honest with me, and here I have that wish come true in Mr Philip Marwood, who has been quite brutally plain about his intentions.

'My mad folly has brought ruination in its wake. Of my own life at the very least, and, it seems now, of those close to me. My dear aunt and my friend Clara Taverner and Lord Winterbourne, too. All are the unsuspecting victims of my foolishness – no! Foolishness is not strong enough a word. My wilful stupidity! My obstinacy! My temper!

'And I don't know how to resolve any of it.' She sat for a long while, bowed down by misery. At last, she raised her head. She spoke out loud, and her voice was calm, and steady.

"Philip Marwood will have me in his power forever if I give way to him now. The only way I can save myself is to bluff it out. Yes; I shall deny all knowledge of Captain Death and denounce Philip Marwood for a liar!" She rose to her feet, but with her hand upon the doorknob, she paused. 'But if I do, then Lord Winterbourne will call him out. He is known as a good shot. And although Philip Marwood is a villain, he speaks the truth! Do I want to make Lord Winterbourne a murderer? Or see Philip Marwood triumphant, and Richard Taverner with a bullet in him?

'Can I truly leave Captain Death to pay the ultimate price for my pride? See him and his men sent to the hangman's noose purely to save my reputation? 'How could I live with such a burden upon my conscience? It is unthinkable. Whatever happens now, it will bring disgrace and shame raining down upon me and all those around me.'

Tears were running, unheeded, down her cheeks. I can't do it. I shan't. I must save Captain Death if I can. And then I shall leave a note for my aunt, to most humbly beg her forgiveness, and return to St Cloud, to spend my days in the countryside and my evenings beside my fire with a good novel, and I believe I shall be content enough.'

'It will break my heart to do it, but I am decided. When the sun rises in the morning, I shall be far away.'

CHAPTER 28

John was in the yard, saddling up his horse. He stopped quite dead at the sight of her. "Miss Violette! What do you do here?"

She flung open the door of Flambeau's stall. "Help me with the saddle! I'm riding to Sumbourne Cove. Major Jennings is gone for Captain Death, with a loaded pistol and a company of his men. And he must be warned!" She stopped. "But what of you? What are you about?"

"The same as you, Miss! Not for Captain Death, who he is and what he does I care not, but along with him are local men – men I have known since boyhood. But you must not go! In your finery, without a cloak to cover you, and from your own ball? No miss! I shall go, but you must not!"

"I couldn't fetch a cloak without arousing suspicion, and I am going, John, and that's an end to it. Now hurry! The Major has thirty minutes or more upon us. I fear we have little time!"

It was a still, cold night. John leading the way, they kicked their horses to a gallop and went flying away over the hills, Violette's dove-coloured gauze streaming out behind her. The sky at her back was a dazzling blaze of stars and sparks and streams of fire as the firework display reached its glittering crescendo.

They reached the plateau where Violette had first caught sight of Winterbourne Hall, all those months ago. Now she reined in her mare and wheeled to a stop. She looked back down the valley at the house that might have been her home. The velvet blackness of the sky was transformed one last time, as a final explosion of emerald and gold and ruby turned the heavens into a lake of fiery gems; and then they were gone. Winterbourne Hall was once more as pale as a pearl, glimmering faintly in the dark.

'Those fireworks are like my engagement. A glittering show that has burned out as quick as it started, leaving the sky blacker than it was before. I cannot carry it on, deceiving those around me month upon month, no matter that it is with the best of intentions.

'I am broken-hearted to do it. Lord Winterbourne has come to have such a hold upon me that I cannot deny it. Yes! – I admit it! I should have liked to have been married to Richard Taverner. I had begun to hope that the long months of our engagement may have softened his heart towards me, and I believe I understand something of the mystery that has plagued me ever since I met him;

that concealed beneath his arrogance and his condescension is something more. I see that where there is conceit there is also kindness, and that his air of languid disdain hides a loving heart.

'But it is not filled with love for me. And any kindness he might have felt towards me will be gone in an instant, when he realises what I have done.

'I can only hope that Major Jennings and Sir Harry Gray will have the courage to rescue the women they love from the degradation that will surely follow from their association with me. But I must save Captain Death." With this, she turned her horse's head away from Winterbourne Hall for the last time, and followed John down onto the coastal path.

They rode fast against a stiff breeze blowing off the sea, with a fine spray of icy droplets thrown into the air by the waves that crashed against the rocks below. After twenty minutes or so, John reined in his horse to a gentle trot, and then a cautious walk. Violette did the same, and they dismounted in the cover of a small stand of windbent trees. Violette's teeth were chattering in her head, and her gown clung to her, saturated by the salt spray.

John shrugged off his greatcoat and put it round her shoulders, his finger to his lips. Violette was too cold to argue.

To their right, the land rose sharply upwards, and above their heads reared The Dragon, silhouetted against the stars. To their left the land sloped steeply downwards. Violette took a few cautious steps across the damp grass and peered over, to find that the shore was no more than a hundred yards below, the cliff edge fallen away to the tumble of rocks she'd observed when she was on the beach with Lady Clara.

Just at that moment the clouds drifting across the moon parted, and in its light Violette could make out a narrow sliver of darkness half-concealed by the fallen stones. 'It's the entrance to a cave! I swear I never saw it when I was down in the cove before. It must only be visible from up here on the cliffs, and even then, only if you are looking in a particular direction."

John joined her, and motioned to her to look out across the water. There was the black outline of a ship riding at anchor, hardly distinguishable from the indigo sky behind it. There was a sudden flicker of light, instantly gone. And from somewhere close at hand came the faint snicker of a horse.

John put his lips close to her ear. "There's someone on the top of the cliffs, signalling with a dark lantern to the men rowing ashore. I'm going to find him, and tell him to change the signal, and send them away. Go back into the trees, Miss, and stay hidden, I beg you!" He sped away into the darkness.

All was silent but for the gentle shush of the waves breaking upon the shore. Violette strained every sense, listening fearfully in the dark. Gradually she became aware of the muted splash of oars, and there was a muttered oath, instantly silenced. There was the scrape of a boat's keel on the shingle. With horror, she knew that John had failed, and they were not warned off. 'We are too late! He will be taken – !'

Her scream rang out across the water. "Go back! Go back! It's a trap!"

There was an answering shout from somewhere higher up the cliff. A dog set up a volley of furious barking; there was a smash of glass – 'the lantern!' guessed Violette. The scrubby dry grasses that grew along the cliff edge blazed up momentarily, and in their light Violette could make out a solitary boat not ten yards from the shore, its occupants already disembarked and waist-deep in the water as they urged the heavy-laden craft forward across the shingle. Close behind were another half-dozen rowboats sitting low in the water with men straining at the oars.

Violette flung off her shoes and stockings and lowered herself over the cliff edge, her fingers digging into the grass and mud of the cliff top as she felt for the rocks with her bare feet. She clambered down into the cove, panting with fear as her feet slipped from beneath her, but at last she was down.

The men in the first rowboat were fighting to clamber back on board and turn themselves about and head back out to sea, but the incoming tide and the wind were against them. Racing across the beach towards them came the handful of Excise men who had been concealed in the shadows. Down the steps from the inn came swarming a dozen more. There was the flash of a pistol followed by the booming noise of the shot; another after that. Then the Excise men were grappling with the smugglers at the water's edge.

Someone grabbed Violette's arm. John's voice was in her ear. "Come away Miss! – there's nothing else we can do here!" There was another man with him, with a sack slung over his shoulder. They disappeared round behind the rocks and into the entrance to the cave that Violette had seen earlier, and she followed them in.

It was as black as pitch. They stopped for a moment to listen for the sounds of pursuit, but there was nothing; only their rapid breathing. Something scuttled over Violette's bare foot. She let out a muffled squawk of terror. And in the darkness, someone reached out and took her hand, and there was a voice in her ear; raspingly low, amused. "It seems that I continue in your debt, Miss deVere."

"Captain Death!"

"At your service. And now we must move, and swiftly. The way through these caves is treacherous. We will be travelling in darkness, and in places the path falls away, so keep close to the wall. Do not fear, I will help you, and John is here, your faithful servant. Come."

The back of the cave narrowed into a tunnel which twisted upwards, away from the shore. A mile or more they went, travelling by feel alone. In some places the roof was low, and they had to stoop. In others, the walls closed in so that there was hardly room enough to squeeze through, but they travelled always on.

The air was still, and stale, and there were places where water ran down the walls and across their feet, to splash into some unseen pool far below. Violette edged her way along the path, whimpering with fear, expecting any minute to lose her footing and go plunging away into the depths.

Just as she thought she could go no further, she felt the welcome relief of cool air, fresh upon her face. She stumbled, and cried out as she knocked her shins painfully against a sharp edge – a flight of steep, narrow steps, leading upwards. A hand reached down to her from above to steady her and she emerged, blinking, into the shaded light of dense woodland in the early dawn.

They were surrounded by thick undergrowth of brambles and ferns. A bird, roused from slumber, gave out a sleepy chirp or two. It was answered by the distant gentle whinny of a horse and the stamp of its hoof. John busied himself pulling brambles across the trapdoor to conceal it, and Violette took a cautious step towards where the trees began to thin a little. There was a tumble of stones – the remains of a low wall – and beyond it was an orchard with row upon row of apple trees. In the near distance she could discern some low outbuildings.

Another few steps and she saw before her the stables of Sumbourne Manor, her very own house.

She turned to look at the figure beside her, stooping to untie the sack that he had carried upon his shoulder. A red knitted cap was pulled down low upon his brow to hide his hair, and a spotted kerchief was knotted across his nose and mouth.

She stared at his bent back, appalled. It was Kit Taverner.

Kit Taverner! Her breath caught in her throat. It was so obvious! His love of the sea, his athletic exploits; his adventurous nature; she remembered Clara laughing at the scrapes into which her twin had led her in their childhood. With that came the memory of the dreams she'd had of his naked body pressed against hers, of clutching at him in the stables at Winterbourne Hall and her frenzied, desperate kiss. His words to his brother; "If I were of an age, I'd play for her myself."

If I were of an age …. he was no more than a boy. A burning agony of mortification swept through her, from the tips of her toes to the crown of her head.

At that moment he stood and upended the sack, and something went bouncing and skittering across the grass at Violette's feet. She looked down.

Captain Death let out a low laugh. "Can you guess, Miss deVere? Tulip bulbs! I thought to place them at Major Jennings's door, and would have greatly enjoyed to see his face when he recounted the story!"

With that, he pulled off his knitted cap with a flourish, and ripped away the kerchief that covered his mouth and jaw. Unshaven, his jaw was stubbled black; his hair was as pale as the early morning clouds in the sky above.

Violette looked Captain Death full in the face for the first time.

"Lord Winterbourne!" she said.

CHAPTER 29

Lord Winterbourne? How could it be?

He raised a quizzical eyebrow; a broad smile upon his lips, his face alight with mischief.

Violette sprang at him. She administered such a slap across his face that he quite staggered back, and her own hand stung with it. Tears of fury stood in her eyes. "How *could* you? Oh, how *could* you! *Damn* you to hell and blazes, Richard Taverner!

"As if I had not scandal enough to contend with! I thought that if it was discovered I had abandoned my own engagement ball, I would be laughed at by my neighbours and sentenced to a life as a foolish old maid, but I was reconciled to it! And then I encountered Mr Marwood –."

"Marwood? What the devil?"

Violette was too agitated to explain. "He threatened exposure of the worst kind, and even *then* I risked not only myself but all those I loved to save your life, *yours!* Or at least – that of Captain Death! And you did not deserve it!

"The agonies I have endured! You wretch, you abominable –! And now it will appear that we have run away together from our own ball! It will be said that we have eloped! Dear God, we have loosed a veritable storm of scandal that will sweep through town and country alike, and we shall never live it down!

"And our engagement, what of that? We cannot break it, now. Oh, what shall we do – what *shall* we do?" She turned this way and that, twisting her hands together in an agony of fear and indecision. "We must get back. Maybe Mr Marwood said nothing. If you were not there, if he could not find you!"

With this, another thought seized her. "But you *were* there. I saw you when I left – in your costume, watching the fireworks! Oh but - it was your brother! You swapped over your costumes! Or at least, he put on your cloak and mask."

She stopped for a moment, and slowly added, "So he's known all along, what your secret was. And if he was convincing … I suppose we might have got away with it. If Mr Marwood held off. And they might all be still asleep and none the wiser."

For a moment she ceased her pacing, but then her thoughts came crowding in once more. "But your clothes? And my mare is still down at the cove. And I was going to leave! I was decided!"

Lord Winterbourne caught her by the shoulders and forced her to be still. He looked down at her with a smile playing about his lips. "My darling girl," he said – and his voice was not the measured, dismissive light drawl that she disliked so very much, nor Captain Death's throaty rasp, but was something deep and warm, with a hint of laughter at back of it. "My darling girl, we chose to be engaged to avoid one scandal, and now it seems we must be married as soon as maybe to avoid another. But 'pon my oath, I care nothing for what town and country might say, as long as you are my own!"

This declaration quite stopped Violette in her tracks. She stared at Lord Winterbourne in great confusion. "But I don't understand. I heard you say yourself, that you would never marry me. You told me plain, that I had forced you into acting against your will, and you wished you had never met me, and cursed the day that you did. You were so angry! But now – how is it, now, that you say quite the opposite?"

"How can I explain it? You've had me turned about from the first moment I saw you. You threw yourself into the Winterbourne to save my dog, and in doing so you threw yourself into my heart. Yes – I say it – entirely into my heart, and never out of it again.

"But as you see, my whole life is a lie. Lord Winterbourne by day and by night Captain Death. All who are involved in my life are in danger and at risk of disgrace. How could I put you into such a situation? I could not. You suspected me, I knew it – of something, but what I could not tell. And I was desperate to tell you my secret. To confess all. To be my true self.

"You cannot know the cost of fighting that temptation. A poor job I made of it, I think. There were times when I wanted to laugh aloud with the joy of simply holding your hand in the dance!

"Oh, my dearest love – can you forgive me? Now you know all, and there shall be no more secrets between us! And in any event," he passed his hand across his jaw, with a rueful grimace, "I would not dare do anything more to cause you distress, and chance such a slap again!"

He opened his arms, and Violette stepped into them. And John, who had been standing at some distance, seemingly highly interested in a crop of wizened apples upon the boughs of an ancient tree, suddenly developed a greater interest yet in another crop more distant still, and moved away to investigate more closely.

After a moment or two, he cleared his throat loudly. The engaged couple, both a little dazed-looking around the eyes, stepped away from one another, and seemed to recollect their circumstances.

Violette was the first to speak. "All the same. We must return to Winterbourne Hall as quickly as we can. If we've been missed, my poor aunt will be worried to death. Oh – but your clothes – and my carriage is there, and our horses at the cliff top. There's only the pony and trap here to take us back!"

"Then the pony and trap it is. We shall go bowling up to the Hall in sight of all our guests as quite the country couple, my darling, and I care not one jot for what they might say to it. And as for my clothes – I agree that appearing in this rough garb might give my guests a shock, and the arrangement of my hair will certainly give them a fright!" He laughed. "I have my riding cape here, and it will conceal me well enough until I can get to my rooms and change into something more suitable."

"So this secret passage on my land, within sight of my house, is how you travel from one life to the other? It appears you must owe me a goodly sum in toll money, my lord."

"I am certain I do, and shall repay you in full, my sweet! Yes, indeed, I leave the Hall as Lord Winterbourne, and enter into these woods, and along the secret passageway to emerge at Sumbourne Cove as Captain Death. It is quite the silliest name! But I adopted it when I was a roistering lad of not yet sixteen and full of bravado and swagger. It has stuck with me, and served me well enough. And I have not forgot what it is, either, to be that lad!"

He pointed to a window set high into the eaves of Violette's house, and bent his head close to hers, and whispered in her ear. "For these past months I have often seen a light in that window, and imagined you there in your bedchamber, and tormented myself with the thought of climbing up the ivy to snatch a kiss from you!"

Violette could not help her blush, but her voice was steady enough. "I am sorry to disappoint you, my lord," she said, demurely, "but in that room you would have found Miss Sally Jennings in her curl papers, and that would have been enough to dampen your ardour, to be sure!"

Richard gathered her into his arms once more. "I would have braved even that dragon for you, my darling!"

John had occasion to clear his throat yet again, and the lovers stepped reluctantly apart and made their way towards the house

John took Lord Winterbourne's chestnut and departed for the cliff top to fetch the other horses, and Violette slipped up the stairs to change her dress and put on a warm cloak, and off they set in the pony and trap.

After a while, Violette spoke. "What of the men who were with you in that boat? The Excise will have taken them, for sure. What will happen to them?"

"They will be put into the lockup for a few weeks and their case will be heard by the local magistrate at the quarterly sessions – none other than Lord Winterbourne! They must be punished, there is no help for it, but as for hangings and deportations, that will not happen. A few months in gaol, but knowing that their families will be provided for, will not be so great an ordeal."

"I still don't truly understand," she said, slowly. "I might not have recognised your face – for I was ill with a fever for some weeks and could hardly trust my memories of that night at all; indeed, I thought I remembered that you – that we – -." She stopped, blushing hotly once again, and unable to meet his eyes.

"You were shivering with cold, and burning with fever, and crying out in your sleep. I knew then and there that I had quite lost my heart to you, and it seemed the most natural thing in the world to lie beside you and put my arms around you to warm you, and hold you close to my heart to comfort you. Don't forget, we had Loki there to chaperone us, and Captain Death might be a rascal, but never a scoundrel!"

"Oh no, I never for one moment thought … and anyway," she cast him a sideways glance below her lashes, "anyway – I liked it!"

Lord Winterbourne dropped the reins and pulled her into his arms once more. There was a long pause while the pony, left to his own devices, stopped pulling the trap and investigated a juicy-looking patch of grass.

After a while, Violette was able to speak. "But afterwards. It seems so foolish, now, that I didn't see what was so plain before my eyes. But your voice and manner? They seemed so changed!"

"Why would you, or anyone, seeing me in lounging disdain in a ballroom, ever have reason to think me a notorious ruffian of a smuggler, doing business in the back rooms of low taverns and rowing out to sea on a moonless night? The more that men like your Major Jennings despised me for a milksop, the better." Lord Winterbourne smiled. Who would suspect a weak-voiced Exquisite with no concern for anything but the fall of his neck tie? And the more aloof and disdainful I was, the less anyone would dare to quiz me as to my movements. I'd dance the requisite couple of dances to begin, and then make my way to the card room; and then leave the card room, and no-one would notice my absence or remark upon it."

"At first it was the greatest adventure, to act one thing by day and another by night, and I thought myself a cunning fellow indeed. I did not foresee that there would be no end to it. That these two separate lives would become so closely entwined that I would become consumed by the fear of forgetting which person I was supposed to be, with disastrous consequences for myself and those I loved.

"And then it was made a hundred times worse. Suddenly there you were, looking me full in the face with your tale of the Winterbourne in flood! You cannot imagine the fright you gave me. I thought that poor dandyish Lord Winterbourne was in imminent danger of the gallows! So I was quite extraordinarily rude to your aunt – poor lady, she had done nothing to deserve such treatment – and I could do nothing but insult you, too.

"I was desperate to escape you! I couldn't even meet your eye, for fear that some spark would pass between us and you would know me straight away. But I hope the gown made up for it. I truly could not bear to see you in anything as monstrous as your aunt's suggestion. Pea-green satin? I shuddered at the thought of it!"

Violette burst out laughing, and he laughed with her. "It is a beautiful gown, the nicest I have ever owned. And my aunt's eventual choice was just as hideous. I don't know why I agreed to it."

"Because you are kind, and I was rude to her. You had not the heart to contradict her, I am sure of it. And then I wished to see you in it, so I persuaded my poor sister to sit through the tedium of the Spanish Quartet at Mrs Fitzallen's, and she has an absolute horror of musical evenings. She only went on the promise of an ice and Mrs Fitzallen forced so many of them upon the poor child that she was positively bilious afterwards! The worst thing was when we were dancing. The fear and excitement of a midnight trip across the water with pistols drawn was as nothing compared to the terror of taking your hand in the dance and seeing your eyes fixed upon mine!"

"A little less life-threatening, though," observed Violette.

"It did not feel it at the time!" came the answer. "But confess. You suspected me – did you not?"

"Only that you never seemed to be where you should. I suppose these were the times when you were engaged in the – as you put it – smuggling trade. And not at the Gentleman's Bathhouse in Drury Lane!"

Lord Winterbourne laughed so hard at this that he had to quite pull the pony to a halt once more, and search through the numerous pockets of his driving cape to find his pocket handkerchief.

"I had cause to speak a little with Sir Harry Gray," said Violette, slowly, "about – well, about his godson, Mr Marwood, who had – who has caused me some disquiet." She would not mention Philip Marwood's campaign of terror against Lady Clara, nor his reasons for it; it was Clara's secret to tell, and not hers. "Sir Harry mentioned that he knew you a little, and told me something of your father, and the building of your house. He was admiring of you, as a young man managing to support your family. I suppose you took up smuggling for that reason."

"At first, I merely allowed the smugglers to store their goods in the outbuildings at the Hall, and they made me some little payment for that, but then I joined a crew to cross the Channel to help spirit away the family of a gentleman who'd felt the breath of Madame Guillotine at his neck. He and his wife and children needed somewhere to hide when they landed in England, for there were spies in this country ready to take them back at pistol point. And there were empty rooms enough at Winterbourne Hall for a dozen fleeing Frenchmen and their children.

"I was paid in what seemed to me a fortune in jewels – enough to pay off some of my father's creditors and keep the rest quiet for a month or two. We set off again, and again after that. When Madame Guillotine was finally sated and the blood of enough men and women had been spilled, the cargo became kegs of brandy and bales of lace and sacks of sugar, and so it went on; and soon I had amassed enough money to purchase boats of my own.

"I never thought to keep at it all these years. It's a young man's game. But the house," his face darkened, "that house is a bottomless pit that swallows money. And I could not sell it, nor the London property for it would have given rise to speculation as to my financial affairs, and I could not risk it.

"I have servants looking to me for their livelihoods, and I had to make good the damage done to the farming families who had depended upon the common land for generations until my father deprived them of it with the enclosures and bled them dry.

"I could not let my mother die in penury. Our cousins in Scotland were kind and took her in, but even so I could not let them do it for charity's sake alone; there was the cost of nursing and nourishing food and good fires, and those little comforts of books, and writing paper and ink for her correspondence.

"There were my sister and brother. A decent tutor and university for Kit ; a governess for Clara, and clothes and an allowance – do not doubt, Violette, that I love them dearly, but it never stops!" His voice shook, and he passed his hand across his eyes.

Violette's voice was very gentle. "But you could have given up Captain Death on the instant, by marrying any woman for her fortune. No-one would have blamed you for it."

"I would not have married a woman I did not love for her fortune, be she never so rich and I never so desperate. I saw it at first hand, how that circumstance leads to nothing but despair and degradation."

"But you might have married me for mine! For you say that you – you love – me." Violette hesitated to say the word; it seemed so strange, and even now she could hardly believe in the events that had befallen her in just these few short hours. "But I heard what you said to your brother; and I confess, it near broke my heart to hear it!"

A shadow passed across Lord Winterbourne's face. "That I would not play for you, for I couldn't bear to look at your face over the breakfast table? I didn't mean it as Kit understood it!

"I saw *you*. Violette deVere. Not your fortune, but *you*. A woman of great compassion and courage, loving and kind. It was my greatest wish to see that dear face smiling across the breakfast table! But I dared not think it. You would have found me out for a liar, someone who married you in circumstances so steeped in deception that you would never trust me again.

"I was counting the months off on my fingers – for Clara to make a marriage, for Kit to take his commission. And then I intended to be done with Captain Death, and come to you humbly and sincerely and confess all, and throw myself on your mercy. And if I had done so? What would have been your answer – if I had come to you, and implored you upon bended knee to be my wife? For circumstances have been such that I did not really ask you at all."

Violette opened her mouth to reply but whatever she was going to say went flying out of her head. For at that moment, they crested a rise, and came upon a scene of unimaginable horror.

CHAPTER 30

Winterbourne Hall was alight; a shining ball of heat challenging the risen sun in its brilliance.

Above the house the air shimmered and roiled. A stream of thick black smoke curled sullenly into a sky which was once more alive with showers of red and golden sparks.

From their vantage point, Richard and Violette could see men at the stables, pulling the terrified horses from their stalls and smacking them upon their rumps to set them galloping away across the gardens, or pushing carriages beyond the reach of the flames. Lord Winterbourne's pack of hunting hounds were barking and howling as they ran free across the park.

Serving girls – some in their caps and aprons, some still in their nightgowns – and men in their livery, and even guests still in their evening finery had formed a chain sending buckets down to the river and back but it was clear that it was too little – the fire could not be checked.

Lord Winterbourne whipped up the pony. The yelling of the men and the women's screams, the frantic neighing of the horses and the dogs barking, and over all the hellish roaring crackle of the flames whistling and crashing through the building grew louder and louder as they raced down the hill towards the inferno that was, once, Winterbourne Hall.

Lord Winterbourne flung himself out of the pony and trap and into the melee of servants and guests. "Come away! Come away – there's nothing more to be done!" he shouted. "Clara! Clara! A servant went running past, Lord Winterbourne grabbed him by the sleeve. "Where's my sister?" The man was filthy with soot and sweat. He turned a blank face towards Lord Winterbourne and shrugged, and ran on.

"Richard!" Violette clutched at his sleeve. "Over there – look!" She pointed to the terrace. Tongues of fire were licking around the ballroom windows. One exploded with a sound like a volley of shot, and another after that, flinging a whirling cloud of splintered glass across the lawns. Blackly silhouetted against their brilliance was the figure of Philip Marwood. One hand was twisted in Clara's hair, and in the other was a knife.

Lord Winterbourne sprinted towards the terrace, Violette at his heels. Through the broken windows, the fire could be seen licking up the painted walls. Waves of flame were rolling across the ballroom ceiling. There was a thunderous crash as one of the crystal chandeliers came smashing down to the floor.

Clara was still in her white silk, all smeared with smoke and ash, and her crown of flowers had slipped over one ear. Tears had traced a pathway through the smuts on her face, which was as white as her gown, and blood trickled down her cheek from a cut on her temple.

"You stay there, Winterbourne!" yelled Philip Marwood. He was wild-eyed, and laughing. "Look around you! This is what you deserve!" He waved the knife around, to indicate the building burning behind him. "You had everything, and I had nothing! I vowed that I would see you reduced and I have! Winterbourne's Folly? Folly seems too gentle a name for what your father did to mine. But I have my revenge! And I'm not finished yet!"

"He's demented!" cried Violette. "Philip – Philip – I beg you! Let Clara go! She has done nothing to hurt you!"

"Nothing to hurt me?" His voice was a screech of pure rage. He shook Clara by the hair, as if she were a doll. She screamed. Violette started towards her, but Richard pulled her back. She should have married me – that was what I planned – and once she did, Winterbourne, I'd have got this place for my own, and seen you off, you might be sure of it!

"And as for you, you blowsy scut! Running off to my godfather and tattling against me like some schoolroom miss!" So enraged was he, that he flung Clara from him, and made as if to run at Violette.

There was a flash, and the sound of a shot. Sir Harry Gray was at the foot of the terrace steps, his pistol smoking. Philip Marwood stopped in his tracks, and laughed. "Betrayed, by God! By some jumped-up miner's boy; not surprising that you prove a poor shot with a gentleman's pistol, sir! I imagine that a pick and shovel is more your weapon of choice!" He turned this way and that, as if not sure what to do next. Richard and Violette were at one end of the terrace and Clara at the other, Sir Harry in between, leaping up the steps two at a time towards him. Philip stood for a moment, irresolute. Then he turned, and plunged into the ballroom.

Richard made as if to go after him. Violette caught at his arm. "No Richard! You can't go in there – he's mad to have done it! Come away – come away!" Even above the roaring of the fire, they could hear people screaming, "The roof! The roof!"

Sir Harry swung Clara into his arms, and all of them ran from the conflagration. And it was just in time.

Flames were shooting from the roof, as if reaching up to the heavens. There was a great groaning boom that reverberated right across the valley and came echoing back from the hills. For one terrible moment, the entire roof appeared to rise up as if propelled by a giant hand. Then it gave way, and came crashing down through the body of the house. A gargantuan choking cloud of smoke billowed forth. The flames were extinguished in an instant; and now what was left was smouldering rubble.

Violette looked away from the ruin of Winterbourne Hall, and looked at Richard Taverner, and he at her.

"It's gone." His voice was curiously flat. "Gone. Thank God for it. Thank God, I say!" And he lowered his head, and wept, quite unashamedly.

Violette turned away. Here was her aunt, Miss Jennings, silent for once, beside her. "Aunt! – oh, Aunt – you're safe, thank heaven!" Violette threw her arms about her.

"Violette! Where have you been? I thought you, oh, I thought – no-one could find you, and I imagined all sorts." She was overcome, and could not speak for weeping. Violette looked at her aghast. Miss Felicia was barefoot in her nightgown, her nightcap missing and her hair streaming down across her shoulders.

Hill was with her and spoke through her own tears. "We were a-bed and roused by screams, and the servants running through the house banging on the doors. It was coming up sunrise, most of the guests were gone. It was only the house guests remaining, and I think all got out safe enough. Though I cannot find John, and we could not find you, and thought you both perished!" At that, her resolve deserted her, and she broke into a flurry of gasping sobs.

Miss Felicia put her arms around her, and hugged her close. "Oh Sarah! Don't cry! We shall find your brother, never fear!"

"Not perished! Quite safe, Hill – quite safe – and your brother with me!" cried Violette. "Look! Here is John with the horses. He shall help you back home to Sumbourne and I shall see you very soon! Aunt, Aunt – take my cloak, I beg you!"

John helped the ladies into the trap and settled himself with the reins. Miss Felicia hesitated for a moment. She looked back at Violette.

"But where were you? For we could not find you at all! I ran into your room – your bed was not slept in.

"And yet here you are – with Lord Winterbourne and in our pony and trap!" She wiped her hand across her eyes and turned her head away. "Oh, I can make no sense of anything!

"Take us home, John, I beg you!"

CHAPTER 31

"… quite astonishing, for I am convinced they hardly were acquainted at all, and I was under the impression that his lordship was most unwilling to enter into any sort of engagement and had been forced into it by her behaviour at Lady Hertford's ball.

"And as for dear Lettie, why, she had said to me most emphatic that she would not have him in any circumstances. But here they are – married at a moment's notice and off to Scotland for a walking tour of the Highlands for their honeymoon. So very quiet a ceremony, too – no time to make arrangements of any sort. Just family there – myself and Lord Winterbourne's brother and sister. No flowers. No cake!"

"That *is* a shame. I have a fondness for wedding cake."

"As do I, my dear, as do I!"

To compensate for the lack of wedding cake, Mrs George helped Miss Felicia to a second slice of almond tart. "And no gown, you say? I suppose there was not time to get one made – marrying in such haste, as it seems."

"No indeed! She wore an old gown – a gown of champagne crêpe de chine, that she'd already worn to a number of entertainments. Not even trimmed up with flowers or a frill or two – for it is an exceptionally plain garment. And what is odd, my dear," Miss Felicia leaned forward most confidentially, and Mrs George leaned in to hear her, "what is odd, is that she wore a most beautiful costume of dove-colour gauze for their engagement ball. With a little adjustment it would have been very suitable for a wedding. I thought it must have been lost in the fire, for everything else was burned to a crisp. But no! It was at Sumbourne all the time! How that came about I cannot tell. I came across Hill trying to mend it, for it was stained something terrible, and sadly torn!

Both ladies were quiet for a moment, considering how a gown could be in a place it was not supposed to be at all and filthy and torn, and the subsequent haste with which the happy couple had made their marriage vows.

Mrs George changed the subject – but only very slightly. "And since we are speaking of weddings... ."She left a telling pause, hoping for news of another wedding. She was not disappointed. Her friend was positively bursting with weddings, and couldn't wait to describe the next.

"You would have heard of the marriage of Lettie's new sister. Lady Clara Taverner, that was. A pretty girl, and a beautiful bride to be sure. All in blush-colour silk, with an overlay of embroidered nets, and a train ten foot in length. Her bonnet was trimmed with Honiton lace that was said to have cost quite twenty guineas!"

"For just a bit of lace on her bonnet? Goodness me!"

"Expense was not spared, my dear, not one farthing was begrudged; for Sir Harry Gray seems to have the knack of making money – quite the Midas touch, I have heard it said!"

"He's a deal older than Lady Clara, I understand?"

"He is. A gentleman of one and forty years, and she but eighteen. But a fine figure of a man, fond of outdoor pursuits and dancing, quite the Corinthian in his youth, I believe. A doting husband with a house in Mayfair, and a free hand for the young bride to make it as she likes. His wife died very young, and his house is said to be something of a gentleman's residence, if you understand my meaning."

Mrs George did. Her own dear husband had been an intrepid and adventurous traveller, and had an instinct for the skins of tigers he'd shot in his youth, and the heads and horns of deer he'd shot in later life. His idea or comfortable living was a wall filled with hunting spears and shields and clubs, and chairs that were as ugly as they were creakingly comfortable and caught the dust.

Upon his death his widow had enjoyed the luxury of choosing prettily gilded chairs and charming chintzes and had consigned the dead tigers and deer heads to the attics.

Interesting as this wedding was, Miss Felicia seemed strangely reluctant to mention the last and most intriguing. Mrs George gave up being tactful and approached the subject straight out. "So tell me, my dear, for I am desperate to know – how did your own wedding come about? And how is it that you are removed so sudden to Bath? I could not be happier to see you once more in my drawing room … unexpected though your call is, it is most welcome!"

"It is a very long story, Mrs George." Miss Felicia hesitated, hardly knowing where to start. "I was sorry to learn that you were taken with a cold, and durst not journey into Kent for the ceremony; though the weather has been very bad these last few weeks in any event, and the roads poor. But perhaps just as well. For things did not turn out at all as I expected."

Mrs George nodded. "I shall ring the bell for more coal for the fire and more tea, and I think there might be buttered muffins. And you shall tell me all!"

"A few days after Lady Hertford's ball we left for Kent, and I confess I was in the very lowest of spirits. Not because of Lettie's circumstance, you understand – hasty thinking on the part of Lord Winterbourne seemed to have averted disaster, so that they were known to be engaged, though Lettie seemed very cast down by that turn of events.

"No; it was Miss Jennings. Much as I had tried to make good acquaintance with her, a more meddling woman you could not imagine. She had her nose in everything; quizzing the servants, looking over cook's shoulder, and demanding to see the account books.

"I had thought that upon our journeying into Kent she would return to her house in Oare. My dear Mrs George, I was counting the minutes! But she did not go. And as for her brother, why, Major Jennings established himself at The Dragon, but he spent more time at the Manor than anywhere else. He took it upon himself to walk in quite as he chose, and to order the fires blazed up with coals heaped upon them, and no thought to the expense. All his conversation was of Captain Death and these smugglers, and his plans to catch them and what would happen to them when he did. It was really quite bloodthirsty – hangings, you know – a conversation hardly fit for the dinner table.

"Dear Lettie found it most disturbing, I could tell, and at moments looked quite pale, but he would not be turned, no matter how much she spoke of her plans for the garden – a pretty design of tulips – or if I asked his opinion on the baked onions."

"Onions?" queried Mrs George.

"Yes; he was very interested in onions, the first time we dined with him. He was very fond of his glass of port, as well, and would sit over the decanter for an hour or more, before coming roaring into the drawing room where Lettie and I – and Miss Jennings, of course - would be sitting after dinner and drinking our tea. And when he was not speaking of the smugglers, he was complaining about John. He'd quite taken against him after the – the," Miss deVere lowered her voice to a whisper, "*Vauxhall Gardens*, you know."

Mrs George was acquainted with the sorry tale of Vauxhall Gardens. It reminded her of something else. "What of that unpleasant young man? Mr Marwood? What's become of him?"

"Quite vanished, my dear! Some say he has been sent away somewhere – the Indies, or the islands of the Caribbean, I believe. Somewhere very hot, anyway. Arranged by Sir Harry Gray, in furtherance of business matters, or so it is said, though I suspect it was to avoid the law. There was always something about that young man that spoke of ill-doing, though what precisely he had been up to, I do not know. But most seem to think he perished in the fire. It is said that it was he who set Winterbourne Hall ablaze, though why he should do so I have no idea! It was a most terrifying circumstance, Mrs George. Even now it makes me tremble to think on it! The whole house burned down to the very ground."

"Lord Winterbourne must have been distraught at the sight!"

"I think he must have been," said Miss Felica hesitantly, "That is – well, yes, I think he must. He

322

was delighted to see his sister safe of course, but it hardly explains …"

"Explains?"

"That as we drove away, he was – he was laughing! Positively laughing! Though I was so confused, I hardly knew what I thought.

"I never have discovered how it was that Lettie and Lord Winterbourne and John, too, were there with the pony and trap from our own stables. Or, for that matter, how it was that we all were in our nightclothes, or evening dress still – but they were not! Indeed, Lettie was in a print morning dress, quite an old one. it was almost as if she had gone home and changed her clothes. But why would she have done so – and in the company of his lordship? Unless they left the ball before the fire started, and went to the Manor together and then returned at dawn this morning, but then that would suggest - it would suggest that they spent the night …. ." She felt she could not continue the thought without arriving at a very unwelcome conclusion, and took an absent-minded bite of almond tart, and chewed it reflectively.

Mrs George tactfully changed the subject. "But you were saying – about the Major?"

"Yes – so, to go back - we returned from London with Lettie engaged to Lord Winterbourne and I thought Miss Jennings would depart to her own house at Oare but she did not, and seemed quite deaf to any suggestion that she should. And then things came to a head with the tea."

323

"The tea?"

"I ordered Orange Pekoe, and it never arrived at all, and when I questioned cook, she said that Miss Jennings had been outraged at the price, and ordered Bohea instead!"

Mrs George fell back in her chair at this. What an imposition! To countermand an order for tea! It had clearly driven her friend to distraction, and even just at the telling of the tale Miss Felicia's voice quavered, and she dabbed her handkerchief to her nose. But she was checked for a moment only, and pulled herself together enough to continue with her account.

"I pointed out that once Lettie was married, she would be off to live at Winterbourne Hall, and I would be once more a single lady living alone, and perhaps it would be not quite proper for the Major to spend so much time at the Manor. Major Jennings did not leave. Rather, he took my words to mean that we should marry forthwith, and set the arrangements in hand, quite without consulting me!

"Then of course it was the night of Lettie's engagement ball. Now, Major Jennings had gone to great lengths to trap the smugglers and boasted to us, saying that the night of the ball would see the end of Captain Death for once and for all. There was talk of a substantial reward for his capture, and it is my belief that the Major was so certain of the result that he had borrowed money against the bounty; for he was certainly spending free enough. Port, my dear, positively crates of it! In any event, something happened to thwart his plans, and he was enraged to a terrible degree. He cared nothing for the dreadful events of that night – that I had been in the most fearful danger, and his sister too – but only for his own concerns! He caught it into his head that someone had betrayed him.

"He stormed about, and accused all and sundry. He came so near as blaming dear Lettie as makes no difference! You can imagine how Lord Winterbourne felt about that. I thought it would be pistols at dawn, or at the very least one of that gentleman's scathing put downs, but he merely laughed in the Major's face, and made some jest about tulip bulbs, which seemed to inflame the Major all the more. But I must say that Lettie has been a most improving influence upon his lordship! His manners are so changed you would not know him for the same man, and a kinder and more generous soul you could not wish to meet."

Mrs George nodded. "A gentleman's spirits can be vastly improved by the acquisition of a wife with a fortune," she observed, sagely.

At this moment, the maid entered with the muffins, and having placed them upon the table, proceeded to heap the fire with coals and wield the poker pretty vigorously. Miss Felicia took this opportunity to compose herself. For although the telling of her story was light-hearted enough, and her friend a most sympathetic listener, it was difficult to explain just how oppressive the situation at the Manor was become under the reign of Miss Jennings and her brother.

Violette's arrival at Sumbourne Manor had been the start of a brief period of great happiness for Felicia deVere. It had been a reminder of the joyous days of her girlhood, when her circle of acquaintance was wide, her invitations plentiful, and she had danced the nights through with one attentive gentleman after another. In those days she'd had the expectations of any girl her age; that life would carry on in this vein, though with the addition of a kind husband, a home of her own to order as she liked, and the joy of children. And when she met Major Jennings – Lieutenant Jennings, as he had been then – ardent and handsome in his regimentals, she had thought that this life would be made complete by the addition of love into the mix, and a degree of adventure. She imagined herself an army wife, and thrilled at the prospect of travelling to countries unknown to her.

It seemed that she shared the same spirit of adventure as her brother, but her brother's spirit of adventure had trumped her own. While Felicia had merely dreamed of love in a distant climate, her brother had acted, and had decamped with his ballet girl. Enraged beyond reason and unable to force his will upon his son, Sir William had enforced it double upon his daughter.

She was ordered to give up the balls and the pretty clothes and her hopes of marriage. His son may have abandoned all thoughts of the duty owed to a parent and to the honourable name of deVere, and to have fallen into the clutches of a fortune-hunting harpy, but his daughter would not be permitted to throw caution to the winds in such a way.

Sir William gave orders for the London house to be sold. He would return to Kent and his daughter with him and there they would stay. He emphasized his determination by suffering an apoplexy, and subsequently assumed the mantle of an invalid, moving only from fireside to bed and back again, and feeding his temper and his gout with a rich diet of game and port.

Felicia deVere's first instinct had been to throw away reputation and fly across the border with her Lieutenant to marry at the blacksmith's forge. But a strong sense of duty would not allow her to do it. Mindful of the demands of society, she had said goodbye to her dreams, and settled into a quiet life in the Kentish countryside, alleviated once a year by a month's visit to Bath for her father to take the waters for his gout or his dyspepsia.

"I was so thrilled to meet Major Jennings once more – and it was beyond romantic, to learn that he had never forgot me, and carried with him the ring he would have given me. But I came to think I was too quick in agreeing to marry him. It was for nostalgia, perhaps. A memory, no more, of happy days that had passed.

"As for Miss Jennings, I remembered her as a girl, lively and pleasant enough. I did not see that we were grown into very different people; and by the time I did see it, it was too late. I could not break my engagement. Break the Major's heart as I had done once already, and the scandal that would follow? I could not bear it."

These had been Miss Felica's thoughts, and for several long weeks she had turned them over and over in her head. 'Sumbourne Manor has been my home all my life, but now it feels more like a prison than ever it did before,' she reflected. 'I have but two choices – to live here married to Major Jennings, and with the constant presence of his sister, or to break my engagement and remain an old maid who threw away her last chance of marriage and her reputation with it.

'I was lonely before Violette came. When she is married and gone to her new home, I shall be lonely once more. I could settle back into that life well enough I suppose; but added to that I should be a laughing stock. I could hardly hold my head up in the street. What little acquaintance I had would be within their rights to shun me altogether."

So she had agreed to set a date for the wedding, and Major Jennings had obtained the licence. And then John had come to her to take his leave.

Miss Felicia rose from her chair by the fireside, and crossed to the window, to look out into the street. The afternoon had faded into dusk, and a heavy frost silvered the pavements. The door of the house opposite opened. Out came the footman with a taper to light the lamps, and in their glow the steps down to the pavement turned to sparkling gold.

Her friend had not yet rung for her own footman to come in to light the candles, so the room was illuminated only by firelight. Miss Felicia welcomed the shadows that hid her face, for the next part of her story was difficult to tell.

"I was not aware that Major Jennings had told John that upon the occasion of our wedding, he would need to find other employment. John had come to the Manor when I was but a child still in leading strings, and his sister when I was grown enough to need a maid of my own. I had known John – both of them – nearly all my life. He it was taught me to ride, and my brother too.

"He was most sober in his speech. He said he was sad to leave, but that I was not to worry. He had been prudent all his life and had saved up his money and invested with a person here in Bath engaged in building houses. It had shown a great return, and now he was become of independent means. Upon leaving Sumbourne he would be taking up his residence in Bath, and his sister would be coming to keep house for him.

"I hardly knew which was worse, losing John, or the loss of Hill. She was more than my maid. She was my dear friend, too. I did not know how I would bear it." Her voice broke, and she choked back a sob.

"It was my wedding day. I had not slept, but lay awake all night. Just before dawn, it began to rain.

Hill came to help me dress. She fastened my cloak for me, just as she had when we were girls together, as caring for me as a sister would be; and she tied my bonnet strings beneath my chin, as if I were a child, still. It was a beautiful bonnet, to be sure, with a trim of velvet fruits upon it; dear Violette had purchased it for me as a gift. She – Hill – tried to be merry; but all the while tears were running down her face at the thought of leaving me.

"John drove me to the church. There was no-one waiting for me. Lettie was away on her honeymoon, and there were no guests invited but you, and a colleague or two of the Major's, so there was no-one to escort me. The churchyard was empty, but for the graves of all the dead souls, and the rain had stopped, leaving a lowering grey sky reflected in great puddles of water lying along the path to the church door. The lychgate – through which I was to pass to my new life as Major Jennings' wife – was half hidden in the gloom of an ancient yew tree. You could not envisage a scene more desolate.

"John stopped the carriage, and came round for me. He opened the door and put the steps down, and held out his hand to help me. I took his hand. I could not let it go. I said to him, 'John, I can't do it. I can't marry the Major. And if you leave me, I don't know what I shall do.' I burst into tears.

"And John put his arms around me, and kissed the tears from my cheeks, and said –," she hesitated, and then continued, in a rush, "he said, well, in that case, maybe I should like to marry him. He said,

'Dear heart, I have been waiting long enough!'" Her voice wobbled, dangerously. "And he said – he said – 'that is far too pretty a bonnet to waste upon the Major!' So I said I would."

Mrs George had abandoned all thoughts of teacups and buttered muffins, and been listening with her mouth quite open with shock. "You bolted! And left the Major jilted at the alter!"

Miss Felicia could not look at her friend. She shut her eyes, and pressed her hot forehead against the coolness of the window pane. When she spoke again, her voice was little more than a whisper.

"I understand if you do not wish … that is – I know that behaving so despicably will have cast me adrift from society. And then to run away with the groom from my own stables!" She was openly weeping now. "I could not help myself, Charlotte. I could not. I love him so very dearly. And I will be so very sad to lose your friendship over it. But I do understand if you feel that it's not appropriate for us to remain friends …" her voice trailed away.

There was a silence in the room, other than the crackle of the fire. Dabbing at her eyes with her handkerchief, Miss Felicia finally turned away from the window to find her friend with her face buried in a cushion, and her shoulders heaving.

"Oh, Charlotte, do not cry, I beg of you!" she started, only to see her friend jerk upright with her face bright red, and to hear her let out a most unladylike snort of laughter. "Felicia deVere – or

331

should I say Mrs Hill? For I assume you have married the fellow!"

"Certainly I have!" Righteous indignation chased away the tears. "And I cannot help but think of the poor Major standing at the altar waiting for me in vain." She paused, but could not help herself. She gave a little gurgle of laughter. "And Miss Sally Jennings, wearing a very ugly gown of tomato-colour sateen, no doubt spluttering at his side."

This was altogether too much for Mrs George. She let out a great screech of laughter, gasped and coughed, and gulped at her tea. She jumped up and ran across to her friend, and took both her hands, and clasped them warmly to her. "My dearest, dearest friend! I have known you since we were quite little children, Felicia, and you were then the most adventurous, the wickedest, the funniest girl I ever saw!

"I was sorrier than I could ever say, to see you fade away to live such a very quiet, dutiful sort of life under your father's shadow, while your brother went on to live an outrageous life himself. It seems to me that your brother – and, indeed, your niece! – were strong enough to grasp happiness when it was held out to them, and why should you not do the same? You have married the man you love, and come to live in Bath which was your dream, and I could not be happier.

"As for society gossip – pooh – who cares a fig for it? It will take but a single turn in the Pump Room in the company of Lord and Lady

Winterbourne for you to be welcomed into society with open arms!" Mrs George was quite rapturous with delight. "I congratulate you, my dear, with all my heart.

"It is the very happiest of endings, to be sure!"

FROM THE AUTHOR

Gentle reader, I hope you have enjoyed the love stories of Violette and Miss Felicia deVere and their friend Lady Clara Taverner.

If you have (or even if you haven't!) I would love to read your review on Goodreads or Amazon. I *do* read *all* my reviews; of course it's wonderful to see kind comments and they encourage me to keep writing. But a critical review is useful, as I know there is always room for improvement in my work.

If you would like to know more about my writing, please visit my website for information about new novels in progress or to sign up for my monthly newsletter.

Thank you!
VIVIENNE
https://www.vivienneshannon.com

Printed in Great Britain
by Amazon

42448738R00188